Every Witch Way but Ghouls

Magical Misfits Mysteries - book 1

K.E. O'Connor

K.E. O'Connor Books

EVERY WITCH WAY BUT GHOULS

ISBN: 978-1-915378-42-2

Written by: K.E. O'Connor

Chapter 1

A fiery encounter and a prickly problem

"These prickled hogs are a pain in my behind." Zandra Crypt skulked beside me in the late evening gloom. The stars were out, and we should have finished work three hours ago, but these magically enchanted hedgehogs we tracked had a different idea. They weren't giving up their freedom without a fight.

"We're close. I can smell them." I lifted my perfect pink-tipped nose and breathed in the chilly evening air. It was tinged with eau-du-hog. Spicy with a bit of musky sweat. The faint sparkles in the air from the noxious gas they emitted when startled also helped with the tracking.

"They definitely came this way." Zandra slowed to inspect small tracks in the dirt on the path we followed through Crimson Cove woods. "These are the right sized prints for hogs."

I sniffed the tracks and nodded. My cute little booping snooter was excellent at picking up smells.

"The scent is fresh. They must have been here less than five minutes ago."

Zandra looked around and sighed. "I'm sure we've come this way before, though. These critters are sneaky. It wouldn't surprise me if they're leading us in circles just for fun. Twisted little spiky monsters."

There was a scuttle of tiny feet up ahead, and we froze. My hackles lifted, and Zandra clenched her hands.

"Juno, did you see where that came from?" Zandra was crouched as if ready to pounce, but I'd warned her several times about not grabbing our prickled challengers. These magically enchanted hedgehogs had poisoned prickles that would shoot out. Get those stuck in you, and you were in a world of hurt.

"No sign of them yet." I didn't feel the cold, thanks to my magnificent white fur, but Zandra was shivering, and her breath plumed out of her. The last thing I wanted was for my witch to get a cold. She was a grump when sick.

"Let's keep moving. They must tire soon." She rubbed her hands together and blew on them.

I didn't like to point out we'd had four nights of endless tracking and hog hunting, and we'd yet to capture these critters. Who knew magically enchanted hedgehogs would be so difficult to detain? They were small, noisy, and indiscreet. This should have been an easy win.

But I was still deliriously proud of my witch, since this was the only assignment we'd failed to complete. Four days on the job in animal control, and everything was ticked off our list.

Our new boss, Barney Hoffman, had been giving us other tasks during the day, since these hedgehogs were nocturnal. We'd mainly checked households to ensure the families followed the familiar care rules and provided suitable enrichment for any tame magic creatures they kept. Animal control was particular about how magical critters were looked after, and sometimes, people got sloppy.

Other than the checks and reminders issued, Zandra had been learning the ropes of her job as an assistant animal control warden, and I was alongside her as her trusty familiar to make sure everything went smoothly. Apart from these pesky hedgehogs, it had been a perfect start to our new careers.

Zandra shivered again and rubbed her arms briskly.

"We could always try again tomorrow," I said.

"No way! These hogs are going down tonight. If I don't catch them, Barney will figure out we lied to get this job."

"We didn't exactly lie. We showed how excellent you'd be in this role."

"You pretended you were a crazed, possessed magical being, and I fake captured you. That's not at all lying."

"You'd have been able to do that with any magically crazed being. There just weren't any around when their services were required. I stepped up. Besides, Barney likes you. He won't fire you for one tiny fabrication."

Zandra ducked, shoving her dark hair tighter under her hat. "That bush moved! It must be the hogs."

She stalked forward before I could stop her, so I sprinted to keep up. "Ten more minutes, then we're calling it a night. Barney doesn't have the budget for overtime. He's always telling you that."

"There won't be any regular time if we don't pull this off." She pressed a finger to her lips. "They're so close, even I can smell them."

"It isn't hard with all that stinky, sparkling gas they keep parping out of their tiny behinds."

A small black blur shot out of the hedge and whacked the side of Zandra's head.

I launched into the air, my claws exposed and a murderous growl shooting out of me, but I was a second too late. The hedgehog pinged off Zandra's cheek, leaving behind several poisoned quills.

She went to touch her face, but I sprung up and knocked her hand out of the way. "Get on the ground. I'll extract the quills before the poison spreads."

"But... the hedgehog! It's getting away. This is as close as we've ever gotten."

"Down! Now! If that poison gets into your system, you're toast."

Zandra dropped to her knees, and I hopped my front paws onto her shoulder and grabbed each quill between my teeth, yanked it out, and spat it on the ground. It must have hurt, but my brave witch didn't protest.

She grimaced as the last one popped free. "You done?"

"One more thing. Think sparkly, happy thoughts." I latched onto the side of her face and sucked the poison from each hole.

Zandra shrieked, since there was nothing I could do about my fangs, so she got a few extra holes in her face. But poison bested cat fangs, so she'd have to endure the pain.

Only when I was certain the foul taste of rotten eggs was no longer present on her skin did I stop sucking.

Zandra gingerly touched her swollen cheek. "I know I should thank you, but that burned like dragon's breath after a spicy curry."

I licked her cheek, then trotted off and lapped from a slushy puddle to clear the foul taste of poison from my mouth. By the time I was done, Zandra was pulsing a healing spell over her cheek. It took a few minutes, but the swelling faded and the holes closed.

"I see now why Barney doesn't want to deal with these hedgehogs himself." Zandra got to her feet and brushed dirt off her knees. "Or maybe this is hazing. All the new recruits get the lousy jobs to see if they can handle the pressure."

"Barney wouldn't do that to you. He's a gentleman."

"The others might."

Zandra often reacted like a startled, magically enchanted hedgehog in circumstances she found uncomfortable. She'd fling out prickles and verbal barbs when trapped in an awkward situation. And when she'd met the rest of the team in animal control, things had been a little strained.

"They'll come around once they get to know you." I wound around her legs several times until she let out a sigh and petted me. "And although I'd rather these hogs were in their cages safely under lock and key, I admire their spirit. They've beaten us for days." I walked along beside Zandra, sniffing the ground and hoping to find a fresh hedgehog trail.

Zandra scooped me up and settled me on her shoulder. "I sort of agree. We need a new approach, though. This stealth tracking isn't working. The hogs must be able to hear us approaching. Even your delicate paws cause a vibration."

"What do you have in mind?"

"Automatic traps. The hogs come in different sizes and have different food preferences, so we'll need a variety of traps and treats. We'll place the traps around the woods, since this is their favorite spot, and wait for them to fire."

I booped my nose against Zandra's healed cheek in approval. "You're sure you don't want a break? There are snacks in the van and a thermos of coffee. We can get everything we need and come back tomorrow evening."

"Snacks and rest later. That'll be our reward once we've caught the hogs."

It took an hour and a trip to the local store to grab food the hedgehogs would eat, but four traps were finally planted around the woodland, complete with tempting treats to entice our spiky nemeses.

We hunkered down in the van at the edge of the woods and waited. Zandra had set up a four-way receiving camera linked to the mobile snow globe network to remote monitor the cages. She had her mobile globe open and was flicking between the images.

"Come on, hoggies. You must be hungry. All that running from me and Juno has burned up calories," Zandra muttered.

My nose was distracted by the meaty cat treats in the glove box. "Give them time. They'll be nervous of the traps."

"Not that nervous. I've got movement on one camera." Zandra grinned at me.

I gave her the cat version of a smile, which was more of a whisker twitch with a tail flick. If I tried to smile like her with my teeth, I looked like I was about to attack. When I'd been turned into a cat, it took me a while to unlearn how to smile and a good year to learn the fine art of cat body language. Use the wrong ear twitch at the wrong moment, and I could have all-out war on my furry paws.

"Look! A hedgehog is going to the smallest cage." She tilted her mobile snow globe so I could see what was going on.

I forced myself not to keep sniffing for treats and focused on the image. Sure enough, the smallest hog we'd been tracking was creeping toward the cage. It sniffed for a good five minutes before slinking inside.

"Is that a hat on its head?" I said.

"Not sure. It's got something on its head. Maybe it's a leaf? Any second now," Zandra whispered. "That baby is ours."

The hedgehog hesitated, then darted forward, mouth open, revealing sharp teeth. The second it got to the food, the trapdoor triggered, and it snapped shut.

The hog twirled around and charged at the door, but it was too late to get out. The critter hit the door several times, quills shooting out in self-defense and pinging harmlessly through the bars, but there was nothing the little prickled spud could do to escape.

"Woo-hoo! It's our lucky night," Zandra said. "Two more hedgehogs are going after the other cages."

"That still leaves three out there," I said. "The family unit. The mamma and her two babies."

"They'll go for the largest cage," Zandra said, surety in her voice. "I reckon the rest are males. We've got the boys, but of course, mamma hog will be cautious and smart. She won't lead her babies into danger."

"If only we could make them believe they weren't in danger from us, but they won't listen to reason."

Zandra petted my head. "You tried talking to them, but they told you to get lost."

"Their language was coarser than that. It involved sticking their prickles where the sun doesn't shine. Repeatedly. And sideways."

She grinned. "You did your best. Some critters just won't listen to reason. They think animal control is all about capture and destroy."

"Once we have them, they'll have a safe place to sleep and all the hedgehog food they can handle, and no one will report them as a nuisance once they're in a sanctuary." I leaned in for more pets. "Like many of the animals we've dealt with since starting this job, they don't trust us."

"Animal control hasn't got the best reputation. Someone needs to do a positive PR spin. It would make our lives easier."

I nodded as I watched the action via the camera. We'd been in this job for less than a week, yet had heard alarming prejudice about animal control.

Sure, there was a misguided assumption that all we did was hunt innocent magical creatures and put them to sleep, but Barney was a decent boss and as animal crazy as Zandra. He advocated kindness first. The animals got compassion and understanding. Even the hedgehogs who poisoned Zandra got a second chance, and I was always unforgiving when anyone hurt my bonded witch.

We watched for another ten minutes before all but one of the traps was filled. The hedgehogs were raging mad about being captured, shooting out quills and parping sparkly gas, but eventually, they settled in and ate the food. And why not? Why fight something when you know you've been defeated?

Zandra bounced in her seat. "It's the family! They're approaching the largest cage. Any minute now, we'll have a full house of hedgehogs."

"Are they wearing hats, too?" The feed from the camera wasn't clear thanks to the magical distortion–magic and electronics did not play nicely together–but I was certain the family of hogs were wearing tiny pointed hats.

"Yeah, they are. Where are they getting those from?" Zandra tried to unblur the image, but it wouldn't get any sharper.

We watched in silence as mamma hedgehog tentatively approached the large cage and sniffed around. The two smaller hogs were eager to go inside, but she kept nudging them back with her nose and nipping them if they disobeyed and tried to dodge past and grab the food.

The view from the camera wavered for a second, then it blacked out before coming back online.

"What's wrong with this thing?" Zandra said. "Don't fail me now. I need to see when the hedgehogs are trapped. If we move too soon, they'll run again."

"It could be magical atmospherics." Barney had come up with a range of clever inventions to ensure most of the vehicles and equipment worked with minimal disruption, but they still weren't perfect.

"This feed runs through the snow globe network. There shouldn't be any interference." Zandra jiggled her mobile snow globe.

The camera image wobbled again and went blank, but not before I spotted a large shadow looming over the hedgehog cage.

Zandra jerked in her seat. "You saw that, right? Someone had better not be messing with my equipment or my hogs." She jumped out of the van and raced toward the largest cage, and I was hot on her heels.

We made it halfway to the capture site, when there was a roar, and a bright light lit the gloomy trees.

Zandra's eyes widened, but she kept running. We entered the clearing, where the large cage was located, and stopped.

Inside the cage was not only the three hat wearing hedgehogs cowering in one corner, but a magic user who looked to be part dragon. His red arm scales flared brightly, and flames flickered from his mouth.

His yellow eyes darted our way, and he roared again before emitting a jet of flames that burned through the cage bars.

"Hey! Stop that!" Zandra yelled above the roar of the flames. "That's the property of animal control."

"I don't think he cares about who owns the cage," I said.

Zandra didn't appear to have heard me. She stalked toward the cage, magic sparking on her fingers.

The part dragon looked at the three hedgehogs. He grabbed each one and swallowed them without chewing.

"Oh, no, you didn't. You did not just eat my catch and ruin my cage." Zandra ran at the melting cage, magic flaring around her in bright red, dazzling swirls.

I gathered my own ancient magic. Although my power was dull and reluctant to perform, I'd force it to life to protect Zandra.

Panic seized my silken tail and tugged it. Nothing happened. My magic refused to function.

My witch was about to go head-to-head with a smoldering, hog eating dragon, and I couldn't help her.

Chapter 2

A close encounter of the dragon kind

The part dragon roared again and pulled apart the damaged cage, rending hot metal with his bare hands as he stepped out to confront Zandra.

I leaped between them, and finally, thankfully, my sluggish magic flared to life. My white fur puffed up all over my body, and I bared my teeth at the part dragon and hissed.

He looked down at me, and a smirk crossed his face. "Bit small to go up against me, aren't you, fluffy? Not worried I'll eat you, too?"

"Give me back those hedgehogs." Zandra stood just behind me, rage radiating off her in red waves of magic.

The part dragon shifted his smirk to her, but he pulled his shirt sleeves down to conceal his scales as soon as he realized they were exposed for scrutiny. He was stocky, his face broad and flat, and now he was in control of his dragon side, the yellow faded from his eyes to reveal they were dark with a few lines in the corners.

"Those were your hedgehogs?" the part dragon said. "Tasty."

"No! Not mine, but they were in my cages, so they technically belonged to me." Zandra huffed out a breath and straightened her spine, pulling back her magic a fraction so it didn't ping against me so violently. "They've been causing trouble around Crimson Cove, and I've been looking for them. I can't believe you just ate them. Why do that?"

"I was hungry. What was in the cage barely touched the sides, and there's a lot of me to fill out." He patted his flat stomach.

"That wasn't for you, and you know it. I should arrest you for damaging animal control property."

"Animal control, huh! You must be new to the job, since I haven't seen you around before."

"It doesn't matter how new I am. You just broke the law."

"And working in animal control gives you the right to arrest me?" The guy arched a brow, still looking too smug for his own good.

I hissed another warning as I shuffled back and sat on Zandra's feet. She could be a hothead, and her temper had gotten her in trouble in the past. I didn't want her tackling a part dragon who freely shot out flames with so little regard for safety.

After a minute of glaring and no one backing down, I decided to be the better cat and extend the fluffy tail of peace. I smoothed my fur to look less intimidating. There was no point in needlessly terrorizing anyone. "We've gotten off on the wrong paw. I'm sure you didn't mean to interfere with animal control business, and you'd have never touched the food or the cage if you'd known better."

The part dragon looked down at me again. "True enough. But you get all kinds of crazies out here. Some people trap animals for fun. How was I supposed to know animal control was involved in this capture? Just last month, I removed two illegal traps from these woods. Some idiot started a rumor about a hybrid unicorn in the area, and we all know how much unicorn horn is worth on the black magic market."

I cocked my head and gave him a thorough scrutiny. Although his initial appearance was that of an out-of-control individual with delusions of grandeur, if he cared about animals, there may be a thread of decency running through him.

"Maybe you planted those unicorn traps," Zandra said.

The guy gave a vehement shake of his head. "Never going to happen. It seems we're on the same side, although you forgot to show me your credentials, so you could be lying to me. How about you show me yours, and—"

"Here." Zandra thrust out her wallet, showing her assistant animal warden badge with the picture of her looking cross-eyed. Still cute with her dark eyes and ever so slightly wonky mouth, but she hadn't been sure where to look when the shot was taken, so the picture made her look quirky.

"Looks legit to me." The guy raised a hand. "Hey, Zandra Crypt. Nice to meet you."

Her eyes narrowed. "It is legit. Who'd fake an animal warden badge?"

"Weirdos. Creeps trying to catch the unicorn hybrid. There are plenty of weirdos around Crimson Cove."

"Including you?" I said.

He chuckled and went to pet me, but a sharp hiss had him retreating. Sensible move. "I have my moments. Want to hear about my weirder ones?"

"We don't need to know anything about you. Just don't do this again." Zandra waved a hand at the ruined cage.

I circled around her legs and nudged her with my head until she took a few steps back, recognizing my cue to talk.

She kneeled, her gaze still on the guy. "What's the matter?"

I placed my paws on her thigh, which was another signal I'd taught her that meant I wished to be picked up. As usual, my wonderful witch obliged, and I was soon nestled on her shoulder. "We should rethink this situation. He could be useful."

"Doubtful. And I don't trust him," Zandra muttered.

"I can hear you," the guy said.

"You were meant to. What were you doing skulking in these woods, anyway?" Zandra moved away from him.

"I wasn't skulking. I was walking. It's not late, and I like to work up an appetite before dinner."

"You clearly did that."

I nudged her ear with my face. "If he's a friend of the animals, he could have insider information. It would make our job easier." The more I studied this mysterious part dragon, the more interested I became in him. He was attractive, not my type, but when you're an ancient demi-goddess, tastes evolve over the centuries, and he had everything in the right place. And when he wasn't smirking, he had a pleasant smile. A touch self-confident but not repulsive.

Yes, there was definite potential here. Zandra needed to date more. She wasn't big on social interactions and hated small talk. But Mr. Smug Part Dragon and Zandra could talk about their love of animals.

He belched. "Those little hogs were spicy. They're not sitting too good."

"Serves you right. And in case you're interested, their quills contain poison," Zandra said.

"That's not a problem for someone with my constitution."

I crinkled my booping snooter. We needed to work on his arrogance if he was going to fit into our lives.

"Are you sure about that? You're looking a little green," Zandra said.

"Maybe they're not as good as I thought. Hold on. I have a solution to my gas issue and your lost hogs." He grimaced, thumped his chest several times, and spat up the hedgehogs.

I stared at them. They were intact and moving! They rolled away, curled into tight balls, their prickles soggy. I leaped off Zandra and rolled them into the damaged cage. They didn't fight back. They must have been too shocked. After a check to make sure they had no injuries, I sealed the cage with a temporary holding spell, so they couldn't escape through the hole.

"Good work, Juno." Zandra jabbed a finger at the part dragon. "Although that was disgusting, I appreciate the return of the hogs."

"Hold on. There's something else lodged down there." Mr. Part Dragon coughed and out came three tiny hats. "Huh! Were they wearing those?"

I sniffed the hats. "Oh, I know where these came from. The gnomes. The hogs have been trashing yards in Crimson Cove with resident garden gnomes. They must have taken souvenirs to wear."

Zandra shook her head in bemusement while Mr. Part Dragon simply looked confused.

He coughed a couple more times and thumped his chest again. "You were right about those hogs. Not dragon compliant. Weird. My constitution is usually cast iron."

Zandra simply smirked and crossed her arms over her chest.

He shifted his weight from side to side. "I... maybe I was hasty when going after your catch. I've had a bad day and haven't eaten much. I was starving, and my dragon side took over. It does that sometimes. You know how it is. Or maybe you don't. I'm guessing you're all witch?"

"You guessed right."

I didn't correct her. Zandra was mainly witch, with a hint of imprisoned demon, but the demon part was so tiny, he was barely noticeable.

"Zandra is an unusual first name, although I recognize your surname. Any connection to the witches over in Willow Tree Falls?" Mr. Part Dragon said.

"Possibly." Zandra looked down at me, and I nudged her leg to encourage her to keep talking. She was the worst at making polite conversation, but Mr. Part Dragon had overstepped, so a dash of coolness should be expected.

She rolled her eyes when she realized I wanted her to make nice then glanced at the guy. "I'm kind of related to them. My dad married a Crypt witch. He took her surname, and I took the Crypt name. That's it."

He nodded. "I'd do the same if I got hitched to a Crypt witch. Those ladies have power. But I have a question."

"Make it quick. You've left me a mess to clear up, and I have more hedgehogs to see to."

"The Crypt witches deal with demons. Why are you catching hedgehogs and not demons?"

"Demons aren't my thing. And I like animals." Zandra smiled at me and winked.

He nodded, his gaze full of interest. "Me, too. I've even got a couple of barns at my place set up to look after any injured animals I find when out walking. I hate to see any creature in distress. You must be the same when you come across animals in your work. It's a tough job."

Zandra uncrossed her arms and checked the hedgehogs. "I guess so, but I've only been doing this job for a few days."

The guy stuck out his hand. "Well, new girl, let's start over. I'm Torrin Conner. I own the repair garage on the edge of Crimson Cove. Have you seen it?"

Zandra hesitated but finally took his hand and gave it a single shake. "I've driven past. I know someone who lives in Crimson Cove, so I often visit."

"You're not new to town? Pity, I was going to suggest we get a drink and I show you around." Torrin gave her an easy smile that made my tail twitch. This part dragon was flirting with my witch.

Zandra stiffened. "I don't need showing around. I know everything about Crimson Cove."

Torrin pursed his lips. "If you've got a local job, does that mean you're moving here?"

She went back to studying the hogs. "You ask a lot of questions."

"I'm a curious guy. And I like to know when someone new moves into my town."

"Your town?" Zandra folded her arms across her chest again. "You think you own this place, do you?"

Torrin chuckled again and rubbed the back of his neck. "Someone has to."

"Why would that be? From everything I know about the place, it's a sleepy town. Nothing happens here."

His easy smile faded. "Who's been telling you that?"

"Just about everyone."

I bit my tongue to stop from correcting Zandra. She was my perfect witch but was a loner and terrible at making friends. Since we'd been here, she hadn't gone out of her way to chat to the neighbors.

Her messy upbringing, thanks to her mother, Adrienne, and the fact Zandra used an aging spell on herself when she was eight-years-old meant she'd missed important formative years. That included everything from education to dating, and her social skills left a lot to be desired.

It was also why I was keen on my witch getting safe experience with a guy who wasn't a toad in disguise. Of course, I'd keep an eye on any bow-chicka-meow-meow going on and bring out my murder mittens if anyone overstepped the line, but we all had to learn. The best way to do that was by doing. Practice made perfect.

Torrin rocked back on his heels. "I don't want to scare you, but you shouldn't believe everything you've been told. Sure, Crimson Cove is cute, but like every place full of magic, it has its secrets."

"Care to share those secrets?" Zandra said.

"Happy to over a drink. We can get dinner, too."

"No, thanks."

"You don't eat dinner?"

"Of course. But I need to take that ruined cage back to my boss and explain what happened. He won't be happy."

"Barney Hoffman?"

"That's the one."

"Don't worry about old Barney. I know him. You tell him what I did, and he can bill me. He knows where I work, and it won't be the first time I've messed with one of his operations." Torrin looked highly amused with himself.

Zandra didn't look impressed by his bravado, and she had good reason not to.

She needed to make a good impression with Barney, so we kept this job and could keep looking for Adrienne, who was missing under suspicious circumstances after leaving an odd message, a letter, and a chest full of magic for Zandra. Adrienne was the dictionary version of a hot mess, and

I was determined Zandra wouldn't follow in her peep-toed footsteps.

"I'm not making the best impression on you, am I?" Torrin said after a moment of awkward silence.

Zandra looked at the cage. "Can't say you are."

"It's a problem of mine, especially when the dragon is in charge." He rubbed at his concealed scales. "I blundered in on your operation, ate your hedgehogs, and damaged your property. I'm a jerk."

Her sharp expression softened. "My half-sister had issues with a demon. He'd take control and get her in trouble, so I know it's not easy to balance power."

"No kidding?"

"It's not a problem now." Zandra pressed a hand against her chest. "Her family looked out for her. And I got the hedgehogs back unharmed, and they're contained. That's all I wanted out of this evening."

"Are you sure I can't tempt you to dinner?" Torrin said.

My stomach grumbled rather embarrassingly, and I scurried away to inspect a shadow.

"Your familiar is hungry. I didn't get her name," Torrin said.

"It's Juno. And she's not hungry either," Zandra said.

"I am," I muttered, wondering if a nearby mushroom was edible.

"Besides, we need to take these captives to holding and complete the paperwork. It'll be a late night for us," Zandra said.

"Another time, then?"

"Maybe. I'll see you around."

"Let me give you a hand with those hogs." Torrin walked over, but Zandra was already shooing him away.

"We've got this. Thanks, but you can go." She grunted as she lifted the cage a few inches off the ground.

I dashed over and shuffled underneath, using a little magic to hoist it up. I trotted along with it on my back, taking most of the weight, while Zandra balanced the cage from behind.

"Watch out for any rogue prickles shooting out." I held my breath as a whiff of sparkly hog stink drifted around me.

"The hogs are quiet. Probably still stunned from being eaten by a dragon."

"Hope to see you again soon, Zandra and Juno," Torrin called out.

Zandra grunted a response, while I could do nothing but focus on my magic and hope it held. Otherwise, I was getting squished.

We got to the van, opened the back, and safely stored the hogs. Then we collected the smaller cages and equipment and stacked them away, ensuring the hedgehogs were safe and not too stressed.

My stomach growled again as we got into the cab.

"Sorry about making you miss dinner." Zandra pulled out a soft, chewy chicken stick from the glove box and passed it to me.

I grabbed it and chewed. "We had work to do. Hedgehogs wait for no witch and her magical familiar."

She checked the time. "I'll let Barney know we've finished for the night. Then I promise we'll go home, put our feet up, and pig out."

I sighed as I finished the last of my chew. That sounded heavenly.

Zandra opened a connection on her mobile snow globe and contacted Barney. It rang multiple times before his red face appeared on the screen.

"Zandra! It's late. Is everything okay?"

"It's great. We tracked down the hedgehogs. We've got them, and I'm taking them back to holding."

Barney's image fogged, and he swiped his hand over the globe on his end. "I knew you could do it. Great work." There was a splashing sound, suggesting Barney was taking his call from the bath. "Any problems?"

Zandra hesitated, and I could see her warring with herself over whether to disclose the dragon issue or the fact she got a face full of poisoned quills.

"It went smoothly. A cage got damaged, but the person responsible has agreed to pay for the repairs."

"Excellent, excellent. A good day's work. And you'll be pleased to know I've got a new job for you. I've had three calls about the same household. There's a misbehaving hellhound in residence."

My ears pricked at this news. I'd had multiple run-ins with hellhounds over my time, not just while in cat form, and they could be difficult. Powerful, fire-breathing, unstable fuzzy nightmares. Well, most of them.

"Is it urgent? I can drop by now if you like." Zandra shot me an apologetic look.

"No, absolutely not. You've done enough. Deal with the hedgehogs, get some rest, and you can tackle the hellhound first thing tomorrow."

They said goodbye, and Zandra ended the call. "No hellhound for us tonight. Shall we go home?" She looked at me and smiled.

I nodded. From magic propelled prickles and arrogant half-dragons to furry, fire breathing punks. This new job was proving enlightening. And we'd be ready for it all tomorrow.

Chapter 3

Headless in Crimson Cove

"Everyone has a busy day, and I should know, since I set your work schedules, so I won't keep you long." Barney Hoffman looked at the assembled group sitting at the table in the main office of animal control.

Sitting with me and Zandra were two work colleagues, Glenda Ridgeback and Oleander Yockley. The rest of the team was already out on emergency calls.

"Zandra, you've got the hellhound noise complaint to deal with first thing." Barney looked at the list of jobs on the table in front of him. He'd been doing this job for over thirty years and was a big old grizzly bear of a man with a soft heart and a gruff voice.

Oleander grimaced, his moist lips smacking together. "The last hellhound I dealt with singed my eyebrows. If it weren't for my extensive experience of being so awesome, I'd be dead. I barely escaped with my life. I have a scar to prove it." He pushed up one sleeve to show a freckle.

"You take the job then, since you're so experienced with hounds." Glenda was a tiny slip of a woman, just brushing five feet tall, thin, with high cheekbones and eyes that glinted amber in certain lights.

I couldn't be certain, but I'd have gambled fifty fishy treats there was a dash of werewolf in her family history.

"Nah. We let the new girl take this one," Oleander said. "Barney's been singing her praises so much, she needs to be put to the test to make sure her success isn't just down to blind luck."

"Settle down." Barney gestured for quiet. "We all take turns dealing with the more demanding cases. I expect this is simply a case of the hellhound being left alone for too long. He's probably pining for his owner. The hound is called Archie, and we've been out to this address before. His owner can be... a touch stubborn."

"Archie is pining for a fresh hunk of meat to show up." Oleander grinned at Zandra.

Glenda elbowed him hard in the ribs. "Quit being a jerk, or you'll be picking up extra shifts because Zandra walks. If that happens, you're doing the midnight shift for a month."

"He's not putting me off," Zandra said smoothly. "And I've dealt with worse than hellhounds. My half-sister has a troublesome hellhound as her familiar, so I'm used to them."

Oleander's pale green eyes narrowed. "Your sister is Tempest Crypt, right?"

Zandra nodded. "Her hellhound has issues. He's dangerous."

I briskly washed my face to hide my expression. Zandra often pulled out bragging rights about being associated with the Crypt witches, even though it was through marriage rather than blood. And as for the terrifying hellhound, Wiggles was a miniature talking hound with a gas problem. He was hardly the monstrous creature Zandra made him out to be. But he was a hellhound of sorts, so she wasn't being totally dishonest.

"If you think this task is too much for you, Zandra, I will come with you," Barney said.

"No, I can handle it. And I know you have the inspection report to finish."

"I do. You've got my details, so any problems, get in touch and I'll be right with you," Barney said.

"Juno and I will deal with the hellhound. We don't need any help." Zandra shot Oleander a filthy look, which I mirrored.

Barney didn't hide his relief at getting off hellhound duty. "Depending on how long that takes, I've got another job in that area. A family reported seeing blue-winged scarabs, the ones with teeth that eat flesh. So far, they haven't been a problem, but it's getting close to the full moon, and they cause trouble around that time."

"So long as the hellhound doesn't eat you or burn you alive, it sounds like you're in for another easy day," Oleander said.

Glenda elbowed him again. "Make sure this jerk gets the worst jobs." She looked at Zandra and rolled her eyes.

Zandra flashed up her eyebrows but didn't respond. My witch was still cautious about being part of this team, although Glenda had been an ally since we'd started and was quick to stamp on Oleander when he behaved like a cretin.

I tried not to hold it against him. This team went up against terrifying animals all the time. If you didn't use gallows humor when facing death, you didn't survive. He should just direct his poor quality humor away from my witch.

"Oleander, you've got the job with the clawed owlettes to finish, and there was a report of a pink horned stallion in the woods again. It's the third time this month. There were three separate accounts from reputable sources, so there's something out there, but we've yet to figure out what it is," Barney said.

"Once I'm done with the owlettes, I'll sweep the woods and see if anything shows up," he said.

"Excellent. Glenda, the team in Echo Park could do with backup. They bagged three spiny horned toads, but there are more out there. I've had complaints. They're breeding, so we have to stop that. When they squeal during mating, it pierces eardrums, so we can't have a population explosion in a public place."

"Make sure you don't kiss any toads while looking for your Prince Charming," Oleander said. "I know how desperate you are to get a ring on that finger."

"I won't. I know what a real toad looks like when I see one." Glenda's gaze ran slowly over Oleander several times until he looked away, squirming in his seat.

Glenda smirked. She had his number.

I liked her. She talked straight and meant business. She was a possible new friend for Zandra.

"I've got three calls to deal with this morning and the report," Barney said. "I'll check in with you all early afternoon, but then I'm heading to the Eastward Sanctuary. They're looking to expand and have asked for recommendations."

We all nodded. Barney oversaw animal control for the entire district and was often needed in more than one place at the same time. He was a solid guy but constantly pulled in different directions. He was capable, although a little stressed, and prone to tripping over his own feet, but he had my respect. And he was a steadying influence on Zandra, an almost father figure I approved of.

There were a few more minutes of discussion about equipment and routes to take, then the team broke up.

Glenda patted Zandra's shoulder as she passed her seat. "Don't worry about Oleander. He's having a bad day. Most of his days seem bad, though. You'll be great with the hellhound. I've met Archie a few times, and he's a sucker for a milk bone. Just watch out while you're in that neighborhood, though. It's rough. Make sure you secure the van once you get out, or it won't be there when you return."

"Thanks for the tips," Zandra said. "It's one of the few parts of Crimson Cove I've never visited."

"Any time. Hope to see you with your eyebrows intact tomorrow." She grinned at Zandra, winked at me, then left the room.

Oleander followed her shortly, grumbling to himself.

Barney collected his papers and walked out of the room with me and Zandra. "Sorry if you got a rough ride back there. I've warned Oleander several times about his behavior, but he has such a way with the animals that I can't afford to lose him."

"That's because he's part animal," I said.

Barney chuckled. "Maybe you're right. He's rough around the edges."

I looked up at Barney in surprise. "Oleander has the scent of a golden jackal about him. Haven't you noticed?"

Barney's jaw dropped. "A... golden jackal? He never mentioned being part anything on his application. That should have been declared. Oh! This is bad news. He lied to me."

Zandra pursed her lips and gave me a stare. Had I deliberately landed Oleander in trouble? Was it no more than he deserved for sassing my witch? I made no comment.

Barney scrunched the papers he held. "I should report this. Is there even a record of his animal magic? How could I have missed this?" His gaze went to the floor, and sadness flickered across his face.

"Don't worry, Barney. He's not a complete magical creature. He may only be one-third jackal. I don't think he can change shape." I looked at Zandra and flicked my tail. She had to know I'd defend her from that creep.

"It actually explains a lot. Oleander hates jobs that involve small furries. It must trouble his chase instinct if something small runs from him." Barney shook his head. "I should have noticed. I would have done, if it weren't for..."

We waited for him to continue, but he remained silent.

"He doesn't have a familiar. That's a clue he's different," I said.

"Not every magic user has a familiar," Zandra said. "We don't all find our perfect fit."

I rumbled a purr. I had. Zandra was perfection. "The smell was also a giveaway."

Barney's brow furrowed. "True, true. I thought that odor was because he only showered weekly. It's something he's proud of. He does it to save water."

"Gross," Zandra muttered.

Barney slumped against the wall. "I don't know what to do with this information. He's excellent at his job, but is it safe to keep him on the staff?"

Zandra looked at me and shrugged. "His jibes don't bother me. If Oleander does his job and doesn't cause trouble, why get rid of him? I know you have trouble recruiting to these roles, so just keep him clear of the small furries so his jackal side doesn't come out and bite."

Barney scrubbed a hand down his face. "Perhaps you're right. I wish he'd told me, though. I demand honesty from my team."

"Is that why you were honest with me when it came to the midnight shifts and how crazy hectic this job would be?" Zandra arched an eyebrow and settled a hand on one hip.

Barney had the decency to blush. "Well, perhaps leniency on my part could be extended. But I will speak to him. This will have to go on his record."

"Just keep Juno's name out of it," Zandra said. "She doesn't want Oleander stalking her because he's angry about her sniffing him out."

"He can stalk away. I'd bat him into the ground with a single paw." I slashed a murder mitten through the air.

Zandra chuckled and tickled my head. "I reckon you would."

We collected the information about Archie the hellhound from Barney and left the office. He locked the door and followed us to the van.

"I'm sure you'll be able to handle this case. Archie's owner, Osorin Greenbow, can be difficult, though. He's got a record. Small-scale theft and evading capture by Angel Force. He loves Archie, though. They're magically bonded, so he's not being willfully neglectful, just slow on the uptake. It won't be the first time he's heard from us."

I wrinkled my booping snooter, not sure it would be as simple as that. My dealings with hellhounds often ended in complications, even the smelly miniature talking hound Zandra's half-sister owned.

"We'll work something out," Zandra said. "We all want to do right by our familiars."

A pained look echoed across Barney's face, then he fretted around us for a couple of minutes, checking the van and our equipment, like a dad sending his child off to big school.

I liked his attention, but Zandra was gritting her teeth and bearing it. My witch didn't like anyone making a fuss, but it was nice to see someone caring for her. She hadn't had a lot of care during her early years.

I was certain Zandra would rule the magical community one day, but while she was making her way toward that pinnacle, she must accept her current role, and that was assistant animal warden being looked after by an over-protective bear of a man.

Finally, after several double-checks to make sure we had everything we needed, Barney left us alone.

We hopped into the van. I settled into my specially designed seat with harness and soft cushion, and Zandra fired up the steam powered engine. We didn't go far before she pulled into a parking spot.

"Let's get eats before facing off with this hellhound. How does scrambled eggs and smoked salmon sound?" she said.

"Like I'm in heaven."

Zandra unclipped my harness, and we headed into Bites and Delights. Sorcha Creer was serving, and there was no one waiting, so we got our order in right away.

"I heard you got the job with Barney. Congratulations. How's it going?" Sorcha was a cheery-faced, ginger-haired, part-vampire. Cute freckles covered her nose and cheeks, and she'd been quick to welcome us to Crimson Cove as soon as we'd arrived.

"Still going strong," Zandra said. "We're off to deal with a hellhound."

"I'm still amazed people have them as pets or familiars. I'd pick an adorable cat any time." She tickled me under the chin then washed her hands before turning her attention back to the food.

"We make the best familiars." My nose wriggled with pleasure as the eggs cooked, filling the air with a warm, buttery scent.

"Tinkerbell is at the back of the café if you want to say hi. You haven't met her yet, have you?"

My gaze flickered over Sorcha. Interesting. She must be part-witch too if she had a familiar. A vampire witch was unusual, but if she had more witch than vampire in her, she should be able to bond with a familiar.

Sorcha seemed to read my thoughts because she laughed. "I'm not all fang, sweetie pie. And it's not a true familiar bond, but Tinkerbell showed up one day at the back door, and she looked so forlorn and sorry for herself, I had to let her in. She never left. Just be warned, she has a tongue as sharp as her claws."

"So she's a pet, not a familiar?" I said.

"Nooooo. Tinkerbell is more than a pet. She's my best friend. I spend more time with her than any of my family. And she comes with neat tricks. Go say hi while you're waiting for the food."

I left Zandra and Sorcha chatting and discovered a plump black cat snoozing on a chair. I sniffed around her a few times, but I didn't want to disturb her slumber.

"What do you want?"

I lifted my head to discover one of her eyes was open. "Greetings. Sorcha sent me over."

"I'm sleeping."

"You're talking."

"In my sleep." The eye shut. "What are you doing in my café?"

"Isn't this Sorcha's café?"

Tinkerbell snorted. "I let her run the place. She's dumb enough to think she's in charge, so I let her."

"I don't see you doing any of the cooking."

"Why cook when I have a slave to do it for me?"

This was definitely not a familiar I wanted to spend time with. A key part of being a familiar was that you talked up your witch or warlock. You enabled them to be the best version of themselves, and you never criticized them. Well, rarely, and only when their life was in danger if they did something monumentally foolish.

Tinkerbell's left eye opened again. "I hear your witch got a job trapping animals and killing them."

"If you mean Zandra Crypt, the most incredible witch you'll ever have the privilege of meeting, then yes, she has the title of assistant animal control warden. And she doesn't kill or put anything down. She looks after the vulnerable. She protects them, and—"

"Yeah, yeah. We all know what animal control really does." Tinkerbell made a gagging noise and faked death for several seconds before sucking in a breath. "Monsters."

"You don't, since you have no idea what her work involves."

"I know enough to want nothing to do with her. And she can't keep coming into my café. She smells like frightened animals and unwashed armpits."

I bared my teeth and zapped Tinkerbell with a bolt of magic.

She leaped in the air and howled, her tail smoldering.

"Take that back," I snarled. "My witch smells like heaven."

"Hey! What's going on?" Zandra raced over, Sorcha behind her.

Tinkerbell ran away, her tail down and still smoking.

"Oh, Juno. Did you two fight?" Zandra said.

"She was being disrespectful about you." I jumped onto her shoulder. "I won't allow it. And she's not even a real familiar. Tinkerbell was mean about Sorcha. She called her a slave!"

Zandra turned to Sorcha. "I'm so sorry. Juno's usually great when meeting other familiars."

"You have nothing to apologize for," I said. "I'm within my rights to defend you."

Sorcha looked nonplussed. "Tinkerbell will be fine. She was probably crabby if you disturbed her sleep. I've been on the wrong side of one of her grumps. It's not fun." She rubbed her forearm.

Zandra still looked mortified. "We'd better take our order to go before you throw us out."

"I'd never do that. I'll get it ready for you. Won't be a minute." Sorcha hurried away to collect our food.

Zandra waited until Sorcha was out of earshot before speaking. "Juno, you shouldn't have done that. We've got to be careful. We have to stay friendly with as many people as possible so we can find out about what happened to Adrienne."

"You should have heard her, though." I shook my head, still smarting at Tinkerbell's rudeness.

"Even so, we bite our tongues and smile sweetly. If people realize we're troublemakers, they won't talk. Then we'll never figure out where Adrienne is hiding."

I wanted to protest, but I did as she told me and bit my tongue. But I wasn't apologizing to Tinkerbell.

That cat had deserved a butt shot of magic, and I'd give her another if she was rude about Zandra again.

Zandra paid for our food, collected the takeout cartons, and we hurried out of the café. She drove off, making sure I could reach my delicious smoked salmon and scrambled eggs while she steered.

As we approached our first job of the day, my mood became slightly less sullen thanks to a full belly and the distracting sound of a deep, rumbling bark of despair.

Zandra parked and stared at the house where the noise was coming from. "Someone is miserable."

I waited for my harness to be unclipped and then hurried out of the vehicle with her. The bark was one of distress, and the scratchy roar suggested Archie had been barking for a long time.

"I don't like that sound. It's unstable. We should call for backup." I tried to cut Zandra off so she didn't get closer to the tumbledown house.

"We'll take a look before we call Barney and show him how incompetent I am." Zandra marched through the open gate and headed to the small, single-story house with a faded lawn and broken wire fencing.

I hurried behind her, my stomach tight and my fur on end. There was something in the air that made me want to turn back, but I wasn't abandoning my witch.

There were scorch marks on the grass, suggesting Archie wasn't the best behaved hellhound, and big holes dug in the dirt.

Zandra knocked at the door, and the barking stopped. "Hello. This is animal control."

There was a deep rumbling growl right by the door, and I nudged Zandra back with my head.

She knocked again. "Is there anyone home? We need to talk to you about Archie. We've had noise complaints."

There was a single bark and then a whimper.

"You don't think he's been abandoned, do you?" Concern crossed Zandra's face as she headed to the window by the door and peered through.

Archie appeared, barking and throwing himself at the glass. He was a giant of a hound, with curly dark fur and huge fangs.

Zandra jumped back. "I don't see anyone inside. Let's try around the back. We'll break in if Archie has been abandoned."

I studied the hellhound as he flung himself at the glass, still trying to get us. "He's not angry. He's upset. Look at him." But Zandra had already disappeared, so I raced after her.

She was peering through another window. Her body tensed, and she made a strangled sound in the back of her throat. She staggered back, almost standing on my tail in her haste to get away.

I hopped onto the window ledge. My eyes took a second to adjust to the gloomy interior, but when they did, I spotted a sagging brown chair and a plate strewn table.

And a headless corpse.

Chapter 4

Angel Whip and Tail Nips

The body was on the floor in the living room. I was almost certain it was male. Despite the lack of head, thick hairy arms and a barrel chest were visible. His legs were bent, suggesting the victim had dropped to his knees and slumped against the wall after losing his head. He wore dirty blue jeans and a gray checked shirt.

I glanced away from the disturbing scene to check on my witch. Zandra looked pale and was breathing too shallowly.

"I didn't imagine that, did I?" She drew in a deep, shuddering breath. "There's a body in there."

With a nimble bounce, I leaped off the window ledge and curled around her legs several times, sending calming magic her way. "Yes. There's a body."

"And there was no head on that body?"

"Technically, there are bits of head splattered all around the room."

Zandra groaned and dipped her head in between her knees. "How did that happen? Did Archie attack him?"

"From the splatter pattern, I'd suggest it was an internal explosion rather than an animal attack. And if Archie had attacked him, why didn't he eat his victim? From my quick inspection, I saw no bite marks on the corpse."

Zandra groaned again. "How can you be so calm when talking about something so nasty?"

"This isn't my first dead body."

She looked up at me. "It isn't?"

"I've lived longer than you, so I've seen a few things." Zandra didn't know my true age or form. I'd always planned on telling her once we were settled, but after more than a decade of happiness, I didn't want to scare her away or make her look at me differently. I'd tell her soon. But not now. Not with a headless body to deal with.

A thud against an interior wall made me jump. "Archie hates us being out here. He thinks we're trouble."

"He must hate being inside with that corpse more. Archie might think we killed that person in there and are back to take him out." Zandra gathered herself and slowly stood. She didn't look through the window again. "We can't leave Archie. If that was his owner, then no one's been feeding him or giving him water. He must be so stressed and confused."

"Archie could also have seen what happened, so we need to talk to him."

Zandra grimaced. "Poor hound. No one needs to see that."

Archie thudded against the wall again, making the glass wobble in its frame.

"You'll have to sedate him if we bring him out," I said.

"There are sedation potions in the van. I'll grab one." Zandra glanced at the window, shook her head, then dashed away.

I took a moment to look around the yard while I waited for her to return. The place had an air of quiet despair and abandonment. The owner cared little about his home. From what I'd glimpsed of Archie, though, he looked well fed and cared for.

My gaze shifted from the house to the neighboring homes. Some of them were in better condition, but they all looked tired. Curtains were twitching, but no one had come out to see what we were doing. It suggested poor community spirit. People most likely kept to themselves or preferred to make complaints to animal control or Angel Force.

Zandra returned with a potion bottle. "This'll do the trick. It's super strength and will take down anything. Now, we just need to figure out how to get it on Archie without losing any limbs."

There was another thud from inside the house, a tortured howl, and the hellhound head-butted the glass. A long, thin crack appeared.

"Archie! Calm down. We're not here to hurt you. We're getting you free." Zandra stood in front of the window, her hands out.

Archie hit the glass again, and the crack lengthened.

"Move!" I charged into Zandra just as Archie slammed into the window. It shattered, and glass sprayed everywhere.

The hellhound roared and leaped through the broken pane. He landed with a thud on the dirt, and his crazed eyes rolled around in their sockets.

I stood in front of Zandra, my fur puffed out and magic sparking off me. "Be calm, hound. We mean you know harm. We're from—"

"Animal control," he growled out. His voice was rusty, and he was drooling. "You want me dead, too?"

"No! We're here to help you," Zandra said.

"Put me in a cage, you mean? I'm not leaving my home or my warlock. Have you seen him? He's... he's gone. His head. It vanished. One second, he was pacing and talking, and the next, boom. Destroyed." Archie tipped back his head and howled at the weak sun.

I pressed a paw on Zandra's foot to ensure our magic was connected, and I could keep her calm when faced with such a tortured beast. Although a thread of panic ran through her, she wasn't terrified. She was steadily taking in the situation.

This hellhound needed support. He was terrified, panicked, and couldn't make sense of what had happened. "I'm Juno. This is Zandra. And yes, we work for animal control, but we want to help. What happened in there?"

Archie paced across the dirt, his gaze repeatedly flashing to the broken window.

"Do you know who did this?" Zandra's tone was soft. She only ever used her quiet voice on frightened critters. It soothed them.

Archie shook his head. "Just gone. Pop and he was down."

"He was shot by something?"

"Gunfire didn't cause that fatal injury," I said. "The man's entire head has gone. Maybe a destruction spell, but it would have needed to be powerful."

Archie tipped back his head and let out another painful howl.

I lowered my ears in a sign of sympathy, and we waited while he called out his misery for everyone to hear.

"Archie, that's your name, isn't it?" Zandra said. "Let us help make things right. I've got something to keep you calm."

"You want to drug me, shackle me, and kill me," Archie roared.

I raised my hackles, but before I flared my magic, Zandra hurled the potion at Archie. It hit his side and coated his fur in a sticky dark purple liquid.

He staggered from side to side, his howl weakening. He slumped down and closed his eyes, letting out a throaty wheeze and what sounded like a sob of despair.

We waited a moment to make sure Archie was under then headed to his slumbering form.

Zandra caught my eye, and her mouth twisted to the side. "I know, lobbing the potion wasn't the best move, but Archie was out of control, and I thought he was about to attack. I figured the potion would absorb into his skin. It worked faster than I expected."

"When he wakes, I'll get him to see sense. Then he won't see us as the enemy." I jumped onto the hound's back and licked his head. "He's too insane with grief to understand what's going on. We'll get him out of here, give him time to sleep it off, and then I'll explain everything."

Zandra stared at the broken window. "The trouble is, we don't know everything that happened here. This wasn't what I expected to find when reprimanding someone about their noisy hellhound. How are we supposed to figure this out? And what will Barney say?"

"Barney will understand. He wouldn't have sent you if he expected a headless corpse and an enraged hellhound looking for blood." I kept licking Archie. He tasted like slightly spoiled meat, and he was sweaty, but he'd find the licks comforting, and my tongue could handle the tangy aftertaste.

"Whoever rang in the complaint probably only heard Archie barking and didn't poke around in case they annoyed Osorin. Barney said he wasn't an easy guy to get along with. If they'd seen the body, they'd have called Angel Force and not us."

I nodded but kept licking. After a few minutes, Archie's breathing evened out, and he gave a huge sigh, his body relaxing. "We can move him now. Let's get Archie in the back of the van."

Zandra used a levitation spell to move the giant hound, and within a minute, he was safely secured in the largest cage. He had food and water, and Zandra even tucked a blanket around him. My tough on the outside witch had a gooey marshmallow inside when it came to animals.

She kneeled outside Archie's cage. "Poor guy, to lose his bonded warlock in such a gruesome way. How did it happen? People's heads don't simply explode."

"I've heard of a voodoo spell that can blow someone's head off."

"You know voodoo?" Zandra climbed out of the van and walked away slowly with me beside her.

"I know a thing or two about everything." Being around for over five hundred years gave me plenty of time to pick up useful information.

We went back to the house and looked through the broken window, being careful not to touch any glass.

Zandra swallowed noisily. "There are bits of him all over the room. Even on the ceiling."

"Just like Archie described. Pop and his head disappeared." The smell of putrefying person turned my stomach. Still, I looked around. If I ignored the gruesome bits, everything else was grubby. There were dirty plates on surfaces and many mugs lying around. There was a clear track of dirt along the carpet going from the main door into what was most likely the kitchen.

"Is that a dog's collar around his neck?" Zandra said.

I peered closely at the body. "It could be. It's some kind of leather strap."

"It looks more like a belt than something you'd wear around your neck."

I tilted my head. "Why would a person need a collar? Only animals wear collars."

"Not all of them." She gave me a tart look, which I ignored. We'd had a long conversation about me wearing a collar. Zandra argued that, if I got lost, someone would bring me back thanks to the information on the collar. I'd argued I could find my own way home. The dispute ended with me giving a firm no, and Zandra not speaking to me for a few hours. She didn't like the fact she'd wasted money on buying me a collar with my name on it, but it was purple and sparkly, and I was more of a red velvet kind of cat.

"I need to let Barney know about this." With reluctance, Zandra pulled out her mobile snow globe. "Hey, Barney. Um... we've run into a problem with the hellhound."

My cat hearing easily picked up the other side of the conversation.

"It's Osorin, isn't it? Tell him this is his final warning. He can't keep taking liberties with animal control," Barney said.

"It's not Osorin. Well, it most likely is Osorin. Or rather, it was." Zandra took a breath. "We've had to take Archie."

"Oh! Was he vicious toward you?"

"No. Well, sort of, but I understand why he behaved aggressively." Zandra sucked in another breath. "Osorin is dead."

"Did you say dead?"

"Yes. It was the reason Archie was so distressed. And from the smell, Osorin's been dead for at least a day. Archie was trapped inside the house with his corpse."

There was a long stretch of silence. "Have you called Angel Force?"

"No. I... err... shouldn't you do that?" The unwillingness in Zandra's voice was clear, and I knew why. She had a complicated history with Angel Force, the angels who managed law enforcement around these parts.

"I can contact them. They'll need to know about the body. Even if it was a natural death or an accident, they have to be told."

"Looking at this scene, I'm certain it wasn't a natural death." Zandra tugged on the ends of her hair.

"What makes you say that?" Barney said.

"Osorin's missing his head. Well, his head has been splattered all over the living room."

Barney made a sound halfway between a snort and a yelp. "You think it was a murder?"

"I'm no expert, but I've never seen a natural death like this. I've not seen much death, though, but even a rooky would think this suspicious."

"Then the angels must be informed. I'll contact them. You stay there. How is Archie?"

"He was distressed, obviously. We've got him in the back of the truck, and he's asleep."

"Good. Don't go near the body. If a crime has been committed, the angels will need to assess the situation."

"Of course. I won't go in. I don't want to," Zandra said. "I can see enough through the broken window."

"Oh, this is terrible. You've only just started working for me, and I've given you a dead body. You're not going to quit on me, are you?"

Zandra pressed her lips together. She looked at the broken window and then at the truck containing Archie. "I'm going nowhere. Sure, this was a shock, but my duty is to make sure the hellhound is settled and safe. That's what I intend to do. My job."

The relieved sigh from Barney came through loud and clear. "You're an angel, too. Sit tight. Someone will be with you soon."

Zandra ended the call and put her mobile snow globe in her pocket. "Like I'd want to be an angel."

I nodded along in sympathy. Angel Force had a motley reputation, and Zandra had skated close to breaking their rules numerous times. It wasn't her fault she'd broken a few rules when learning how to be an awesome witch. She'd had no real magical education when young, and no idea how powerful she was. That meant several explosive situations the angels had poked around in and asked questions.

Of course, once I became involved as her bonded familiar, I'd successfully diffused all troubles. And with the support of the Crypt witches, Zandra's magic was stable. With my guiding paw on the magical helm, she rarely encountered a problem with the angels more than once a year.

"What are you doing out here?"

We turned to see a stout woman in a flowered housecoat, her hair in curlers, peering at us over the broken wire fence.

Zandra hurried over. "We're from animal control. Did you call about the noise from the hellhound?"

"Maybe I did, maybe I didn't. You can leave anonymous tips, you know. Did you break that window? I heard glass shattering." She was peering over Zandra's shoulder, having to stand on her slippered tiptoes to do so.

"No. That was Archie. He was distressed about being trapped inside."

"He's not trapped now, is he? I saw you load him into that van. You'll put him to sleep?" The woman's snub nose wrinkled.

"No. We're helping him. And you are..."

"Looking out for my neighbors. Are you really from animal control?"

"Here's my badge."

The woman barely glanced at the badge Zandra offered her. "That looks fake. You don't look like the usual animal loving type."

"There's a type?"

"Yes. Odd looking. Usually needs a good wash. Hairy."

"You're describing a yeti," I said.

The housecoat wearing neighbor marched around the fence and through the gate. "What are you really doing here? Filling that van with Osorin's things, I suppose? Are you stealing?" She scurried past Zandra.

"Of course not. But you shouldn't be here." Zandra dashed after her, but the woman was faster than she looked. She skipped to the window and peered inside.

She yelped and staggered back. "Oh, my word. What happened? Did you kill him?"

"No! We found him like this. Please, go back to your house. You can't help. This is a crime scene, and I'm waiting for Angel Force to arrive. Then they'll deal with everything."

The woman was backing away, her shaking finger pointing at Zandra. "Osorin wasn't the nicest neighbor, but you didn't have to take his head clean off."

"I didn't! I found him like this. Wait, let me explain." She chased after the neighbor, but the woman was dashing away as fast as her slippered feet would allow her.

"I've got this. You stay back and keep an eye out for the angels arriving." I overtook Zandra and dashed after the woman, temporarily distracted by the wobbling bobbles on her fluffy slippers. But I wasn't here to play. I was here to enthrall. It had been one of my talents when I'd been worshipped by the masses. Well, so long as you discounted that goblin jerk, Nalak, who'd turned me into a cat. I could still pull on my ancient power to get people to love me. Although I had to pull hard to make it work.

If that failed, as my magic had a habit of doing, and I couldn't get this pink-slippered screamer to see things my way, I'd knock her out. That was always an effective way to ensure compliance.

She looked over her shoulder and squeaked when she realized she was being pursued by a murder mittened mistress of magnificence. "Hellllp! They're going to kill me."

I raced in front of the woman and made eye contact. "Forget what you've seen. You have no business being here. This was all a dream."

The woman's steps faltered. "But... the body. That witch! She killed him, didn't she?"

"No, you made a mistake." I pulsed power into my words as my pupils dilated, and I tugged the woman into my confidence.

She wobbled and took a step back, her eyes glazing. "What would you have me do?"

It was a favorite question all my worshippers asked, but it had been a while since anyone had said it to me. It felt so good.

"Forget what you saw. Focus on me. Worship and love me."

A soppy smile spread across her face. "I worship you."

"You never saw the headless corpse. You didn't see the witch, or think she was guilty of murder. All you saw was me. Do you understand?"

"No murder, no witch, only you."

"Perfect. Now..." For a second, my tail went numb, then a searing pain rocketed up my spine. I yelped, leaped in the air, and spun around to find a small, sharp-beaked turtle hanging off the end of my perfect white fluff pole. The pain intensified as the turtle tightened its hold. "Get off me, you devil!"

The turtle remained attached to my tail, his evil black pinhole eyes narrowed and his scaled limbs digging into the dirt so he could get a better purchase. Was this monster planning to bite off a chunk of tail?

I swiped at him with my claws, but the turtle was just out of reach, and every time I moved, he moved with me.

An ear-piercing scream shot through my brain. The slippered neighbor was no longer enthralled and was staring at Osorin's house in wide-eyed horror. "You monsters! I'm calling Angel Force. You'll be arrested. Chinook, don't let that cat go." She dashed away.

I couldn't follow her because I had Chinook, my turtle accessory, clamped to me. I bared my teeth and hissed at him. "How dare you assault me. Don't you know who I am?"

The turtle couldn't reply because he had a mouthful of my tail, so I had to assume the answer was no.

I batted my murder mittens at him. "Un-beak me this instant, or I'll turn you into a paperweight."

The turtle spat out my tail. "I know what you were doing with your weird, enthralling magic. You're a demi-beast. Dangerous. Not to be trusted."

"I'm not a beast, you shell dwelling monstrosity. I'm a goddess." I caught my tail in one paw and examined it. It was bleeding. "I was helping your mistress, not harming her."

"Myrtle is a good one. You had no right to glamor her. Evil." The pond scum smelling miscreant hissed at me.

"I'm not a fairy. I don't glamor. Myrtle was under a simple enchantment." I licked my wounded tail. "I'm assuming Myrtle is yours? And you are... Myrtle's turtle?"

"Straight up correct, I'm Myrtle's turtle. The best turtle in the whole of Crimson Cove. I eat concealed demi-beasts for breakfast."

I checked over my tail again. "So I see. Well, Myrtle was panicking, and I had to calm her. You shouldn't have interfered. You've made things worse."

"For you. I was protecting her from you." He snapped his nasty little beak at me.

I licked the wound on my tail again to heal it. Although angry with Chinook, I understood his behavior. I'd do anything to protect Zandra. "You simply misunderstood. This situation is chaotic enough without your bonded witch making a mistake and accusing my witch of murder."

"Maybe your witch is a killer. She doesn't look friendly."

I glanced at Zandra, who was watching the action from a short distance away. "Her resting face is simply a touch on the bitchy side. That doesn't make her a killer." I sniffed the air and got a hint of pond water and death. "You're fortunate I understand your motivation. Otherwise, all that would be left of you would be shell and roasted scales."

The turtle snapped his beak again, not intimidated by my, as he called it, weird magic.

"Is everything okay?" Zandra finally joined us, keeping a healthy distance from the evil snapping turtle.

"We have a situation," I said.

"Uh-oh. You couldn't convince the neighbor I didn't kill Osorin?"

"This miscreant failed my attempt." I jabbed a paw at the turtle, who was scuttling away to Myrtle's house.

Zandra rolled her shoulders and sighed. "Misbehaving hedgehogs, hysterical hellhounds, and now a homicide. We're making a terrible impression in this new job."

"Once we talk to the angels, they'll see sense." A rapidly approaching scuttling noise hit my ears. Unbelievable! Chinook was coming back for a second bite.

I zapped him with magic and raced away, but he kept snapping at me. He was fast for a little guy with stumpy legs. His bad attitude must make him speedy.

"Myrtle is upset and crying inside. It's your fault." Chinook kept running and snapping, so I kept throwing spells and dodging him.

My wonderful witch intervened just before I got another bite on my tail. She scooped me up, gently nudged Chinook away with her foot, and then jogged back to the corpse house.

I hissed at Chinook, who quickly lost ground and stopped his pursuit. After making an obscene gesture at me with his stubby tail, he turned and scurried to Myrtle's house.

Zandra scratched my cheek and rested her head on my side. "That turtle hates you. It's weird, but it feels like trouble keeps following us around."

Having a mangled tail, an insane hellhound to handle, and the unwelcome arrival of Angel Force to deal with soon, I couldn't disagree with her.

Chapter 5

Turtles, lies, and alibis

Ten minutes later, two angels arrived on enormous wings, dressed in white as they descended from the sky. As always, they landed in a showy display of strength and power, their wings outstretched and one hand fisted and resting on the ground as if they were superheroes. Which was impossible. Everyone knows superheroes come with fur.

Zandra's association with them biased my opinion of Angel Force, but I didn't disagree with her that they were difficult to handle. They were bumbling rule followers, slow to react, and generally wrong when making assumptions.

The angels stood, folded their wings against their backs, and took in the scene.

I sat on Zandra's shoulder and felt her muscles tense under my paws. I gave her cheek a comforting lick. She'd always been nervy around the angels, since they often pointed the finger in her direction whenever anything went wrong in our former home of Willow Tree Falls. Maybe some of those wrongs had been her fault, but my witch needed to learn how to use her powers. If one or two trees got blown up or things changed color or vanished while she practiced her magic, it was hardly her responsibility.

The larger of the two angels, surprisingly with sandy brown hair rather than the usual angel blond, stepped forward. Although dressed in the pristine white uniform of Angel Force, he looked rumpled, as if he'd slept in his uniform. He also had a day's stubble on his firm jaw, and his eyes were black rather than blue. Most intriguing. A different kind of angel?

"We had a call about a witch killing someone," he said. "What's your reason for being here?"

"Coo-eee! Over here. I made that call." Myrtle was unhelpfully lingering by her front door. She pointed at Zandra. "She's the killer. Arrest her. And her mangy cat attacked Chinook. He's shell-shocked."

I hissed at Chinook, who was in Myrtle's hand, looking smug and like he needed to be transformed into a decorative box.

The stubble-faced angel focused on Zandra. "Is any of that true?"

She took a steadying breath. "No. I work for animal control. I was sent here because of a noise complaint. When I arrived, I discovered a hellhound trapped inside this house. The body was already in there."

The angel looked at his colleague, who'd been walking the yard. "We'd better check it out, Bertoli."

"There's a broken window around the side. You'll see everything from there if you don't want to mess up the scene." Zandra's hands were clamped behind her back, so only I could see they were fisted.

I licked her cheek again and nuzzled against her ear. "Relax. We've done nothing wrong."

"Tell that to the suspicious angels," she muttered out of the side of her mouth.

The sandy-haired angel paused. "Wait right here, miss..."

"Zandra Crypt."

His gaze went to me.

"I'm Juno. Zandra's familiar."

"Bertoli, you check the window. I'll look around the rest of the house. Don't go inside. Not until we've seen what we're dealing with." The angel marched away, and his colleague disappeared around the side.

"We should leave while they're busy," Zandra said.

"If we sneak off, Myrtle and her irritating turtle will sound the alarm. We stay. It'll look suspicious if we vanish. And we're innocent. We were doing a job and discovered a crime. We were going to call Angel Force, but the nosy neighbor got there before us."

"The nosy neighbor just put me in the frame for this murder." Zandra glared at Myrtle until she went back inside her house and shut the door.

Zandra paced the yard several times as we waited for the angels to return.

Bertoli came back first, and his typically handsome angel face looked drawn. His colleague joined him a moment later. They conferred for several minutes before walking over to us.

"I'm Finn, and this is Bertoli," the angel with the sandy-brown hair said. "You've gotten yourself into a situation, Miss Crypt."

"Not of my making," Zandra said. "Contact Barney Hoffman at animal control. He recently hired me, and he'll vouch for me."

Finn nodded as he jotted notes on a pad he'd pulled from his top pocket. "I know Barney. He's a good guy. Have you got ID on you?"

Zandra pulled out her assistant animal warden badge and showed it to them.

Finn made more notes on his pad.

Bertoli tilted his head as he studied Zandra. "You're not related to the Willow Tree Falls Crypt witches, are you?"

Zandra hesitated, and I understood why. The Crypt witches and Angel Force had a fractious relationship. It had taken her half-sister a long time to win them around, although these days, Tempest regularly helped them with their more difficult investigations. But to begin with, she'd been more of a thorn in their side.

Finn looked up when Zandra didn't answer. "No connection to them?"

"In a way. My dad married a Crypt witch."

"You have much to do with that side of the family?" Finn said.

"Now and again. Is that a problem? Those witches keep the demons off your back."

"They may do, but they also cause us trouble," Bertoli said. "I hope you're not a troublesome Crypt witch. We're already busy dealing with too many cases and don't need more problems coming to town."

Zandra's jaw flexed against me. "I'm only here to do my job. I don't want trouble."

"Don't mind Bertoli being moody. We've got a spate of armed robberies to deal with at the moment, and some creep in a weird mask robbed the hardware store not so long ago. Feathers are flying because we can't figure out who did it," Finn said.

"And it's not helped by this situation," Bertoli said.

"I'm sorry someone lost their head on your watch," Zandra growled out.

"Do you know Tempest Crypt?" Bertoli's tone wasn't friendly. "She's always stressing Dazielle."

Finn chuckled. "Oh, yeah! The stories Dazielle tells about that witch. I never know whether to believe her because they're so outrageous."

Zandra settled a hand on one hip. "Tempest has helped Angel Force solve more murders than you'll ever do. She's a talented witch."

Finn's eyebrows flashed up, but his expression remained amused. "Is that so? You two close?"

Zandra raised her chin and stared at the angels. "She's my half-sister, and I'll defend her against any rumors Dazielle spreads around. They're never true."

Most of them were very much fact-based, but now wasn't the time to disagree over something so insignificant.

Finn nodded. "Good for you. Always look out for family. So, what do you think happened here?"

Zandra blinked. "A guy is dead. That's all I can tell you."

"Talk me through what happened when you arrived. Did Barney send you on this job?" Finn said.

She nodded, and I felt her relax a fraction. That was good. Zandra didn't want to antagonize the angels, or they might go hard on her, especially Bertoli, who was still glowering at her like she'd stomped on his favorite flower.

"This was my first job of the day. I got here with Juno, and we looked around. We could hear the hellhound, Archie, barking as soon as we arrived. I knocked, but there was no answer. We looked through the window and saw the body."

"There's no hellhound inside the house," Bertoli said.

"He broke the window to get out. He was distressed, so I sedated him and put him in my van."

"You can communicate with him?" Finn said.

"Yes, he talks. I understand him."

"Archie is deep in his grief. Familiars take the loss of their bonded magic user seriously. It's like losing a part of yourself." I leaned against Zandra's head, a lump in my throat at the thought of ever losing my witch.

Finn made a note of what I'd said on his pad. He differed from the other angels I'd met. More organized for a start, but also less uptight and adorable looking if you liked feathers, stubble, and firm jawlines.

"Did Archie tell you anything useful?" Finn said.

"He was too upset to make much sense." Zandra rested a hand on my side, and I took a second to feed her calming magic. "He said it happened quickly. One second, Osorin was pacing and talking, and the next, his head was gone."

"How do you know who the victim is?" Bertoli flexed his wings.

"Osorin Greenbow lived here, and I planned to talk to him about his noisy hellhound. Archie is certain the body belongs to Osorin." Zandra half-shrugged. "I guess it could be someone else dead in the living room, but why would Archie make a mistake like that?"

"Why does Myrtle think you killed Osorin?" Bertoli said.

"Because she panicked and wouldn't listen to my explanation. Myrtle saw the body and assumed the worst about me."

"Maybe she didn't. Maybe you did it and then sedated Archie so he couldn't tell us the truth. Is the hellhound even alive?"

"Of course he is." Zandra tensed as she scowled. "I didn't know Osorin. Why would I kill a stranger?"

"That's for us to find out. This looks suspicious. Should we take her in?" Bertoli said to Finn.

I couldn't be certain, but Finn looked like he was holding back a smile. "Let's get some more information. Zandra is being helpful, and she's here for a legitimate reason. There's no point in arresting the wrong person. We don't want to look incompetent, do we? The boss is still smarting over the wrongful arrest of Avis Loolander after she was mistaken for a yeti."

"She was wearing a huge fur coat, and it was midnight! And she had that fluffy hat covering her face. How was I to know she was simply cold?"

Finn patted Bertoli's arm. "If we're going to arrest anyone, we need evidence to ensure we don't get it wrong. Unless you want to take a risk. Are you feeling lucky? Does Zandra seem like a murderer to you?"

Bertoli shook his head, his glare lasered on Zandra. "Let's keep asking questions."

I narrowed my eyes at him. I'd have to keep watch on this angel, in case he caused my witch trouble.

"So, you saw the body, figured it was Osorin, and then what?" Finn said to Zandra.

"Archie broke the window to get out. We kept him as calm as we could and then got him in the van once he was sedated. Then I called my boss."

"You didn't think to contact us?" Finn said.

Zandra let out a soft sigh. "I freaked out. It's not every day you show up to work and discover a headless corpse. I needed to know if there were protocols to follow."

"The usual protocol when finding a body is to call us." Finn lifted a hand. "But I understand if this was your first corpse. You weren't thinking straight."

I bit my tongue. What Zandra was most likely thinking was that she wanted nothing to do with Angel Force and their blunt approach to questioning.

"Right. I'll remember that for next time." Zandra's other hand rested on her hip.

Bertoli spluttered, while Finn simply laughed.

"Please, go on," he said. "What happened next?"

"I spoke to Barney, and he said he'd get in touch with you. Then Myrtle came out of her house. She looked through the window and started yelling."

"Do you know this neighbor?" Finn said.

"Never met her before. Never even been to this part of Crimson Cove until today."

"You're new to the area?"

"No, I've been visiting for a few years. I've got a family member who lives here, but I visit her and then go. This was my first visit to this street."

"And you, Juno?" Finn said.

"Where Zandra goes, I go. Who Zandra knows, I know."

"This is a rough part of town. It's possible Myrtle saw the body and figured you were somehow involved. People rarely visit for the friendly atmosphere," Finn said.

"Then she thought wrong. I can't be of any more help to you, and I've told you everything I know. I need to get going. Archie could wake at any moment, and I don't want him stressed and hurting himself by trying to escape." Zandra took a step back toward the van.

"We'll need to talk to him," Bertoli said. "He could have seen what happened. He'll tell us if you had anything to do with this murder."

"I didn't." Zandra sighed. "Archie won't be of any use to you for a while. We'll keep him at the animal control center until we can find him a permanent home, or Osorin's family can look after him."

"You'll have trouble there. If that is Osorin Greenbow inside, he doesn't have much close family. There's a sister nearby, but I don't think they're friendly with each other. And he's not married, so it won't be easy to find a place for the hound. Is he even safe to re-home?" Finn said.

Zandra tilted her head, her gaze turning interested as she looked at Finn. "I believe he's safe. It was hard to tell because he was so grief stricken, but I'll know more about his condition once he's slept off the sedation potion. My plan is to get him rehabilitated and re-homed."

Finn pulled out a small card and handed it to Zandra. "If things don't work out, get in touch. I can help."

Bertoli rolled his eyes and muttered under his breath.

"Something you want to say?" Finn swiveled his head toward Bertoli.

"No, nothing."

"Then put a sock in it. This isn't interfering in our investigation." Finn's tone was sharp.

Zandra showed me the card. *Creature Comforts Animal Rescue.*

I chirped my approval.

"You're different," Zandra said to him. "Not like the usual angels. Why is that?"

Finn grinned at her. "I'm unique."

We both snorted our disbelief.

He raised a hand. "And part of a special inclusion campaign. The angels got flak for being too strict with their criteria when recruiting, so they had no choice but to let me in or face a public scandal."

"We weren't too strict. There was simply a small misunderstanding of higher angel law when undertaking previous recruitment drives." Bertoli studied his white boots.

"Sure. That, too." Finn's expression was full of repressed laughter.

"I heard something about that. Only angels can still join Angel Force, can't they?" Zandra said.

"Dazielle has deputized Tempest loads of times," I said. "And she's mostly witch with a dash of demon, so there must be the option to relax their rules."

"Yeah, but that was only ever a temporary thing," Zandra said. "Angel Force only recruits full angels for permanent jobs."

"Not anymore. Providing you have a little angel in you, you're eligible to apply." Finn bent at the waist, a gleam in his black eyes. "I'm part angel, part demon."

My jaw dropped at the same time as Zandra's. The angels were fussy, exclusive snobs and didn't tolerate demons. To recruit someone who was a half demon was a shocker. They must have received serious flak to be forced into making that move.

Finn chuckled as he took in our reactions. "I know. Everyone is saying it's a huge leap forward for the angels. And it will be until one of us goes rogue. Isn't that right, Bertoli? I know you've got a little magic hidden under those wings you can use to take me out if I go all evil."

Bertoli grumbled to himself. "I've got no complaints about your methods of working, so long as you're good at your job."

"Was that what you said to our boss? Didn't you barge into her office and say you weren't working with a half-breed?"

"You didn't?" Zandra looked appalled.

"Let's not discuss that now, shall we?" Bertoli looked pointedly at us.

"Oh, let's! I'd love to hear a replay of that conversation," I said.

Finn shrugged as he tucked away his notepad. "If you have a problem with Archie, get in touch. I may have room for him. My rescue is small, though, so no promises."

She put away the card he'd given her. "Will do. Is it okay if we go now?"

"Sure. Thanks for the information, Zandra. And a word of advice: don't look into this any more than you have to. If that is Osorin inside, he was a troublemaker. He's known to us, mainly for petty stuff, but perhaps he got in over his head this time."

"Was that supposed to be funny?" Bertoli snapped, looking like he was still smarting at Finn's revelation of his prejudice.

Finn looked puzzled for a second and then grinned. "Hah! Sorry, terrible joke. What I meant was Osorin always wanted to run with the big guns, but he was lousy with magic and made mistakes. It didn't earn him brownie points with the local troublemakers. Perhaps things went wrong during his last attempt to make a criminal name for himself."

"I won't poke around anymore than I have to. But I have a question. What do you make of the collar around his neck?" Zandra said.

"I noticed that. A fashion accessory?" Finn said.

"It's an odd fashion accessory," I said.

"There's a trend going around involving collars in the bedroom. You know, kinky games," Bertoli said.

Zandra jerked her head back. "A kinky trend?"

Finn smirked. "Tell us more. Have you got experience with these games?"

Bertoli's face flushed scarlet. "Of course not! You... well, you get your partner to gently choke you with a noose or their hands. A belt would also work."

"How is that in any way pleasurable?" Zandra said.

"Um... something to do with being in control. It's powerful to hold someone's life in your hands." Bertoli waved a hand at the house. "I just thought perhaps Osorin had a friend who liked to..." His words failed him, thankfully.

"Drop by and choke him with a belt to get their kicks?" Finn couldn't hold in his laughter.

"He must have had a deeply disturbed partner if they enjoyed games like that." Zandra was also chuckling, and so was I.

"It's a theory. Finn's idea was just as stupid. He said the collar was a fashion accessory. I simply suggested..." Bertoli went back to studying his boots. "Forget it."

"I can't forget kinky bedroom play." Finn nodded at Zandra, his smile lighting up his dark eyes. "Where's the best place to find you?"

"You can try animal control. Or I'm renting Vorana Stowell's basement."

"Hey, my favorite bookstore lady. Perfect. We'll be in touch."

"Don't leave town," Bertoli said. "We'll have more questions for you."

"And we'll be happy to answer them." I resisted the urge to hiss at Bertoli. "We want this mystery solved as much as you."

He didn't look too happy about our cooperation. He was probably hoping for a fight, so he had a reason to arrest Zandra. You lose, buddy.

Finn lifted his eyes skyward then smiled. "Thanks for your time. You're free to go. But just in case you are our secret kink killer, stay around until we've gotten this cleared up."

Zandra sighed, but nodded. "Of course. I have no plans to go anywhere."

That made me happy. Despite the headless corpse and the snapping turtle, we didn't need any reason to leave Crimson Cove. There was too much unfinished business to deal with.

Chapter 6

Something's missing and a bond is formed

Zandra nursed a large mug of caramel mocha coffee while I sat outside Archie's cage. We'd been back at animal control for the rest of the day and most of the evening and had stayed with Archie to monitor him for signs of distress.

I was glad Barney hadn't insisted we go to another job. Although Zandra hid it well, she was stressed by discovering a headless corpse and then dealing with Angel Force. And when my witch got stressed, she needed down time, and she was terrible at taking it. But I'd put my paw down and insisted it was for Archie's benefit we remain here.

After a few protests, she'd agreed, and so had Barney, who'd fretted and worried until I'd hit him with a relaxation spell and gently encouraged him out to get cookies and fresh air.

"Those angels had better not pin this murder on me," Zandra said from her seat opposite the cages.

"They can try, but they'll fail. You didn't meet Osorin until today. Why murder him? And if you did, there would be bits of his brain all over you."

"Gross. I could have made him magically explode from a distance to avoid the brain splatter."

I masked my admiration for her belief in her power. My witch could do anything if she put her magic to it. "You still have no motive for wanting him dead." I focused on Archie as he heaved out a sigh. "He should be waking soon. Then we'll get answers about what happened to Osorin."

"Once Archie is awake, we need to call the angels. They'll want to question him."

I rested my chin on my paw. "The angels will get their chance, but we should help Archie to open up first. He'll trust us."

"He didn't seem too trusting at the house. If I hadn't hit him with the sedation potion, he'd have chewed through our throats."

"Archie would have seen sense before any dangerous chewing happened. He wasn't thinking clearly. I'd be the same if I lost you."

Zandra reached forward and petted my head. "My life before you wasn't much fun. It was kind of scary. You make life less scary. I'd be lost without you, too."

I purred at the compliment. "I spent too long with the wrong kind of magic users."

Her bottom lip jutted out. She knew about my past bondings with other magic users and how badly they'd failed. "They made you do terrible things."

"A few of them weren't so bad, but I've learned to look beyond the initial dazzle of power and seek the goodness in my magic user."

"I never thought of myself as good until you came along," Zandra said. "I was always told I was more trouble than I was worth by Adrienne."

I crinkled my booping snooter. "She only said that because your mother has her own demons to deal with."

"As we're discovering, since there's still no sign of her." Zandra leaned back in her seat. "Whenever I think about her, I get a bad feeling in my gut. Something's wrong, but I don't know what, and the letter she left me was hardly helpful. Has Adrienne run up too much debt in Crimson Cove, so she had to leave? Did her jerky landlord scare her off? And what job did she have lined up to pay for her mystery vacation?"

Adrienne had left so many questions behind when she'd vanished, and it was down to me and my witch to figure things out.

"We'll focus on finding her again soon. Let's deal with Archie, figure out what happened to Osorin, and then we can get back to finding your mother."

"Yeah, good plan." Zandra sipped her coffee. "I know I've asked you before, but why choose only powerful magic users to bond with? Familiars bond with witches of all levels of power."

I wrinkled my nose again as I considered my answer. Was now the right time to tell Zandra what I really needed from her, other than our powerful bond, belly rubs, and a limitless supply of fishy treats?

When I didn't answer, Zandra narrowed her eyes. "You're not a secret bad girl, are you? Have I been living with a dark infiltrator for a decade? What are you planning to do, take over the magic community?"

"Oh no, that's something I expect you to do."

She snort laughed. "I love your confidence in me. I have no interest in ruling over anyone, though. It's too much work. And I bet there'd be a ton of admin with a job like that. It wouldn't be all smiting, fine dinners, and magical clouds of amazingness."

"Perhaps. But I want you to have that choice. You could choose to control everyone with your power, or you could choose not to. Wouldn't that be delicious?"

"It would be stressful, and I want an easy life. All I want is to make sure I have a decent mug of coffee, you by my side, family members who don't cause me problems, and a roof over my head. And maybe free cookies for life."

I hopped up and walked over to her. "You've already got most of those things."

"Not the free cookies, and I still have the troublesome family. Even if I figure out what's going on with Adrienne, the Crypt witches will always be lurking around. Did you see the way Bertoli looked at me when he figured out who I was?"

"That wasn't because of you. Tempest has a reputation. You can't be responsible for her actions." I twirled around her legs. "Don't you want something more?"

"If more means complicated, then no. Why should I? Isn't this enough?"

I lifted my nose and looked around. It should be, and I had a good life with Zandra, but I remembered being worshipped, having power I could wield while barely thinking about it, sitting on a magnificent throne, and dictating what should happen in my Queendom. Once you've had so much, having it taken was traumatic. I wanted it back. But to do that, I needed Zandra's help.

"You know, you can tell me anything," she said softly. "There shouldn't be secrets between us."

"There won't be. Look! Archie is waking." I walked over to the cage but didn't miss Zandra's sigh. She knew I was hiding something, but it was for her own good. Zandra would understand once she knew everything about me.

"Archie, it's Juno. How are you feeling?" I kept my focus on the hellhound. He was our immediate concern.

He whined, and his eyes flickered open.

"I should call Angel Force," Zandra said.

"Soon. Archie's stressed, and bringing in the angels now could make him worse. They'd interrogate Archie and tip him over the edge. You know how fragile familiars are when a bond is broken. It can kill them. You don't want to be responsible for that, do you?"

"Of course not! Way to guilt trip a person. But we'll get in trouble if the angels find out we've questioned Archie without them being here."

"Since when were you afraid of a little angel trouble?"

"Since I became a responsible adult with a job I don't hate, a basement flat of my own, kind of, and a high maintenance cat to spoil."

I snickered. "I've been around for years."

"You're not denying the high maintenance part." Zandra joined me by the cage.

"If I did, I'd be lying." I leaned against her leg. "Leave the angels out of this for now. Archie's a petrified, grieving hound. He needs comfort and support, not quizzing by Bertoli. They can have their turn, but it's up to us to determine if Archie is fit for questioning. It's a part of your job."

"Is that so?" Zandra was smiling as she shuffled closer.

I flicked my tail. "If it's not in your job description, it should be. Barney would approve. Animals first. Always."

"Okay, I'm sold. Let's see if we can help him." Zandra sat cross-legged outside the cage. "Archie, my name's Zandra Crypt. We got you out of your house. Do you remember us visiting?"

He whimpered and hid his nose under one large, grubby, dark paw.

"It's fine to be scared and confused. You've been through a lot. But we need to know what happened in your home," Zandra said.

"It wasn't a nightmare, then?" he whispered. "My owner is dead?"

Zandra's face was full of concern. "We think so. Was that Osorin Greenbow?"

"Yes!" Archie whimpered. "He was so anxious and kept talking to himself. Nothing I could do would reassure him. Then his head... it vanished."

"Did you see it happen?" I said.

His body shook. "I did. I stayed with him because I was worried about him. People weren't kind to Osorin, but for all his issues, he was good to me.

We have a strong bond. Well, we had." A tortured sigh-groan came out of Archie. "The bond was torn away the second he died. It felt like someone ripped off my head, too. One second, the bond was full of life, and then it was stamped on. I'm tethered to no one. I have no one to care for. No one to care for me."

I risked putting a paw through the cage bars and touched Archie's muzzle. His magic quivered under my toe beans like a startled rodent. His heartbeat was fast and thready, and there was an unsteady throb to his power.

With a flick of my ears, I drew back and gestured my head, moving away from the cage. Zandra took the hint and followed.

"Is something the matter?" she whispered.

"It's Archie's magical vital signs. I'm not sure he's going to make it."

"We can't let him die. Not after everything he's been through. We have magic. We'll use it to keep him comfortable."

"Spells and potions will only keep him stable for a short time. He needs a tether."

"How about we sedate him again?"

"That would only be a temporary fix. And if Arche is sedated, he can't answer questions about what happened to Osorin."

Zandra bit her bottom lip. "What do we do? I'm not letting him die."

I looked back at the cage. Archie's eyes were closed, and he was panting. "He could bond with me via our connection. I'll share my power to keep him stable. I'm bonded with you, so I'll offer the same link to Archie. It won't be as stable as if he's bonded with a single magic user, but it should be enough to keep him going until he gets over the worst of his grief and we find him a home."

Her worried expression intensified. "You can share our bond?"

"I can. It won't be a problem." It used to be simple for me to use all magic, but since becoming a cat, my abilities weren't what they should be. Even simple magical tasks were draining. But I'd make things right for Archie.

"I'm happy to share our bond, if you are. Anything to keep Archie alive."

"Give me a few minutes with him. He may resist the bond, especially while grieving for Osorin. If he doesn't want to accept it, I'll have to force it on him, and that won't go so smoothly."

"Make sure he realizes this'll keep him alive. Maybe he won't fight so hard."

I looked back at the whimpering hound. The state Archie was in, I didn't think he wanted to live, but I was determined to give it my best shot.

I returned to Archie and rested a comforting paw over his much larger one. "I have bad news."

His eyes remained closed. "I can't take any more. I don't want to know. Leave me alone."

"You need to listen. Your bond with Osorin has broken. As a result, your magic is unstable. You must feel it wavering."

"All I feel like doing is closing my eyes and never waking up. What's the point of going on if I have no bond with a magic user? My purpose has gone."

"It's hard, but remember the time before you were bonded to anyone. We all had that period in our lives, when we sought the right magic user. Life wasn't so bad. You must have good memories of being a young, single hound."

"I don't. I only remember my time with Osorin."

Archie wasn't making this easy, but I pressed on. "You survived that time with no connection. You may even have had fun. Those days were carefree, and we had no responsibilities. We only worried about ourselves. I had good times when I wasn't bonded to my witch." Times when worshippers threw flowers for me to walk upon and I didn't have to groom myself with my tongue.

Archie simply whimpered in response.

I looked at Zandra, who watched with concern in her eyes. She encouraged me to keep talking to Archie with a gesture of her hand.

"So, Archie, the bad news is, if you don't bond with someone else, your magic is so unstable it will kill you."

"Let it. I'm done with this place."

I gently caressed his paw. "It's not done with you. You were a good and loyal hellhound, and someone else will be worthy of forging a bond with you. But you must stay alive so you can find them."

"I don't want anyone else. Just Osorin." Archie huffed out a hot, breathy sigh. "And I know that's not possible. He's gone."

Sympathy and patient explanations weren't working, so I'd shake up this cowering pooch and get his furnace hot. "Don't you want to stay alive and find out who killed Osorin?"

He grunted.

"Someone wanted Osorin dead. You could have information that'll help us figure out who killed him. Wouldn't you love to stop the bad guys? See a little justice handed out paw-style?"

I got another grunt, but Archie's ears were up and forward. He was interested.

"Don't you want to avenge Osorin?" I whispered.

His eyes opened, and he stared at me for a long, silent minute. "I do. They must pay. Osorin had his faults, but I adored him. He didn't deserve to have his head go boom."

"Then let's get a bond formed. My witch is strong and can handle partial bonds with an infinite number of creatures. And I'm not without power."

Archie blinked once. "I sense it. You're not your average familiar, are you? Neither is your witch an ordinary magic user."

"Oh, you sweet thing, there's nothing average about me or Zandra. And the bond we'll forge will be magnificent. You can be part of the team for as long as you need until you feel ready to move on. So, how about it? Want to join my gang?"

Archie let out a long, shuddering breath. "So long as you find out what happened to Osorin and let me eat the killer."

"You have my paw-felt word. My magnificent witch will hunt them down and obliterate them."

Zandra loudly cleared her throat and gave me the stink eye. "No killing, and no eating the suspects."

"Of course. Archie, the avenging and chomping must be done in a completely legal way." I winked at him.

He stood on shaking legs. "Let's do it."

I looked at Zandra and nodded at her. She gave me a thumbs-up. I took a moment to center myself and draw out my ancient power. I didn't dive deep into the well of energy often. I had so much missing that, when I felt for my origin power, it was weak and misshapen, as if someone had taken a club to it and bent it out of shape with too many blows.

But that would change. My witch had pure, untapped power. She was extraordinary, and with her help, one day, I'd have it all back. One day, I'd be complete and rule again.

"Hey, is everything okay?" Zandra whispered. "Should I feel something when the bond forms with Archie?"

"Give me a minute." I forged the shakiest link I'd ever made. Every time I tapped into my magic, it got a little harder, but I wasn't giving up. "You should feel the change any second."

Zandra opened her mouth as if she wanted to say more then simply nodded. She trusted me.

A few hundred years ago, forging this bond would have been as simple as clicking my fingers, but I made do with what I had. It was good enough.

My power trickled through Archie, and a weak bond twirled around us in a spiral of green magic. It drifted to Zandra, and she closed her eyes and let the bond in.

She opened her eyes, her brow furrowed. "Huh! I thought that would be harder or feel more... magical. Are you sure the bond formed right?"

"It's there. I feel you and Archie. It's perfect." It was as shaky as a drunk mouse being chased by a leopard, but it was holding.

"How do you feel, Archie?" Zandra said. "You're okay with this?"

He barely nodded.

The poor hound. At least we were now bonded, his magic would be stable, and he stood a better chance of surviving. And we needed him focused. We had to get sense out of Archie and figure out how his bonded magic user lost his head.

"Archie, are you up to answering questions?" Zandra came back to the cage and sat in front of it.

He shook out his fur. "I want to help. Juno said you'd get revenge and destroy the killer for me."

"Um... sure. We'll figure something out."

I got another stink eye from Zandra, which I ignored.

"Tell us about Osorin," she said to Archie. "You said he was agitated just before he died."

"Before he was killed." Archie growled. "Not a death, a murder."

"You saw it happen," I said. "What was Osorin doing just before he was killed?"

"He was talking to himself, and he wasn't making much sense. I kept trying to understand what the problem was."

"What time was that?" Zandra said.

"He left early and was back by ten that morning. He exploded just before eleven."

My heart clenched. This sad hound had been trapped with his dead owner for almost a day. No wonder he'd been so frantic.

"Osorin was worried when he got back from his trip?" I said.

"Yes. He was pacing and complaining and kept sending messages on his snow globe. He was also looking for a place to stash the money. And he had the strange face."

"What money?" I said. "What face?"

"Osorin brought home a bag. He said it had a prize inside. Of course, I thought he meant the big ball of raw mince and peanut butter he gave me, but there was something else in there. I think that's what he was worried about. He said it wasn't enough, and they wouldn't be happy. They'd know the truth. I didn't know who he was talking about, though. He also said they wouldn't let him down and would be in touch. Everything would be sorted."

"Was it a family member or a friend he was trying to contact about this money?" Zandra said.

"I don't know. Osorin didn't have much family. He had friends, but he'd sometimes go out for hours and not take me with him. I hated that. Everywhere he went, I wanted to go, too, so I could protect him. You know what our magic users can be like." Archie shared a shrewd look with me.

I chuckled. "They get themselves in trouble."

Zandra poked my side. "You get yourself in a fair amount of trouble too if I don't watch you."

Archie whined and dropped back onto the floor of his cage. "You're so happy together. I miss Osorin."

"What did you mean by the strange face?" I said.

"I don't know. Nothing makes sense. I want him back."

It took me a moment to stabilize our bond. The connection was so weak, I was worried it might break. Archie wasn't fighting, and he had to fight if he wanted to live.

"Remember what we're doing. Osorin's murder must not go unpunished," I said.

Archie slowly got back up. He nodded. "I'm doing this for him."

"Was Osorin's behavior unusual on the day he was murdered?" Zandra said. "Or was he often anxious about things?"

"He lived on his nerves, but I hadn't seen him that bad for a long time. And he never got up early. That was strange, too."

"When was the last time he behaved like this?" I said.

Archie cocked his head. "Just before Angel Force arrested him. He'd gotten in with a bad crowd and was trying to prove himself to them. They made him steal the statue outside the front of the Angel Force building. It was a test to see what he'd do for the group."

"How did he expect to get away with that?" Zandra said. "The angels love those dumb statues."

Archie gave the hound version of a shrug. "I loved Osorin, but he didn't use his brain too often. The angels saw him do it. He ran, but they knew where he lived. That was the last time I'd seen him so panicked."

"Which suggests he did something illegal on the day he died. Something that would bring the angels to his door," I said. "Do you think he stole the money he brought back?"

"I... maybe. Osorin had a habit of stealing."

"Is the money still in the house?" Zandra said. "I don't remember seeing a bag next to Osorin, but then there was a lot of... well, other things to look at. I was distracted."

"There wasn't a bag," I said.

"I think Osorin hid it. He fed me my peanut butter and meat treat and stashed the bag. Although I didn't see where he hid it." Archie grimaced. "My stomach feels bad."

"It's the grief. It can make you feel horrible." I massaged his paw gently to get him to relax.

The door opened, and Barney walked in. He slowed as he took in the scene. "Zandra, what are you doing?"

"Oh, nothing." She scrambled to her feet, her cheeks flushed. "Good news. Archie is awake."

"And you're questioning him?" Barney's forehead furrowed.

"Just asking him a couple of things. I needed to see how he was doing."

"And work out how to find Osorin's killer and smoosh him into the ground like a slug." Archie stamped his paws, making the cage shake.

"Err... we may have talked about something like that, too." Zandra's cheeks grew even pinker.

"You should have contacted the angels the second Archie woke. They need to deal with this." Barney hurried over and peered in at Archie. "You look better."

I nudged Zandra with my head. We were making progress with Archie, and that would be lost when the angels blundered in and took over.

She nodded at me and winked. "Archie is still distressed. Would it do him good to be questioned by strangers when he's so vulnerable?"

"That's for the angels to decide, not us. We're the experts in animal retrieval and care, not in figuring out murder suspects. You could get in trouble for interfering in an investigation," Barney said.

"Archie needed to talk," I said. "This is good for him. It won't cause any trouble for Angel Force. You always say animals first."

Barney was shaking his head. "We have a responsibility to do our job, but this sounds like a difficult case. We can't have the angels thinking Archie got odd ideas from anyone."

"We were just talking," Zandra said.

"About squashing the killer like a slug?" Barney pursed his lips.

"That was my idea to get him motivated," I said.

"Well, it's worked, but that's enough. We need to get Archie stable and then find him a home so he can settle."

Archie whined. "I don't want a new home. I want my old one."

Zandra leaned in close to Barney. "No one will take him while he's in such a vulnerable state."

As if on cue, Archie keeled over and panted. His eyes rolled back and his long limbs quivered.

Barney studied Archie, concern etched across his face. "Perhaps you're right. For now, he can go into a holding pen we use for strays. They're nicer than the cages."

Archie whimpered, and the bond we'd forged almost broke as his misery took over, and the faint flicker of hope I'd fanned faded.

I hurried over to Barney and stomped on his booted foot. "He won't survive alone. We have a duty of care to protect him."

"I agree with Juno," Zandra said. "Perhaps we could find a family member who'll take Archie. Even if it's only temporary. He needs people he knows around him."

"He's really that bad?"

"Look at him. He could die," I hiss-whispered. "We must save Archie."

"Well... Osorin had a sister, Monika. I don't think they spoke much, though, so there's no guarantee she'll take Archie." Barney rubbed the back of his neck. "And it's getting late. Archie can go in a holding pen overnight. One night will be okay."

Archie whimpered again, I wrinkled my booping snooter, and Zandra frowned.

Barney raised a hand. "The holding pens have warm bedding, light, food, and other animals to keep him company. He'll be fine overnight."

"It'll take me less than an hour to contact Monika and arrange everything," Zandra said.

"I can't have you eating into more overtime. My budget won't stand the strain."

"Then don't pay me. I'm happy to visit Osorin's sister on my own time."

Barney patted Zandra's shoulder. "Your enthusiasm is appreciated, but don't get too involved with every case, or this job will eat you alive. I'll transfer Archie to a pen. You go home and rest. In the morning, we'll figure things out."

"Are you sure I shouldn't visit Monika this evening? If she lives in Crimson Cove, it won't take me long," Zandra said.

Barney paused. "I know Monika, and she's a tricky character. I doubt she'll be friendly if she gets an unannounced visit from animal control. Stay out of her way for now. It'll be safer for everyone."

"Safer? Is she violent?" I said.

Barney tilted his head from side to side. "No, but she can be abrupt. Now, off you go, and I'll see to Archie. That's an order."

With much reluctance from both of us, and after reassuring Archie everything would be okay and Barney was a safe pair of hands, we left.

"I hate leaving Archie," Zandra said. "What if we haven't done enough to keep him alive?"

"The bond we've forged will help, and Barney will look after Archie. He's one of the good ones."

"He is, but Archie needs stability. We must move fast to get him the help he needs."

My ears pricked. Zandra had that look in her eyes that meant business. "What are you planning?"

"First thing tomorrow, we're locating Monika, asking her about Osorin's money issues and why anyone would want to blow his head off, and finding out if she's got room in her life for an adorable giant hellhound with a slight drool problem."

I purred and rubbed against her leg. Of course, my witch had the perfect solution to any problem.

Chapter 7

Just because they're family...

We were up early the next morning. So early, Vorana, our bookish, food-obsessed landlady, hadn't even risen to make Zandra's usual delicious pancake breakfast.

I snuck off as Zandra brewed her coffee. After yesterday's stressful events, she needed a treat, and I had just the delicious, vole flavored treat in mind.

After a silent creep around the yard, I found the vole in its nest. "Sorry, my little friend, but your death will serve a greater cause. My witch needs this."

I made it quick and painless then dashed inside and placed the warm little body on the top of Zandra's purse. She could thank me later.

After Zandra poured her coffee into a takeout mug, we headed to the door. She grabbed her purse and shoved her hand inside to get her keys. She froze then squeaked and tossed her purse across the room. "Juno!"

I winced. My cat side sometimes got the better of me, and I forgot my origins and obsessed over the small furrries. "I thought, after yesterday, you deserved something nice."

"So get me a box of chocolates or a scented candle. Don't leave bodies in my purse."

My nose wrinkled. Such a waste. I hadn't even seen where the vole had gone. I could sniff it out, but...

"Juno! I'm not joking."

I raised a paw as the squeak of Sage's wheels signaled her approach. At least someone would get to enjoy my gift.

Zandra sighed. "Let's get out of here before Vorana throws us out for destroying the local wildlife."

I wanted to protest, but I was a touch embarrassed about letting my feline side dominate. I needed better control of my hunting instincts. Perhaps I should try a mole next. Zandra may simply want something with a bit more meat on it... no. No more vermin hunting.

We slipped out of the house and hopped into the work van to drive to Monika's house just as the sun came up.

Zandra had discovered where Monika lived from Vorana, who'd also advised caution when dealing with her. Apparently, Monika kept to herself, hated strangers, and was light fingered. Just like her deceased brother.

"The money Archie mentioned yesterday has been on my mind," Zandra said. "It could be the reason Osorin was killed, especially if he stole it."

I stifled a yawn and focused on the murder. "Given his track record, that seems likely. And there must be someone else involved if Osorin was trying to reach them before he died. Maybe he had a partner or a lookout when he burgled places."

"And from what Archie said, Osorin sounded worried. Something could have gone wrong with his last job."

"We need evidence and suspects before we go much further in this mystery." I rested my chin on my fluffy bed. "Osorin could have been bullied into stealing the money as a show of loyalty, just like when he stole the angel statue. It sounds like he was always trying to prove himself."

"Knowing where that money was would be helpful. We could trace the source."

"The angels must have found it when they searched Osorin's place."

"Let's hope so." Zandra didn't sound too confident in Angel Force's ability to do a thorough job.

"We should mention it to them. You know what the angels can be like. Clues get missed, and innocent people get accused of crimes they didn't commit."

"You read my mind, but if we do that, we'll have to spend time at Angel Force." Zandra drummed her fingers on the steering wheel. "But you're right. If they don't know about the money, they need to. We want nothing overlooked. Not if it'll help get Archie closure."

I looked over at her. "Bertoli was a jerk, but I didn't mind Finn. He was helpful. And he has that animal sanctuary, so he can't be all bad."

"I wasn't wild about either of them. The less we have to do with Angel Force, the better."

"You liked Finn, didn't you?"

Zandra arched an eyebrow but kept her attention on the road. "He wasn't terrible, but then he isn't all angel. I'm still surprised Angel Force is letting demons work for them. It goes against everything they stand for. They're here to protect the world from demons, but now they're recruiting them to the team."

"Keep your friends close but your enemies closer," I said. "At least, some of the time. I don't think you're my enemy, and I keep you the closest."

"I'm glad to hear it." Her gaze flicked around. "I don't think much of this neighborhood."

The row of small, tired houses we drove by weren't welcoming. There were abandoned cars and tires on the roadside, and stacked up bags of trash overflowed out of several driveways. The place looked sad and unloved.

"This is the one." Zandra pulled up outside a two-story house in desperate need of a paint job to conceal the crud brown peeling walls. There was a rusting bicycle in the front yard, and weeds were the dominant flower of the season.

"This isn't far from Osorin's house," I said. "It's on the edge of the same neighborhood."

"Which suggests neither of them had much money. It's another reason for Osorin to steal. He could have been behind on the mortgage or rent and had no one who could help him."

After Zandra unclipped me from my harness, I got out and sniffed for danger. The overwhelming scent was decaying food and ripe nappies, but there was no whiff of demon or dark magic. “It’s all good. But let’s not hang around for long.”

We headed through the yard to the front door. Zandra knocked, and we waited. After a minute of waiting, she knocked again.

“The curtains are drawn. They could still be asleep,” I said.

Zandra started knocking, and she didn’t stop.

I joined in, bumping my paws against the front door in a staccato rhythm, getting into the groove and adding my tail, too.

My paws were throbbing when feet stamped toward the door. It was yanked open, and a thin, wrinkled woman with a clove smelling cigarette hanging out of one corner of her mouth glared at us.

“What do you want?”

Zandra lowered her hand. “I’m Zandra Crypt, and this is Juno. We’re from animal control. Are you Monika Greenbow?”

“What if I am? We don’t got no stinking animals here. I got rid of the last cat after she puked on the rug too many times. You’ve come to the wrong place.” She tried to shut the door, but Zandra pressed a hand against it.

“We’re not here about a complaint. We’re here about Osorin’s familiar, Archie.” Her tone stayed friendly, but there was a note of steel running through it.

“Oh. This is about Osorin, is it?”

“That’s right. I want to know if—”

“Pluto! Get your flabby butt out here!”

My ears rang at the scratchy shriek from Monika, and I lowered my head. I looked up at Zandra, and she gave a small shrug.

"What are you yelling about, woman?" A scruffy guy with several days' worth of beard, wearing baggy gray sweatpants and a vest on inside out, stumbled into the hallway and joined us at the door. His hand went inside his pants, and he scratched around.

"More problems with my loser brother. It's his mangy hound this time." Monika sucked on her cigarette.

"What about it?" Pluto adjusted the waistband of his sweatpants, flicking at a stain on his vest.

"This woman claims she's from animal control."

"He's bitten someone, I suppose?"

"No, Archie is in the safe care of animal control, and he hasn't hurt anyone." Zandra paused. "You are aware of what happened to your brother, aren't you?"

"Sure. The angels turned up yesterday and gave us the news. Idiot gone and got his head blown off." Monika chuckled, and Pluto joined in.

Zandra cleared her throat. "I'm sorry for your loss. Following Osorin's death, we took Archie into our care. He's grieving for his bonded magic user."

"And?" Monika said.

"That guy was a dummy. Always acting like the big man. He was a joke. No one took him seriously," Pluto said.

Monika nodded along as Pluto spoke. "Osorin stumbled from one disaster to another. He was a waste of space, just like that hound."

"Someone thought Osorin was worth bothering with," Zandra said. "They killed him, so he must have had something they needed."

"Nah. Osorin wasn't important enough to notice. And he owed me money. There'd better be something worth selling in his place. He may be dead, but the debt needs to be repaid. I know my rights." Monika jabbed her finger as she talked.

"You'll have to speak to Angel Force about that." The disdain in Zandra's voice was clear.

Monika nudged Pluto in his flabby gut. "We should get what we're owed. Check if Osorin had anything worth pawning or selling."

"His house is a crime scene," I said. "You'll have to wait to get your hands on his things."

She looked down at me and scowled. "I need my money. As you can see, we're not living in a palace. Osorin owes me, and he's dead, so he won't miss what we take. If we don't get in soon, the place will be overrun with squatters, or the landlord will dump his stuff and the vultures will pick it clean."

"What about making some money from the hound?" Pluto said.

Zandra stiffened, and my hackles rose.

"What are you thinking?" Monika sucked down another lungful of clove smoke.

"He must be worth something."

"That mean old thing is almost blind in one eye and farts more than it blows flames. Who'd want that? It's as messed up as Osorin."

They laughed again.

I bit my tongue and held in my magic to avoid blasting them. You didn't disrespect a familiar. We were loyal, trustworthy, and we enhanced our magic user's life.

"We should leave." Zandra stepped back. "I didn't mean to waste your time."

She must have the same idea as me. This was the wrong place for Archie.

"Wait a minute. We could spruce up the mutt and sell it," Monika said. "Is there still a market for familiar fights?"

We both gasped at that heinous comment.

"Nah, they closed the last place a year ago. It's a tragedy. I always loved betting on who'd survive and who'd be ripped apart," Pluto said.

Zandra and I scowled.

"It's too much trouble to start up a fight ring. What about dog meat? We could sell the mutt to a processing factory. Although I doubt we'd get much. Osorin kept the thing well fed, though." Monika's cold gaze settled on Zandra. "What do we have to do to claim the hound?"

Zandra hesitated, and I was glad she did. These people were appalling and didn't deserve to be anywhere near Archie.

"I didn't think you wanted him," she said.

"You don't tell me what I think." Monika sniffed. "It would be an easy way to get my money. We'll figure something out."

"It wouldn't be easy. There's paperwork to fill in," Zandra said, "at least ten copies of everything. You don't want to trouble yourselves with that."

Monika's eyes narrowed. "We want the hound. Osorin owed me. If all I can get for now is that hound, then I'll take it."

"He's a biter," I said. "He almost chewed through my tail. We had to use strong sedation on him before he'd cooperate. The hellhound is dangerous."

"Osorin wasn't firm enough with the mutt. We'll whip it into shape," Pluto said.

I couldn't help the growl that escaped.

Zandra covered it with a cough. "We're not here to see if you want the hellhound. Simply to let you know... he's been tagged as dangerously unstable. He may even die because the familiar bond was severed so abruptly. We're putting him out of his misery. It's the kindest thing to do."

"All of Osorin's property comes to his closest relative. That's me. I'm his sister. That hound is mine."

"You don't want him. Archie's gas is something else," I said. "I passed out twice while dealing with him. Do you want that polluting your home? He parps every other step."

"It probably don't smell any worse than Pluto," Monika said.

Pluto rubbed his stubbled chin. "There's nothing wrong with my stink. And you're almost as bad after a bowlful of hard-boiled eggs and that tinned spam you're always frying in lard."

Monika tried to stub out her clove cigarette on his arm then shoved him away.

We stepped back as Pluto got Monika in a head lock, and she screamed until he let her go.

"We should leave you to it." Zandra turned to go.

"No! I want that hound." Monika glowered at Pluto as she gave him another shove. "And it's mine.

You don't get any of the money I make from selling the thing."

"Babe, I'm your guy. We share everything."

I nudged Zandra with my head. We had to escape and make sure they never got their grimy hands on Archie.

She gave me a nod. "Even if we could get him stable, which won't be possible, Archie would need several walks a day and expensive veterinary treatment. It could cost you thousands to keep him. That's if he's safe enough to bring home."

"The mutt doesn't need treatment. It just needs to toughen up," Monika said.

"It would be a condition of you taking him," Zandra said. "You'd have to agree to finance his treatment and his feeding schedule. That would be accompanied by weekly checkups from me and other members of animal control. We'd also need to spend the day with you to monitor Archie. Taking on someone else's familiar is challenging, and given his instability, we'd have to double up those visits, just to be on the safe side. I'd hate to have anything bad happen to you and your charming partner."

"We don't want busybodies poking around in our business," Pluto muttered. "I've got my game coming up. The boys won't come around if this nosy witch shows up. It's high stakes, so I have a chance to win big."

"Or lose big," Monika snapped.

"My visits would also be unannounced," Zandra said. "I'm within my rights to show up between the hours of seven in the morning and midnight. It's best that way for the animal. I'm sure you understand."

"Monika, the game," Pluto whined. "I'm having a lucky streak. When I win—"

"If you win."

"Babe, I will. But we can't be disturbed. The hound isn't worth the hassle. I'll make more on the game."

Monika glowered at no one in particular, her gaze flicking around as she inhaled a raspy breath. "Get rid of it. I'll wait until I can get into Osorin's house to take what I'm owed."

We let out relieved sighs. We'd come here, hoping to find a benevolent family to take on Archie, not these scruffy nightmares who thought about profit over pups.

"I'm sure you'll get what you're owed soon enough." Zandra looked like she wanted to leave but hesitated. "Did the angels say when they're releasing Osorin's property to you?"

"They didn't tell us much. I'd planned to wait a week anyway, just in case," Monika said.

"In case of what?" I said.

"In case whoever blew off my idiot brother's head is still about. They did it for a reason, and I don't want them coming after me if they learn we were related."

"What could that reason be?" Zandra said.

"I reckon the Shadow gang whacked him." Pluto tugged at his sweatpants again, his hand inching in, suggesting he was going for another scratch.

Monika smirked. "They wouldn't waste their time on Osorin. My brother was a nobody, and the Shadow gang only have big hitters on their crew."

My ears perked at this information. "Osorin was involved in a gang?"

Pluto shook his head as he scratched. "Nah, but he was always trying to get in with them. The last time I saw him, he was lying about them taking him on a job, and he reckoned he was gonna be the right-hand man to the top guy."

"Osorin was a liar, which was why I didn't like him coming here and filling your empty head with garbage. You always knew you were in for a couple of hours of over-the-top rubbish whenever he was around." Monika lit another clove cigarette in a well-practiced move. "That was my brother. Full of trash and no good to anyone. The Shadow gang took one look at him and saw the truth."

My heart sped up, and I leaned against Zandra. It was clear she was also excited by this information because she was shifting around and her pulse was fast.

"I'm new to Crimson Cove, so I know nothing about that gang," she said. "They're bad guys?"

Monika drew deeply on her cigarette. "They're the people to go to if you need a problem sorted and you have enough money to pay them to do it. They take on any job, no questions asked. And I'm not talking about the cleaning kind of job. Although they probably have a guy to hide any spillages."

"Osorin reckoned he was in with them. Poor sap. He never stood a chance," Pluto said. "I almost feel sorry for the guy."

Monika elbowed him again. "Why bother? He's dead."

I was nudging Zandra, eager to leave. With this information, we had a firm lead on who killed Osorin.

She backed away. “Thanks for your time. And again, sorry for your loss.”

“It's no loss. So long as I get what I'm owed.” Monika slammed the door.

“We have to find out more about this Shadow gang,” I said as we dashed to the van.

“My thoughts exactly. Although, you know what that means.” Zandra opened the van door so I could get in.

I nodded. “We need to talk to the angels.”

Chapter 8

Revealing the shadows

Zandra had half a strawberry and vanilla cream mini sponge cake in front of her, provided by Barney. I'd been gifted a delicious chicken flavored chew. I preferred fish but appreciated the effort he'd made in getting it for me.

They were rewards for doing such a good job with Archie, although I got the impression Barney felt bad about not letting Zandra have her own way yesterday. Despite his gruff, bearlike exterior, he was a softy.

"I have a confession." Zandra leaned forward in her seat by Barney's office desk.

He dabbed at the cake crumbs on his lips. He'd gifted himself a chocolate cake. Barney was a man who loved his sweet treats. "You haven't changed your mind about staying in the job?"

"No! I'm not leaving. I like this job."

"That's good. I expected you to resign. After everything that happened yesterday, I wouldn't have blamed you. Not many people would be thrilled about finding a headless corpse. Many of them would run away as fast as they could." He picked up his cake then set it back down without taking a bite. "I spoke briefly to Finn from Angel Force."

"He checked in with you that I wasn't lying about working here?"

"He did. I said nothing but positive things."

"Why would you say anything else about my wonderful witch?" I said.

Barney's cheeks glowed, and he finally took a bite of his cake. "Absolutely. So, what's the confession?"

"I went to see Osorin's sister before work. And before you mention the overtime, I did it on my own time, to make sure we could get things arranged for Archie as fast as possible." Zandra waited a second for Barney to challenge her, but he didn't. "Monika wasn't helpful. She wanted to use Archie as either dog meat or in a fight ring."

Barney almost choked on his cake. "You didn't agree to hand him over, did you?"

"I strongly discouraged her from taking him. I may even have stretched the truth about the monitoring and paperwork to put her off. Then I made an excuse, and we left as quickly as we could. Monika and Pluto aren't having Archie. They don't deserve him," Zandra said.

"Not if they're talking like that. Disgusting. You did the right thing to discourage Monika. Archie will need careful handling for months. I've checked on him several times this morning, and he's eaten. He's still sad but is responsive. He keeps talking about Osorin. He's also complaining of stomachache."

"Grief can make you constipated," I said.

"Among other things." Zandra gave me an odd look. "Have the angels been to see Archie yet?"

"They're coming this afternoon. I took your advice and suggested they leave him for a while. It seemed the kindest thing to do." Barney dabbed the last of the crumbs up with his finger and sucked them into his mouth. "I've also put out a call to our specialist fosterers. Most of them are busy, but there may be a space for Archie. It could take a while to find one, though. And while he's so focused on what happened to Osorin, it's better he stays in a pen. We can't afford to have a hellhound go rogue. That would result in an order to have him put to sleep, and that's never something I want to issue."

"I'd have him, but there's no room in the basement at Vorana's house. Well, there is, but it would be a squeeze," Zandra said.

"We can visit him while he stays here," I said. I didn't want Vorana's hospitality stretched too far. She already made most of our meals and was charging us barely anything for rent. I got the impression she liked our company, though, so it was a good arrangement for all of us.

Barney's mobile snow globe buzzed, and he checked the caller. "I'd better take this. Your jobs for the day are on your desk. And try not to worry about Archie. We'll see him right." He hurried out of the room.

"I don't like Archie being stuck in a pen like he's a criminal. None of this is his fault," Zandra said.

"It's not ideal, but the bond we have with Archie is helping him," I said. "I can sense his mood."

"You can? I'm not feeling anything. I feel our connection as strongly as ever but figured, since we were all joined, I'd pick up on how Archie was feeling, too. I'm not even aware of him. You're sure the connection worked?"

"You doubt my magic?"

She scratched behind my ears. "Never. And I've never been joined with two familiars, so I don't know what to expect."

I pretended to be offended, but I felt concern. My power was weakening, but I had to hold on. I couldn't let Zandra know I was incomplete. Not yet.

After the cake and meaty chew were finished, we headed into the back room where the pens were kept.

Archie was alert and watched us approach. He even gave a small wag of his tail. "Have you found Osorin's killer?"

"Not yet," I said. "But we're looking. And we've made progress."

"Can I help? I want to. I need to be useful."

Zandra settled in front of the pen. "Then talk to us before Barney catches us again. What can you tell us about Osorin and the Shadow gang?"

Archie whined. "A gang! Osorin wouldn't be part of a gang."

"You mentioned he didn't always take you with him when he went out," Zandra said. "Could he have met the gang, then? Have you ever heard him talk about the Shadow gang?"

Archie swung his head from side to side, drool spraying around. "He said he wanted to be just like them, but if he couldn't, he'd form his own crew. I said I'd be a part of the crew, but Osorin laughed. He said I was too good to be bad. I wasn't sure what he meant. I'd be anything he wanted me to be."

"He probably wanted to keep you out of trouble," I said. "This Shadow gang sounds like bad news."

"We don't know much about them, other than what Monika and Pluto told us," Zandra said.

"Monika!" Archie's ears lowered. "You're not going to make me live with her, are you?"

"Definitely not. That's not even a suitable home for a dead sea sponge," I said.

He puffed out a plume of smoke. "I'd rather stay in this pen for the rest of my days than go there. She's mean."

"Barney is looking for a foster home for you, but while we're working things out, it's best you remain here," Zandra said. "You'll get walked and plenty of food."

Archie whined again.

I rested a paw on his. "You'll be safe in here. And we have our bond, so you know you're not alone."

"I want Osorin back, and I want to be in my home."

"We'll figure out what happened to him and find you an amazing home. I promise." I sent that promise over with a dash of magic, so Archie knew my word was my bond. "You'll always miss Osorin, but you could find someone else. A new person to bond with. I've done it many times. It's difficult, but once you find the perfect magic user, it'll change your life."

"I had my perfect person, and then his head exploded." Archie slumped down.

I poured gentle, calming magic over him and then looked at Zandra. She gave me a determined nod. After attempting to comfort Archie some more, we had to admit defeat. And we had work to do.

We headed to the van and settled in. Zandra took a moment to check the schedule. "Two stops about noise complaints, three familiar monitor checks, and a look around for those blue-winged scarabs, and then we'll visit Angel Force."

"Agreed. But first, food?"

"You just ate the two chews Barney gave you."

"They were small and chicken flavored."

She shook her head, smiling as she started the van. "A quick stop at Bites and Delights. We can grab takeout and see if Sorcha knows anything about the Shadow gang."

Zandra drove into town, parked in a spot outside the café, and we got out.

Sorcha waved as we came through the door. I looked around for her grumpy sort of familiar, Tinkerbell, but she was nowhere to be seen. Good, I didn't want to get into another fight and be scolded for defending my witch.

We headed to the counter and placed our order. Salmon for me, mocha coffee for Zandra.

Sorcha leaned against the counter as she buttered a bagel. "Rumor has it you found a headless corpse."

"Is that so?" Zandra raised an eyebrow. "Who have you been talking to?"

"Everyone's talking about it. Osorin Greenbow lost his head. Is that right?"

"It was him. We only found him because we investigated his noisy hellhound. We got to the house, looked in the window, and discovered Osorin. The angels are looking into what happened."

Sorcha grimaced. "That can't have been fun. They have any idea what happened?"

"Not sure. Although I want to ask you about something that could be connected to Osorin's death. Have you got time?"

"Ask away. I'm the conduit for town gossip. Everyone comes in here wanting to chat while I make them food. If I know anything that can help, I'll let you in on it."

"The Shadow gang. That name has come up in connection to Osorin. Do you know much about them?"

Her eyes widened, and her mouth formed an O of surprise. "Unfortunately, yes. And if they're involved, you need to take care. And stay out of it."

"What have they done that's so terrible?" Zandra said.

"It's more like what haven't they done. If there's a crime to commit, they'll do it."

"Who's in this gang?"

"The gang members are fluid, but there are a few key figures that stay constant. One of them is Anan Shadow. He's the guy in charge, along with his brother, Koku. Anan is a seriously unpleasant guy. I've banned him from the café."

"I bet he loved that."

"He threatened to burn the place down."

"You weren't worried he'd carry out that threat?"

"Fortunately, half a dozen people heard him make it, so he's not dumb enough to carry it out. People love my muffins too much to stand back while this place burns." Sorcha thumped down the butter knife. "For a while, he was sending nasty little packages through the post, though. Anan loves to intimidate people."

"What was in the packages?"

She rolled her eyes. "Fake body parts covered in sugar syrup blood. The guy's a sadist and gets a thrill out of upsetting people. It happened for a month, but then he must have gotten bored because the packages stopped arriving."

"He's never been back to bother you?" Zandra said.

"He leaves me alone. It helps I have these." She flashed her fangs. "I'm not afraid to go into vamp mode and bite that sucker if he kicks off. I could take Anan in a fight."

"Let's hope it never comes to that," I said.

"Me, too." Sorcha winked at me. "And I hope you're not planning any more fights with Tinkerbell. She complained about you for hours after you left."

"So long as Tinkerbell remains civil, so will I." That cat was a disgrace to the familiar community.

Sorcha chuckled. "Good luck with that. I don't know what's wrong with her, but she's barely talking to me these days. I wondered if there was a fault in our partial bond. I tried to strengthen it, but she's still being sharp."

I was tempted to tell Sorcha what Tinkerbell really thought of her, but would it do any good? It was hard to break a bond with a familiar. Both parties had to be willing, and there was always magical weakness following a break. Sorcha needed to keep her magic in top form, in case the Shadow gang came after her again.

"Where can I find this gang?" Zandra said.

"We're going after them?" I said before Sorcha spoke. "Is that wise?"

"They could have answers about what happened to Osorin." Zandra petted me.

"I'm with Juno on this. Leave the Shadow gang to the angels." Sorcha handed over our food and coffee. "You don't want to get on their wrong side, or you'll get fake body parts through the post, too."

"Juno promised Archie we'd find his killer." Zandra looked at me and shrugged. "I didn't miss that little declaration at Archie's pen."

"I said I'd do it. You don't need to snoop around a criminal gang."

"What do you always tell me? Where I go, you go. It cuts both ways."

Sorcha giggled. "Familiars are funny. Although it's been a while since Tinkerbell has wanted to go anywhere with me. Maybe she's sick."

"You should take her to the vet for a physical. She needs a full exam." I flicked my tail.

"Juno, don't stir. Tinkerbell would hate to be poked about if there's no need. You wail if I even suggest you get your teeth scaled." Zandra gently chided me, even though she was smiling.

"My teeth are perfect, as is the rest of me." I didn't miss the eye roll Zandra made at Sorcha.

"Did you ever see Osorin with any of the gang members?" she asked Sorcha.

"No, but I didn't have much to do with Osorin. I think he was lonely, though. He didn't fit in anywhere. His family wasn't kind to him, and he never married or settled down with anyone special. He was a drifter."

"We know about his sister. We've met Monika." Zandra's top lip curled.

Sorcha wrinkled her nose. "Then you know what I mean. He never had a support network, so he was always looking for one. Maybe that was why he got interested in the Shadow gang. They're a twisted version of family. Once you're in, they look after their own. I wish you luck if you have to speak to them."

Zandra paid for our food, and we headed outside.

We walked to the van and settled in to eat.

"We should stay away from the Shadow gang," I said.

"You don't think we can handle a bunch of thugs?"

"I could. You could, too, but why should we?" I slurped down a strip of smoked salmon.

"Because they're bad guys and could have killed Osorin. And you're the one throwing out promises to Archie that we'll solve this murder."

"I overstepped." I didn't want to put Zandra in harm's way, and the more I learned about this Shadow gang, the less I wanted her to have anything to do with them.

"Right now, we can't think about the gang. Finish your food. We'll get these noise complaints dealt with, and then we can have a fun visit to Angel Force. If luck is on our side, they'll have already solved this case."

I snorted a laugh. "Is that likely?"

Zandra started the engine. "I think I just saw a pig fly."

The work was done, and with only two minutes left before the end of our shift, Zandra drove to Angel Force. Their offices were housed in a large white building in the center of Crimson Cove. There was an angel statue outside, and glass double doors led into a quiet reception area.

I was settled on Zandra's shoulder to make sure she didn't get stressed while dealing with the angels. They had a habit of jangling her nerves. She was tense but kept it together. I was so proud of my witch.

An angel I didn't recognize was looking after the front desk. She was big, blonde, and beautiful. We gave our names and asked to see Finn, and she disappeared out the back to get him.

A moment later, Finn appeared, still looking rumpled and smelling slightly of toast and marmalade. Odd thing to eat this late in the day, but I was always partial to breakfast food and could think of worse smells.

He nodded a greeting. "Hey, how are you after yesterday?"

"I'm good," Zandra said.

"Seeing a headless corpse didn't rattle you?"

"It did some."

Finn grinned. "I sense you're a lady who doesn't rattle easily."

She shrugged. "Not when you have a family like mine. I was interested to know if there'd been any progress in the case. Barney said you'd planned on interviewing Archie today. How did that go?"

"Not great. That hound is a mess."

"He gets stressed every time he talks about Osorin," Zandra said.

"No surprise. Any joy in getting him a home?"

"Nothing yet. Barney has put out feelers to local fosterers, but he'll be tricky to handle while he's so vulnerable."

"My offer stands. I can make room at my place. The rescue is small, and it's just me at the moment, but I don't like to turn an animal away. I tag team with a couple of other people in the area, so we always find space. And that hound needs help. A cage at animal control is the wrong environment for him."

"I'm not arguing that point. If I can't figure something out, I'll take you up on the offer, so long as Archie and Barney are in agreement." Zandra twisted her hair around her hand.

"Was there something else?" Finn said.

I nudged her with my nose then hopped off her shoulder onto the reception desk. There was no point in keeping secrets from the angels, and we could be useful to each other, providing Finn continued to be competent and helpful.

Zandra sucked in a breath. "Two things. Did Archie tell you about the money Osorin had with him before he died?"

"He mentioned it, but we found nothing at the house other than a jar of coins. We searched, but it wasn't there. Maybe Archie made a mistake about the money."

"Archie was convinced Osorin came in with a bag of money just before he lost his head. He said he stashed it somewhere in the house," I said.

"He told me the same thing, but after Osorin's body was removed, we did a search. It's standard procedure after finding a body. The place was a dumping ground, so it wasn't easy to look through everything, but no bag of money showed up," Finn said.

"Then what happened to it?" Zandra said.

"Maybe it never existed."

"If it wasn't money, maybe it was something else." I inspected a tray of papers and decided they would make an excellent bed while I listened to the conversation.

"Like what?" Finn said.

I didn't have an answer, so I simply swished my tail and performed a perfect circle. I didn't think Archie had made a mistake. I focused on the soft crinkle of paper under my toe beans. So relaxing.

"Whatever it was, it had Osorin worried. Archie said Osorin was concerned and was trying to reach someone on his snow globe, but they weren't picking up," Zandra said.

"I quizzed him about who that could be. The snow globe was destroyed in the blast, so we can't check who he contacted. Osorin must have dropped the globe when... well, you know, he lost a vital body part. As it stands, we're assuming there wasn't any cash and Archie got confused. Not a surprise, given what he witnessed."

Zandra crossed her arms over her chest. "Huh! Is that so?"

"If we didn't find a mysterious bag full of money, it doesn't exist."

Or the angels hadn't been thorough when they'd searched the house. I was as puzzled about this missing money as Zandra. Had Archie gotten it wrong, or had the angels missed something important? Given my knowledge of their practices, it wouldn't be the first time a vital clue was overlooked, although Finn seemed more competent than most angels. His partner, Bertoli, not so much. He could have overlooked the money.

"We did find something useful in the house, though," Finn said. "A mask."

I flicked my tail. "Oh! The strange face. Archie mentioned Osorin had a strange face."

"Been talking to my witness, have you?"

Zandra glanced at me and winced. "Only to see if we could help, not to cause any problems."

Finn chuckled. "It's fine, so long as it does Archie good. And I don't think you're the bad guys, so I have no problem with you poking about. After all, you were first on the scene. Your curiosity must be raised."

"Err... it is. You really don't mind?" Zandra said.

"So long as you don't hide evidence or lie to me, we're good."

I gained a new level of respect for Finn. He was one of the good guys, despite having a demon side.

"It took me a while to piece things together, but the mask connects Osorin to the armed robberies in Crimson Cove, especially the most recent one at the hardware store," Finn said. "The owner confirmed the mask worn by the robber was a match for what we found in Osorin's house."

"So where is the money from these robberies?" Zandra said. "It can't all have vanished or been spent."

"We're looking into it. The discovery of the mask has made Bertoli happy, though. He's announcing to everyone he cracked a major robbery case."

"You don't sound so certain."

Finn leaned against the desk. "Osorin could have done those jobs, but the guy lacked drive. And as you said, where's the cash? I'm not sure what's going on, but I don't think it's as simple as that."

I nodded along. There were interesting puzzle pieces in this mix, but I didn't know how they all fit together yet.

"What was the second thing you wanted to tell me?" Finn said.

Zandra stood up straight. "I visited Osorin's sister. Her husband, Pluto, mentioned Osorin was interested in joining the Shadow gang. Did he achieve that goal?"

Finn's eyebrows flashed up. "You're kidding? It's not on his record he was in that gang. And we'd know. We keep an eye on what Anan and his band of motley troublemakers are up to."

"Maybe he wasn't, not officially. But according to Monika and Pluto, he was trying to get in with them."

Finn rubbed his stubbled chin. "That's interesting. It's not come up on our radar while we've been investigating. If Osorin did something to annoy the gang, they wouldn't hesitate to kill him."

"Do they usually blow up people they don't like?" Zandra said.

"They're more subtle. If there's someone on their hit list, the person simply vanishes." Finn's expression turned pensive. "We've tried to bring down the Shadow gang dozens of times, but they're always a step ahead of us. And I don't know how they do it, but if they want someone gone, all traces of them are erased. It's like they wipe their memory and turn them into someone else. It's creepy how they manage it."

"You should have a word with them," Zandra said. "Find out if Osorin worked for them. Maybe he messed up a job, and they got revenge with a new method of extermination."

Finn pulled out his notepad and made a few scribbles. "Thanks for the tip off. I'll do that. Although that weird collar around Osorin's neck means Bertoli is still convinced it was a kinky game gone wrong. He wants us to bring in all the night walkers to see if Osorin paid someone to choke him." He chuckled, and Zandra joined in after a few seconds of stunned silence.

"I suppose you need to investigate all the avenues," she said.

"The kink angle is on the murder whiteboard, so it hasn't been dismissed. I wish it would." Finn shook his head. "I'll have my wings clipped if this murder was because of a kinky game gone too far."

Zandra grimaced. "You should take that back. Weirder things have happened."

"I'm not a fan of flying. Being only half-angel, it takes effort. And it's cold up there. Full angels barely feel the chill, but I have to use a little demon heat to make sure it's bearable. You can imagine what the angels think of that." Finn quirked an eyebrow and raised two fingers to show devil horns.

"I've got to say, I'm still stunned you're officially part of Angel Force."

He glanced over his shoulder. "Just between us, so am I. And I have my moments when I wonder why I bothered joining. I've got nothing against Angel Force, but they move slowly, and they take everything so seriously. What's wrong with having fun while you work, provided you get things done?"

"I couldn't agree more," Zandra said.

As they chatted, I studied Finn and Zandra. She wasn't tense, and he was smiling. I didn't object to him. He was handsome, had a steady job, and must keep on the right side of the law if he worked for Angel Force. Perhaps Zandra would like a bad boy in her life.

I wouldn't mind a man in my life either, but I'd never liked lots of hair on a guy. And that was a big problem. As a cat, all I got was fluff, fluff, and more fluff. That meant I either put up with the fur or remained in my current state of abstinence, which was far from ideal and on the wrong side of frustrating.

Suitable men for both of us would be agreeable. But before romance, we had a mystery to solve, and I had to keep my witch from going after the Shadow gang without backup.

Chapter 9

A family mystery and brownies

I was settled on a soft cushion on the floor next to Zandra. She was muttering as she sorted through yet another box of her mother's things she'd salvaged from her apartment, just before Adrienne's mean landlord threw it all out.

"There must be something here to give me a clue about what Adrienne is playing at. We've been here almost a week, and there's been no word from her. And that letter she left me shows something went wrong. A mistake caught up with her. What if she has to keep running? She may never come back." Zandra dumped a pile of old postcards back in a box.

I flopped onto my side and exposed my belly for a tickle. "Maybe she's keeping below the radar for a few weeks until the trouble blows over. This disappearing act could be about the debts she's racked up in Crimson Cove. She won't know you're here paying them back. Or Lennie, the scummy landlord, could have gotten mean and chased her away."

"I wondered that too, but Adrienne doesn't scare easily and can usually charm her way out of most situations."

"Her charm failed this time, so she had to vanish. She'll come home."

Zandra kept hunting through the box. She pulled out several purses and rifled through them, removing old candy wrappers, tissues, and pieces of paper with shopping lists scrawled on them. "Who needs this many purses?"

"Apparently, your mother. Although I don't see her favorite, that yellow purse with the big tassels." I loved to bat those tassels when no one was watching.

"She must have it with her," Zandra said. "I've counted a dozen purses. I don't even remember packing this many."

"Maybe they've been breeding. Boxes make comfortable nests."

She sorted through another purse and then dumped it on the floor.

"Knock, knock. Is it okay to come down?" Vorana's voice drifted down the staircase.

"Sure," Zandra said. "We're decent."

My nose picked up the sweet smell of warm cinnamon and chocolate. There was also a delicious undercurrent of smoked fish. I hopped up and met Vorana at the bottom of the stairs. She had a plate of brownies in one hand, a smaller plate with smoked fish on the other, and Sage, her cat familiar, was settled in a papoose on the front of Vorana's belly.

"I thought you might like dessert down here," Vorana said. "You sped through dinner so fast, we hardly had time to talk."

"Brownies! You're always welcome if you bring brownies." Zandra stood and took the plates.

"That looks comfortable," I said to Sage as I admired the soft papoose she was snuggled in. Sage had lost the use of her back legs under mysterious circumstances she'd yet to reveal to me. Her tail and paws hung loose as Vorana walked into the basement.

"It's a convenient way to get around, and it's nice to be out of the wheeled harness for a while." Sage's eyes narrowed. "Don't eat all the fish before I get down, though. We're sharing."

"Of course. I'm always happy to share." As much as it pained me, I patiently waited for Sage to be unwrapped from the papoose. Vorana gently set her on the cushion I'd been using and adjusted her back legs until they were in a comfortable position.

"You get started on a brownie," she said to Zandra. "This smoked fish is tough, so Sage will need help to get it down."

"She treats me like a baby," Sage grumbled. "I still have my fangs." She displayed worn yellow stubby teeth.

"I do it because you're my baby, no matter how old and curmudgeonly you get." Vorana kissed the top of Sage's head. "I don't know where I'd be if it weren't for you." More kisses were planted, accompanied by lots of mwah, mwah, mwahs.

Although Sage grumbled, she was purring as she received her kiss overload.

Vorana pushed a piece of fish over to me and pulled apart the other one for Sage until the pieces were small enough for her to eat without much chewing.

She washed her hands in the tiny adjoining bathroom and joined Zandra for a brownie. "You're sorting through your things?"

"This belongs to Adrienne. I was hoping I might find a clue as to her whereabouts. But so far, nothing, and I haven't heard anything from her. She hasn't been in touch with you, has she?" Zandra said.

"No. Have you tried her snow globe?"

"She left it behind and doesn't have a mobile globe. She likes to be disconnected from the world." Zandra sighed dramatically.

Vorana indulged her with a smile. "Your mother always was a fun character. I miss her not being around. I hope she comes back soon."

"Me, too. I figured she'd have left notes about her arrangements, where she was staying, or her travel plans, but I've found nothing. And the note she left me, it got me worried."

"Note?"

Zandra's gaze went to the chest in the corner of the basement.

I looked up from eating my smoked fish. Zandra was always cautious about revealing information to people she didn't know, but I had a good feeling about Vorana, and she'd only been kind to us since we'd arrived in Crimson Cove.

I finished my last mouthful of fish and hopped onto Zandra's lap. I nudged her with my head to encourage her to keep talking.

She took the encouragement well enough. "You may as well look. It's no big deal." Zandra finished her brownie, collected the letter her mother had written her, and gave it to Vorana.

She took her time reading and then looked at the chest. "What sort of things did she leave you?"

"Spell books, potions, old manuscripts. I haven't looked through it all. I've been flicking through some papers in the evenings, though. It's advanced magic. I'm surprised, because Adrienne was never into magic. She rarely used it." Zandra kept her gaze on the chest. "I can't decide if she got lucky with everything she put in the chest, or she knew more than I realized."

"Mind if I take a look?"

"Go ahead. It's not locked."

They headed to the chest and sorted through the contents together.

"Wow! You've got everything you need to go into battle. Spells, potions, even weapons. What did Adrienne think you were going to do with your life?" Vorana said.

"I don't think she gave any thought to my future. She was always too wrapped up in her own problems."

Vorana looked skeptical. "Don't be so sure about that. She must have cared to put together all these supplies. Some of this is expensive. It looks like she wanted you prepared for anything. You've got to be a certain level of magic user to wield some of these spells without blowing yourself to pieces."

"Then you know more about this stuff than I do," Zandra said. "I don't know what to do with most of it. My magical education was... wonky."

"May I suggest spending time in my store? I have answers to all the questions. You just need to find them among the pages." Vorana waggled her eyebrows.

Zandra shrugged. "Books?"

I poked her with a paw. "Books are magic."

"Magic is magic." Zandra hovered a hand over the chest. "But I won't turn down any guidance that'll help me figure out what all this does."

"Magic is like everything else. It takes practice. No one is great the first time they try a spell. I remember when I was in a rush and tried a cleaning spell in the bookstore. The books rearranged with the spines facing the wrong way. It took me a week to get everything back to how it should be." Vorana laughed and shook her head. "The next time, I used the spell on a small section of the store, until I got more confident. There are few magic users who can click their fingers and everything falls into place."

My witch was one of those magic users. She just didn't know it yet.

"I guess so. I never thought about it like that," Zandra said.

I held my tongue. Several of the Crypt witches had repeatedly told Zandra she needed to practice her magic daily to ensure she had a handle on her power. But my witch had a habit of not always listening to sensible advice.

"Where did you train?" Vorana said. "You said you had a wonky education."

"I didn't grow up in a house full of magic, so it feels alien to practice," Zandra said. "I know we should keep trying new spells, that's how you become a great magic user, but there would be weeks when

Adrienne wouldn't use a single spell or potion, so neither did I. She acted more like a non-magical than a witch. I don't think she believed in her own power enough to use it."

I knew someone else like that, but I didn't hold it against her.

"You didn't get much of a magical education?" Vorana thumbed through a spell book she'd lifted from the chest.

"No, and I was partly responsible for that. I mentioned the age-up spell I used on myself when we met, didn't I?"

"You didn't, but I worked it out for myself. Adrienne talked about you a lot and said you grew up too quickly and she lost her little girl before she was ready. You did that to yourself?"

"I needed to. Adrienne couldn't help me. My dad was a mess, and no one would take a dumb kid seriously. I had to get noticed."

Vorana set down the book. "You don't regret it? Growing up so fast? I must admit, there were times in my childhood I'd rather not remember, but I learned a lot from other witches when I was growing up."

"Is there any point in regrets? It's not like I can perform an age reversal spell and live out all my teenage years for the first time."

I tilted my head from side to side. Technically, Zandra could, but I didn't want her getting ideas. We were settled and maturing, and Zandra was almost ready to face her next challenge by my side. Maybe it was selfish to put my needs first, but if I didn't do it soon, it would be too late for me.

"No. Generally, regrets don't make life better." Vorana grabbed two more brownies and held one out. "I live in the moment, while practicing for the future."

Zandra took the offered brownie. "I have nothing to complain about now. I've got Juno, I'm living in your amazing basement, eating your incredible food, and I even like my new job. If I hadn't found a body, things would be perfect."

Vorana munched on her brownie, her gaze intent on Zandra. "Would it be better if you got your mother back?"

"Only so I could keep an eye on her. Do you know what Adrienne meant in the letter about trouble finding her?" Zandra said.

Vorana considered the question. "Nothing comes to mind. She was always having little dramas but never anything big enough that would need her to disappear. How about you? Do you know what she meant?"

"No, but I met her former neighbor, Mrs. December, and she mentioned Adrienne arguing with a guy just before she went on her vacation. He had small eyes and a hand tattoo. Does that sound like anyone you know?"

"A hand tattoo? They're uncommon around here. They're only used by certain people. People you want nothing to do with."

"Who?"

Vorana's face crinkled as her mouth twisted. "It's a tag for any member of the Shadow gang. Ever heard of them?"

My head jerked up, and Zandra sucked in a breath. We were back to the gang again. That couldn't be a coincidence.

"You've seen these tattoos?" Zandra said.

"Sure. The head of the gang, Anan Shadow, insists every member get the same tattoo to show allegiance. It's also a warning mark for anyone who has the misfortune of meeting someone from the gang. If you're not respectful, they come after you."

"I keep hearing about this gang," Zandra said. "You think Adrienne had anything to do with them?"

"Doubtful. And she never mentioned being involved with the gang. Anan is a seriously unpleasant guy, though. He's been running that gang for over twenty years. There's nothing good about him. He loves to cause trouble."

I leaned against Zandra as her pulse picked up. "Your mother might not have been involved with Anan or the gang."

"What about the hand tattoo? If it wasn't a gang member, who was she arguing with?" Zandra petted me as she talked. "If she needed a problem sorted, she could have gotten desperate and gone to them. Monika and Pluto said the Shadow gang will deal with any problem you need, provided you pay them."

Vorana shook her head. "Adrienne got into scrapes but nothing that would need the attention of the Shadow gang. She can't have a connection with them."

"You know the gang pretty well?" Zandra said.

"Only by reputation." Vorana pulled apart the last piece of her brownie. "But I know somebody who has a connection to them. He's not in their inner circle, but he's done business with them in the past."

"You think this guy could get me an in with the gang, so I can speak to them about Adrienne?"

I stiffened. "That's a terrible idea."

"We have to find out if Adrienne was connected to this gang," Zandra said.

"I agree with Juno. This gang isn't to be messed with. They've had their claws in this place for decades. Most of the time, we rub along beside them without trouble. They don't mess with residents, and we turn a blind eye to their shady business dealings."

Zandra's brow furrowed, and she pushed away her brownie.

Vorana pursed her lips. "I get it, and it's not something any of us are proud of, but it's the simplest way to keep the peace. They don't hurt us, so we keep quiet about what we see."

"What if they've started messing with the locals?" Zandra said. "Including Adrienne? Would that change things?"

Vorana was quiet for a moment. "I know your mother sometimes struggled to make enough money, but she'd have known better than to get involved with that gang."

"You don't know her as well as you thought. Adrienne acts on impulse, and she never thinks through the consequences of her actions. Maybe this time, she pushed things too far."

"And you think someone from the gang hurt her?"

Vorana shook her head. "No. She's alive and well. This'll blow over, and she'll come back tanned and excited about her vacation, probably with a gorgeous guy on her arm."

"Just in case that doesn't happen, I need to meet your contact," Zandra said.

There was another hesitation from Vorana. "I'll see what I can do. Meet us tomorrow lunchtime in the café. What time do you get a break?"

"I'll meet you there at one."

Vorana finished her brownie. "I hope you're wrong about this."

"So do I."

I was unhappy Zandra was risking herself by investigating this gang, but if her feckless mother had gotten tangled in their dubious activities, we had to find out. And whatever happened, I'd make sure no one harmed my witch.

"How about dessert?" Vorana said.

Zandra raised her eyebrows. "We've just had brownies."

"Those were the entrée desserts. Second dessert is even more delicious."

"Is it more fish?" I said.

"You and Sage will also get a special second dessert, full of fishy goodness."

I suddenly felt more positive now there were treats upstairs. Maybe these mysteries would be swiftly solved with no gang involvement. Then I could help Zandra with her new friendships, focus on my plan, and ensure my witch followed her passions.

"Second dessert sounds amazing," Zandra said. "Thanks. And thanks for listening to my worries. I'm probably overreacting, but.."

"It's always a pleasure. And we can talk about something other than the Shadow gang, if you'd prefer."

"So long as the talk isn't about books, I don't mind what we discuss."

Vorana laughed as she headed up the stairs. "Where I go, book talk goes. Suck it up and learn to enjoy it. You never know, you could unlock all that hidden potential with the help of a few books."

Chapter 10

A surprise and a treat

After a morning chasing a troop of wild glittery ferrets with red eyes and breath like a unicorn's behind and getting them successfully moved, we were ready for our lunch break. And maybe a shower.

Zandra pulled the van up outside Bites and Delights, and we climbed out and walked inside. She looked around and waved as she spotted Vorana sitting at a table at the back of the cafe. Her contact was with her, but he had his back to us.

Zandra grabbed our food, and we headed to the table.

As I got closer, I recognized the guy's scent, but before I warned Zandra who it was, she'd stopped by the table. Her smile vanished as she looked at Torrin.

Vorana's expression also changed. "Oh! Do you two know each other?"

"We do." Zandra's tone was cautious. "Torrin messed with one of my jobs. He destroyed a cage and ate my hedgehogs."

"I thought we'd established they weren't your hedgehogs." Torrin grinned at her. "They looked free roaming to me."

"They were in my cage when you stuffed them down your throat."

Vorana's eyebrows flashed up, and she burst into laughter. "Torrin! I knew you had exotic tastes when it came to your food, but hedgehogs! That's a stretch even for you."

He laughed, his attention still on Zandra. "I learned the hard way that anything with prickles and poison doesn't make for good eating. I coughed them up, and they were unharmed. How are the little guys doing?"

"Relocated safely. No thanks to you." Zandra looked around as if seeking somewhere else to sit.

Torrin lifted his hands. "It was an honest mistake. You shouldn't leave traps big enough to catch me in, though. I'm a sucker for a good meal, especially when someone else has caught it."

Vorana jabbed him in the arm with a finger. "Behave! And don't eat any more of Zandra's animals. Got it?"

"I'll try, but sometimes the dragon takes over." His eyes changed color before reverting to their normal dark shade.

"Well, it sounds like everything worked out in the end," Vorana said. "Grab a seat, Zandra. We have things to discuss."

Zandra looked torn between making a point and leaving and getting information on the Shadow gang. I held my breath as I waited to see which option she'd choose. In the end, she took the mature route. She placed my food down for me and settled in a seat.

"At least I don't have to make any introductions," Vorana said. "And Torrin is happy to help in any way he can."

"Of course. I want to make sure our new residents feel welcome." He flashed Zandra a smile, which she didn't return.

He was devilishly handsome, but his looks made no impact on Zandra. She was quick to hold a grudge, so it would take Torrin time to get back on her good side.

As I ate my strips of fish, a striking cat sitting in the cafe window took my attention. He was big, with large ears and a fine-boned face with high cheeks. He was also hairless, and his gleaming skin was a beautiful tawny brown.

I was tempted to speak to him but needed to remain with my witch. My breath grew short as his muscles flexed while he washed, seeming oblivious to the attention he was drawing.

"Don't you want your food?" Zandra said to me.

"I do. It's good. I'm just... waiting." I'd been so distracted by the stunning hairless cat nonchalantly licking his face that I'd forgotten my salmon. I was glad I was covered in fur because no one could see me blush, but I was so intrigued, my appetite had gone. Who was this enigmatic stranger? I hadn't seen him in the café on previous days, and he didn't seem to be with anyone.

"What can you tell me about the Shadow gang?" Zandra said to Torrin.

"Vorana's told you the basics about them," he said. "Essentially, they're thieves. And they take anything. Magic, gold, people. Whatever they can sell, traffic, and turn a big profit on. They're nasty guys, and I'm certain they've killed plenty of times, but they always get away with it."

"I've heard the angels aren't big fans," Zandra said.

"The angels are intimidated by them." Torrin shook his head. "The problem with the Shadow gang is not only do they have the muscle, but they also have the brains. They've got some hot shot lawyer who can get them off any charge. Or at the very least, get the charge reduced so they only pay a fine. I think the most any member of the Shadow gang has spent inside is two weeks, and then they got let out early on a technicality."

"They can't be that clever," Zandra said.

"As I mentioned, people look the other way with the Shadow gang. No one wants to become their target," Vorana said. "It means they get away with a lot of shady things and aren't reported."

"What about Sorcha? She told me about the fake body parts when she stood up to the gang. Did no one help her?"

Vorana leaned closer. "Did Sorcha tell you what she found under her pillow one night?"

"Uh, no. She just said she got gross fake bits delivered to her door covered in fake blood."

Vorana's eyes narrowed. "A tongue. Someone placed a tongue under her pillow. And there was nothing fake about it."

That got my attention, and I stopped lusting after the hairless honey in the window. "How did they get inside to leave it?"

"Sorcha wasn't sure, but there was no sign of a break-in. After it happened, she paid a powerful sorceress to place wards around the café and her upstairs apartment. They prevent anyone associated with the gang from entering her property. She gets them topped up every week because she's so concerned they might try again."

"No one saw it happen?" Zandra said.

"If they did, they didn't report it. The Shadow gang has everyone scared. We've all seen what happens if they come for you." Vorana slid a finger across her throat.

"You vanish, just like Adrienne," Zandra muttered.

"Oh! No, I didn't mean... sorry, that was a dumb thing to say. They haven't hurt her, I'm sure of it." Vorana grabbed Zandra's hand and squeezed it.

"You think the gang had something to do with your mother going AWOL?" Torrin said. When Zandra glared at him, he jabbed his thumb at Vorana. "I asked why you were interested in them, so Vorana gave me the back story."

Zandra lifted her chin. "Sure. And I'm not certain, but Adrienne was seen arguing with someone with a gang tattoo not long before she disappeared."

"Vorana said Adrienne left a message about going on a vacation. Why do you think she's lying about that? Why does this have to be gang related?" Torrin said.

"She can't afford a trip to the car wash, let alone a vacation. She also told me not to look for her. And...." Zandra glanced at me, and I nodded for her to continue. It was important Zandra let people into her life, especially those who could help her.

She drew in a breath. "I found a chest of magic supplies she'd left me. There was a letter in there. It said she'd gotten in trouble and had to disappear for a while. She put the letter somewhere it would be hard to find."

"You think she hid it in case the gang poked around her place to find out where she was?" Torrin said.

"It's possible. Adrienne never thinks anything bad will happen to her, but what if she did something that brought her to the gang's attention?" Zandra tugged on the ends of her hair. "Or she was working with them and something went wrong? She could have seen something she shouldn't or overheard a private conversation and got jittery."

No one spoke. No one ate. They all looked worried.

"I don't think the gang took her," Torrin said. "You said she left a message. If they'd abducted her, she wouldn't have done that."

"They could have forced her to do it, so people wouldn't look for her," Zandra said.

Neither Torrin nor Vorana spoke again, although they exchanged a worried glance.

"You think I'm onto something, don't you?" Zandra said.

Torrin sipped his coffee. "Not for certain"

"How do you know the Shadow gang?" I said. "Have you worked with them? I don't see a tattoo on your hand."

"I was never in the gang. They demand complete devotion if you want to be a part of what they do, and I had no interest in that. But I did business with them in the past. It was nothing serious. They needed goods moved fast and discreetly, and I had the means to do it."

"Stolen goods?" Zandra's nose wrinkled.

"I didn't ask any questions. They simply paid me and told me where to take the goods. I wouldn't work with them now. Back then, I needed the money."

"You said they traffic people. You didn't do that, did you?" Zandra said.

Torrin's eyebrows lowered. "I have boundaries. It was a load of boxes. They were sealed, and I didn't look in them, but they weren't big enough or sturdy enough to put people inside."

"It can't have been a one-off job, though," Zandra said. "You wouldn't learn much about their operations by dealing with them once."

"I did maybe a dozen jobs for them over a year, then I had to go away for a bit."

"You were arrested?" I said.

Torrin smirked. "I see how high I am in your estimations."

I gave a little shrug. Torrin had taken money off a dangerous gang. What did he expect me to think of him?

"It was family business that made me leave. I wasn't around, so the gang moved on and found someone else. That was fine by me. I came into some money so I could set up my business and no longer needed to deal with them. I wasn't unhappy about it."

"Why do you want to help me?" Zandra's suspicious side rose. "If the Shadow gang finds out you've been talking about them, it'll look bad on you."

"Maybe it will, but I know Adrienne, and I like her. I want to make sure nothing bad happened to her. And I kind of like you, too, when you're not scowling at me."

Zandra looked away, a faint blush on her cheeks. "Do you think they took Adrienne?"

"I think you've got a right to be concerned, but the Shadow gang doesn't mess with the locals. They work hard to keep the balance right. They know, if they mess with what's going on in Crimson Cove too much, people will turn on them."

"Things change. What they did to Sorcha proves that," Zandra said.

"They knew they'd gone too far with Sorcha. Anan is insane, but he's not dumb. If he'd kept prodding her, he'd have regretted it," Vorana said. "The Shadow gang is intimidating, but if we all stood against them, they'd be in trouble."

"So would Crimson Cove. They'd destroy the place," Torrin muttered.

I couldn't decide if the residents of the town were sensible to find a balance with this gang or cowards. Time would tell.

"Adrienne could have done something to anger them. I need to know if she was involved with them," Zandra said.

"I never saw Adrienne with any gang members," Vorana said. "And she didn't talk about them. She always told me about her work and any guys she was seeing, so I don't think she had a connection to them."

"Maybe she did jobs for them, like Torrin. She could have moved things or stored stuff for the gang in her apartment," Zandra said.

"But why make her disappear?" Torrin said.

Zandra sighed. "Because she messed up. It wouldn't be the first time."

"Or she talked to someone she shouldn't," I said.

"Angel Force?" Vorana said.

I nodded. "Adrienne could have been worried and tried to do the right thing. The Shadow gang found out."

"Pump those fluffy brakes. You're getting ahead of yourself. You don't even know if she's missing or on a vacation. We need facts," Torrin said. "I'll see what I can find out. After all, I want to make sure our newest residents in Crimson Cove are happy."

Zandra ignored his big smile again. She wasn't warming to this handsome half-dragon.

I nudged her leg with my head until she finally acknowledged Torrin. He was putting himself in danger by asking the Shadow gang if Adrienne had ever worked for them, so he deserved a small amount of encouragement.

"Thanks. I just worry about Adrienne." Zandra pulled apart her muffin. "It feels like our roles have always been reversed, and I've spent my life looking after her. Even from a young age, we had this weird relationship."

"You don't have to tell me about weird families," Torrin said. "Mine is the weirdest. That money I came into was because my parents fought each other to the death."

"Whoa! They killed each other?" Zandra said.

"Yep. They challenged each other. It's a dumb dragon thing. They were both part dragon, and their bickering got out of control." Torrin shrugged, but I caught a flash of pain in his eyes. "Neither of them would give up, so they died for honor. My dad survived for a couple of days, but his injuries were so bad, nothing could save him, not even the strongest healing spell. They were too proud for their own good and look where it got them. Their bodies on a dragon pyre, and me with no parents."

"You really do know about weird families." Zandra looked at me, alarm in her eyes.

"Sure do. Listen, Adrienne will be fine. Even if she has gotten herself into a mess, you're here to help her," Torrin said.

"And we're here, too," Vorana said.

Zandra nodded. She relaxed into her seat and ate some muffin.

I was happy Zandra was making friends, even if it was with reluctance. She'd spent too long on her own, struggling to understand her powers and find her place in the world. She needed a family around her. Whether that was a new family she formed herself with help from me or her dad and the Crypt witches.

"How about we meet tomorrow night for a drink?" Torrin said.

Zandra glanced at Vorana, who was busy investigating the contents of the milk jug. "I can't do tomorrow."

"The following night?"

"Why?"

"To get to know you better."

"A date?" Zandra said.

"No, although it could be if you're interested. It could be a getting to know you kind of date," Torrin said.

"No, you're good. Thanks."

"You're seeing someone?"

Vorana chuckled, quickly hiding her face behind her large coffee mug when Zandra glared at her.

Zandra looked at me and winked. “I’m too much in love with myself to have room for anybody else in my life.”

I snort laughed, and Vorana smirked.

“I love a confident woman,” Torrin said, not deterred by Zandra’s rebuttal. “No strings. We could meet, and I’ll give you an update if I have news about the Shadow gang. There’s a bar next to my workshop. It’s a fun place. They do great burgers and fries, and the music is decent if you like rock ‘n’ roll.”

“I don’t hate any of those things.”

“Then it’s on?”

“I’ll think about it.”

“I’ll be there, anyway. I usually drop by after work and catch up with friends. If you’re free, come along, too. You could meet new people and find out more about the gang.”

Zandra nodded, but I could tell she’d committed to nothing.

I settled my tail neatly over my paws while studying Torrin. He was a potential match for my witch, although I wasn’t settled on him. His angry dragon side could be a problem. But I needed to get Zandra back in the dating game before she decided a spinsterly life was for her. My witch was too cute and sassy for that path.

My gaze slid to the enticing bald cat in the window. Maybe it was time I dipped a paw back into the dating game, too.

Chapter 11

It's a date

"I'm impressed." Barney sat opposite Zandra in his office. He had a sheet of papers in front of him, a pen in one hand, and a smile on his face. "You're efficient, and you get results."

Zandra shifted in her seat. "I'm glad you think so. Although finding a body during my first month on the job wasn't something I was warned about during my induction."

Barney's laugh had a nervous hitch. "I'm glad you stayed. I was worried I might lose you over that. What with the hellhound attack and then the corpse, it would be enough to make most people walk out."

"My witch is made of strong stuff." I sat on the edge of Barney's desk as they went through her appraisal. "She won't let you down."

"I'm realizing that. You're both an asset to the team. The others like you, too."

"Because I'm taking all the gross, difficult jobs and don't complain," she said.

"Maybe that has something to do with it. They'll ease up soon. The old guard likes to test new employees. The next hellhound complaint we get, I'll make sure Oleander takes the job."

"I don't mind hellhounds," Zandra said. "Once you've been around them a while, you learn they're not so terrifying."

"That's right. You mentioned your sister has a hellhound as her familiar."

"Kind of. They have a unique bond. Tempest lets Wiggles do his own thing, and he hangs out with her because he likes her. It works for them."

"Well, I'm glad you stayed. And your work has been outstanding. I know when you started, you mentioned you may not stay too long. Have you got a date for when you're leaving Crimson Cove?" There was a hopeful look in Barney's eyes, which suggested he didn't want Zandra to leave anytime soon.

I also wanted us to stay, so I was eager to hear Zandra's answer.

"I'm in no hurry to go," she said after a short pause. "I haven't made progress in finding Adrienne, and until she's back and I figure out what she's been up to, I'm going nowhere. And I like the work. I'm surprised how much satisfaction I get from looking after the animals. I don't even mind gently educating people about their responsibilities. Some owners I've met let their familiars run wild."

"It happens. And it's not always the owner's fault. It's easy for a powerful familiar to get the upper hand if the bond isn't powerful," Barney said. "Sometimes, it takes a few nudges to get owner and familiar back on the right track. You haven't had problems dealing with people, though?"

"A couple of them have been sharp, but they know I have the authority to take their familiar, and none of them want that to happen." She rested a hand on my back, and I leaned into her touch.

"No one wants to be without their familiar." Barney's gaze went to a small empty cardboard box in the corner of the room.

I'd been tempted to try it out for size on several occasions, since it looked to be the perfect fit for a cat, but something had made me stop. And from the way Barney looked at that box, this wasn't just any old box. It was a shrine. A memory of someone who'd been important to him.

Zandra picked up on that too, because she also stared at the box. "Barney, you lost someone, didn't you?"

He cleared his throat and straightened the papers in front of him. "It was a while ago."

"Your familiar?"

Barney nodded, his head down. "She was wonderful. A big, plump black-and-white cat."

"I'm so sorry for your loss. What was her name?"

"Isabella. Izzy for short. She found me when I was a teenager, and we clicked. She had a knack for calming anxious familiars. It was her superpower. She could also neutralize dangerous magic with one touch." Barney's breath shook as he exhaled. "That was how she died."

I stepped over his paperwork and hopped onto Barney's lap.

He looked down at me in surprise, and a single tear slid down his cheek as he petted me. "Izzy was protecting me when it happened. A magic user was stealing familiars. He was a bad guy, heavily into dark magic. He was ripping away familiars, distorting the bond they had with their magic user, and turning them against their bonded owner."

"What kind of monster would do such a thing?" I leaned against Barney's soft belly.

"He was jealous of a family in Crimson Cove. They had a successful business, and he'd worked for them but had been fired because he got caught stealing from the register. So he ruined their lives. Two people died, and several more were gravely injured before we figured out what he was doing. Of course, Izzy was her usual fearless self. We tracked him to an abandoned house and cornered him."

"Where were the angels? They should have helped you," Zandra said.

"They were involved, but there were six trapped familiars we had to get out, and they needed to be handled carefully. Things went wrong. The angels were injured, so it was just me and Izzy left. The guy shot out a killing spell, and Izzy jumped in front of me. She took the full blast. There was nothing I could do to save her." Another tear trickled down Barney's face. "It's been five years."

I licked his hand to give him small comfort at enduring such a heart-rending loss.

"You've never looked for another familiar?" Zandra said softly. "Of course, it wouldn't be easy. I'd be lost without Juno, and my life has been so much better with her in it, but maybe it's time."

"I don't know about that."

"There could be the perfect familiar waiting for you. You have a big heart. Does it have room for one more familiar?"

"That's kind of you to say, but I gave my heart to Izzy. No one will replace her. She was wonderful. I keep telling myself I need to move on and get rid of her things." Barney's gaze went to the box again. "I can't. If I do, it would be admitting she was really gone and I'm never getting her back. And I know she's not coming back, but still, there's that tiny, foolish hope lingering. It's silly."

"Barney, hope is never foolish," I said. "You grieve for Isabella however you want to. She sounds like a magnificent familiar, and I'm sure you have wonderful memories of your time together. She did what all the best familiars do. She protected her bonded magic owner with her last breath." Just like I'd do for Zandra.

"You have a good one here." Barney petted me some more. "Juno is a solid gold familiar."

"I couldn't agree more." Zandra looked on proudly. "I wouldn't be half as good at this job if it wasn't for Juno."

I hopped off the desk and trotted to Zandra to make sure she didn't feel left out of my fluffy attention.

Barney sniffed and looked at his papers. "Well, that's enough of that. And you're welcome to stay here for as long as you like. As far as I'm concerned, I'm not looking for anyone else. The job is yours."

"Thanks. I appreciate that," Zandra said. "When I do plan to move on, I'll give you plenty of notice."

There was a knock at the door, and it was opened a second later by Finn. Bertoli accompanied him. "I hope I'm not interrupting. There was no one out front, and we saw the light on back here."

"No, we're just finishing our meeting," Barney said.

"I thought you'd want an update about the findings at Osorin Greenbow's place." Finn nodded at me, while Bertoli's expression remained sour, as if he was sucking a bitter lemon.

"Absolutely. Take a seat," Barney said.

The angels settled in, and Finn pulled out his notebook. "The body was definitely Osorin. And the cause of death, well, that was obvious. He must have died instantly, given what happened to him."

"Do you know how it happened?" Zandra said.

"Not yet. And we're struggling to figure out if it was an accident, if Osorin did it to himself, or if someone used a spell or potion on him."

"The neighbors didn't see anyone around just before he died?"

Bertoli grumbled under his breath as Zandra asked the question, but Finn seemed happy enough to answer.

"The neighbors saw nothing. And I suspect, if they did, they wouldn't tell us anything," Finn said. "They'd be too worried trouble would find its way to their door if they talked. Not everyone trusts Angel Force to get things done discreetly."

"Which suggests whoever did this to Osorin isn't to be messed with," Zandra said. "Could it be the Shadow gang?"

"We're still investigating that avenue."

Bertoli sharply cleared his throat. "We can't share all the case information with civilians. It could jeopardize the investigation."

Zandra tilted her head. "Do you still think I'm involved because I found the body?"

Bertoli glowered at her. “We’re considering all options.”

Finn’s expression soured. “No, you’re not a suspect, Zandra. And we appreciate you alerting us to a possible connection to the Shadow gang.”

Barney gripped the edge of his desk. “I didn’t know they were involved in Osorin’s death.”

“They may not be,” Finn said, “but thanks to Zandra, it’s a lead we’re following.”

“I have a question about the gang,” I said.

“We didn’t come here to answer your questions,” Bertoli said. “This is a courtesy call since animal control was initially involved in discovering the crime scene.”

“And we appreciate that,” Barney said.

I hissed softly, while Zandra’s expression hardened as she glared at Bertoli.

“Has Archie remembered anything else?” Finn said. “He was still in shock when we talked to him, so the conversation was one-sided.”

“Unfortunately not. Archie has withdrawn and isn’t talking much. We’re still looking for a foster home for him,” Barney said. “He’s under regular monitoring, but it may be too late for him.”

I tugged on the bond I’d formed with Archie. It was barely functioning. I’d taken my eye off the ball, and he was in trouble. “Finn will take him.”

Finn’s eyebrows shot up. “Err... sure. I said I would, and I’ve had hellhounds in the sanctuary before, so I’ve got experience. I’m full at the moment, though, so it won’t be right away.”

“I’m not sure about that,” Barney said. “I know you’ve taken plenty of the smaller familiars, but Archie needs specialist handling, and I don’t want you questioning him about what he saw. It would distress him."

"Hey, Barney! I wouldn't do that," Finn said. "Just like you, it's the animals who come first. I wouldn't run a sanctuary and spend my wages on feed and healing spells if I didn't care about their well-being. If you can't find a place for Archie, send him my way. You know I can handle him."

Barney tapped a finger against his chin. "He has some digestive issues he's dealing with. You need to be prepared for that. And if you took him, he'd need to be supervised by animal control."

"Zandra will do that," I said.

"I will?"

"Yes. It'll be good for Archie to have a familiar face around. We could drop by and make sure he's okay." And while we were there, we could liaise with Finn about the case without Bertoli getting in the way.

Zandra appeared to catch on to what I was plotting, because she nodded. "I don't mind doing that. I could drop by your sanctuary after work and check on Archie."

"I'm fine with that if you are," Finn said. "Give me time to sort out a space for him, though. A guy that size will need plenty of room, so I'll have to move a few of the others around."

"It could work," Barney said. "And I'd appreciate it."

"Then I'll make it happen." Finn grinned at Zandra.

Barney collected his paperwork. "Is there anything else we can do for you?"

"No, but get in touch if Archie reveals anything that'll help with the case," Finn said. "I'm certain he was there when Osorin died but must have blocked the traumatic memories."

"You think someone was in the house with Osorin when he was killed?" Zandra said. "Is Archie a key witness?"

"It would explain the missing money," Finn said. "We went back to the house and had another look, but nothing was hidden."

"What's this about money?" Barney said.

"Archie thought Osorin had a bag of money, but it's missing," Zandra said. "If someone was in the house, they could have taken it. I'm thinking that was the reason Osorin was killed."

"Your thoughts are no good to us. We need evidence that money even existed," Bertoli said. "You didn't take it, did you?"

Zandra stood slowly, magic crackling around her. "Say that again."

Finn leaped from his seat and stepped in front of Bertoli. "No need for that. Bertoli's just having another bad day."

Zandra's magic continued to crackle. "I'm not a thief."

Finn nodded. "Exactly. But that money is a loose end we need to fix."

"And unless you have any useful information about it, you're of no further help to us." Bertoli leaned to his right, his attention on Zandra.

My hackles rose at Bertoli's rudeness.

"Forgive my partner. He didn't get any cake today. We'll leave you to it." Finn stepped back and patted Bertoli on the shoulder.

Bertoli stood, nodded at Barney, and strode to the door. "I'll be outside."

Finn grinned at Zandra and rolled his eyes.

"Barney, are we finished with my appraisal?" Zandra said. "There's something I need to speak to Finn about."

"Of course. I'll write up the report and give you a copy."

Zandra hurried out after Finn, and I followed her, not sure what she was planning. She made sure the door was shut before speaking. "Finn, I want to ask you a question about a family member."

"Uh-oh. Don't tell me the infamous Tempest Crypt is coming to town. Should I call in back-up?"

"No, nothing like that. My... mother lives here. Adrienne. At least, she did until recently."

"Oh, sure. Sorcha said you two were related. How's Adrienne doing? I haven't seen her around much."

"That's just it. She left town in a hurry, and she could be in trouble. Do you know if Adrienne had anything to do with the Shadow gang?"

His eyebrows rose. "Why do you think she's tangled up with them?"

"I don't know for certain she is. You've never had to warn her to be careful around them, have you?"

Finn shook his head. "Nothing like that. I'm surprised to hear you say she could have links to them. I don't know your mother well, but she seems like a sweet lady and not a troublemaker. I mean, there were a couple of rumors about unpaid bar bills, that sort of thing, but she always paid in the end."

"If you hear anything, could you let me know? The more I'm learning about Adrienne's life in

Crimson Cove, the more worried I get. Something is wrong, and I have to know what trouble she's in."

"Of course. I'll keep you informed. But if she has a connection to the Shadow gang, be careful. They don't appreciate being questioned about anything." He slid his notebook back into his pocket. "How about we meet for a drink, and I can tell you if I've found out anything useful?"

"A drink?" Zandra tilted her head from side to side. "I guess that can't hurt. How about tomorrow evening at seven o'clock at the bar next to Torrin's workshop? Do you know it?"

"Sure. I often go there. It's a date."

"A date? If you say so." There was a mischievous look on my witch's face I'd seen plenty of times before. She was up to no good.

I waited until Finn had headed out after Bertoli before confronting her. "What are you doing?"

"Nothing! Well, nothing wrong. Everyone keeps asking me out for a friendly drink, and they're all being so selflessly helpful, so I need to see how genuine they are." She grinned at me.

"You're planning on meeting Torrin and Finn at the same time and at the same place?"

"Why not? They claim they just want friendship, so let's get them together and see what their true motives are."

I purred my approval. My witch was not only clever and resourceful, but she was also a little devious. I loved it.

Chapter 12

Poop showers

"Come on, buddy. This cage has your name written all over it. Back at animal control, there's food, bedding, and a safe place to sleep. And we have sanctuaries. We'll find you the perfect place where you can chill, fire off your magic, and no one will stop you." Zandra spoke gently, her hands out.

Her persistent encouragement wasn't convincing the sparkly red panda with the white stripe on his back, who was huddled in a damp, muddy hole. We'd been chasing this stubborn critter for hours. We were tired, I had several magic burns to deal with, and the panda had used a gross shower of poop to cover Zandra in a less than fragrant odor. I also had a dollop of poop on my tail. It stank.

The panda bared his tiny pointed teeth at us. "Danger."

"There's no danger coming from us," I said. "I trust my witch to do the right thing by all familiars. Where is your bonded magic user?"

"Gone. Missing." The panda was so panicked he could only use single words, his frantic black gaze shifting around, looking for an escape.

"We'll help you find him, but you can't stay out here on your own. It'll get cold soon, and you're frightening people with your unstable magic and poop showers." I lifted my once pristine white tail to show him exactly how nasty they were.

"Back!" Another shower of panda poop got flung at us.

Who knew such a little guy could be so prolific in the pooping department?

"What if someone thinks you're a danger and hurts you?" I inched closer to the panda. If I had to, I'd subdue him by force.

"Back! Back! Back! Danger. Pain. Taken. Go."

"No, we're here to help. And we're going nowhere. Not without you."

The panda lunged at Zandra, but I was quicker than this fluffy bundle of red rage. I grabbed the panda's scruff in my teeth and wrapped my legs around him. He was bigger than me, but I was stronger and had more motive to succeed. If he got hold of Zandra, she'd be covered in something far worse than panda poop.

I couldn't be certain, but this critter was tainted with something dark. The magic he'd hit me with still stung and throbbed through my bones, so I wasn't letting it touch Zandra.

"Excellent. Hold him, Juno. That's it. You've got him." Zandra zapped the panda with a light sedation spell. He struggled for a few more seconds, but his magic weakened, as did the blows he rained on my legs with his hard little paws.

It took another minute of tussling before he admitted defeat. He sagged against me, his breath heaving out and his grip slackening.

"This guy is a bundle of anxiety. What a state to get himself in." Zandra stood over me and the slumbering, drooling panda. "He was terrified of us. And what was he talking about? It sounded like his bonded magic user is missing."

I rolled away from the snoozing panda and shook out my fur, dislodging the clump of drying poop from my tail. "He was just panicked. He probably thought we'd put him to sleep. That's what you thought you'd be doing when you first heard about this job."

"Maybe I did, but I've learned a few things since then. Sensational news and rumors are always so popular, though. Bad news makes a better headline. Although I always thought it should be the other way around. Animal control should be celebrated because of all the animals they help every day." While Zandra talked, she gently lifted the panda, and we walked back to the van.

"You should start a good news only channel," I said. "I'd watch."

"You may be biased about that, since you'd watch me paint a wall and find it interesting." She placed the panda in a cage and secured it. "We'll have to locate his owner."

"He could have been abandoned. It happens. Some magic users are monsters." I sniffed around the cage.

"If he has an owner, we'll find him. And if this guy has been abandoned, we'll make sure the owner knows it's not okay and slap them with a huge fine." Zandra wiped her hands on her jacket and grimaced. "He sure knew how to put us off. This jacket needs to be burned. These stains aren't ever coming out."

I glanced at the time on her watch. "If you're going to make your double date with Finn and Torrin, you need to hurry. We have to be at the bar in half an hour."

"That'll have to wait. I need to take this little guy back to base, get him secured, and do the paperwork. They won't mind waiting." Zandra headed to the driver's seat, and we climbed inside the van.

"Before the date, you need to go home, shower, and change. I adore you, but you stink."

Zandra chuckled. "There's no need for that. And the panda crud is mainly on my jacket. I got a bit on my pants, but that should wash out."

I stared at her. "You're going on the date dressed like that?"

She started the engine, and we headed back to base. "As I keep telling you, this isn't a double date. Though I suppose, if we're going strictly by numbers, it should be called a triple date since there are three of us. Or does there have to be three couples to make it a triple date? Anyway, it's a drink with two people who want to help me. That means they shouldn't care what I look like."

"They might care what you smell like, though. We'll get the poopy panda secure, then you head to Vorana's. You have a five-minute shower while I pick out something for you to wear."

"That's not happening. The last time you were in charge of my outfit, you tried to get me in a little black dress with a plunging neckline."

"Everyone needs a little black dress to show off her assets."

"Even you?"

"Especially me."

"You'd have to cut a hole for your tail if you wanted to wear a fancy gown." Zandra laughed as we headed through the light traffic back to animal control.

I sighed. I used to have magnificent closets full of clothes. A whole room dedicated to the finery I'd drape around my body. A demi-goddess had to look her best, no matter the occasion. And I loved clothes. I'd felt naked for a long time with only fur. My white fur was magnificent, but it was no match for a fitted cream silk gown with a draping train and a lace edging.

"Hey, Juno, I'm teasing. If you want a dress, I'll get you one. It's trendy to dress up animals. I've seen it on social media," Zandra said. "Personally, I'm not a fan. But we could look into getting you something suitable. A cute sweater, maybe?"

I wrinkled my booping snooter. I'd seen enough pictures taken of animals wrapped in tight sweaters with hats stuck on their heads to know it wasn't for me. I needed the finest fabrics, not a mass produced, scratchy sweater with *small but sassy, bros before bones,* or *merry pawmas* printed on it.

Zandra giggled at my expression. "We'll put that idea on the never to be attempted list, shall we?"

"No outfits for me. My fur does me proud."

She reached over and petted me. "It does. It's beautiful."

I looked her over one more time. If Zandra wasn't showering, I'd need to lick off that bit of dried panda poop on her cheek before we got to the bar. Providing we left the jacket behind and she sponged the poop off her pants, she'd have to do. Hopefully, Torrin and Finn liked the lived-in look in their dates. And even though Zandra didn't consider this a date, I did. She may not think romance was on the cards tonight, but how could they not fall in love with her?

After settling in the still slumbering panda, getting the paperwork ready to complete in the morning, and after a brief debate, I'd convinced Zandra to clean up in the staff washroom.

It took her ten minutes, and she smelled sweeter and looked presentable as we arrived at the bar, only fifteen minutes late.

The interior was modern chrome and wood, a rock song blasted from behind the bar, and there were several groups of people enjoying themselves. Some had food, nothing fishy smelling, but most were simply drinking alone or chatting to friends.

Finn and Torrin were already there, although sitting separately.

I waited to see who Zandra went to talk to first. That would show her preference.

"You go get Torrin. I'll say hi to Finn." She pointed at the bar.

An interesting choice. A half-angel, half-demon was her preferred potential mate. This could get spicy.

I trotted to Torrin and nudged his leg with my head. "Zandra Crypt wishes for you to join her and her companion."

Torrin looked down at me and smiled. "It's Juno, isn't it?"

I nodded. "And you should hurry. She's not a witch you should keep waiting."

He chuckled. "I imagine she's not. Trap any innocent people who were out walking in the woods today?"

"That was hardly my witch's error. You stuck your snout in a loaded cage. What other outcome could you have expected?"

"The food was worth it. Who's the companion?"

"My witch will be attended to by two gentlemen this evening." I walked away, confident Torrin would follow. The thud of his boots behind me showed he was doing exactly that.

Zandra was at the bar, chatting to Finn. She looked up as we approached and smiled.

"Hey! What's going on here?" Torrin said. "I thought it was just the two of us?"

Zandra's smile widened. "I figured I could meet you at the same time. After all, you both said you wanted to help. Is there a problem with Finn being here?"

The guys stared at each other for a tense few seconds. Then they laughed.

"No problem with me," Finn said. "We hang out together all the time."

"Well played, Zandra," Torrin said. "Sure, let's have a *friendly* drink together."

"That's what I was thinking," Zandra said. "Finn is buying the first round."

Finn shrugged, an amused look on his face as he called over the bartender.

I was impressed with how my witch was handling things. Zandra had experienced a few missteps in her past relationships, mainly through lack of experience, but I always set her on the right path. Although I was yet to decide which path she should follow in Crimson Cove. The rugged half-dragon or the dashing half-angel? Maybe tonight would provide that answer.

Once the drinks were served, we found a table and settled in away from the music. I had a bowl of mineral water, which I gently lapped while I waited to see which gentleman would make the first move.

"I've been asking around about Adrienne's connection to the gang," Torrin said.

"You're involved in that, too?" Finn said.

Torrin nodded. "I have connections. I figured they could be useful to Zandra."

Finn's eyes narrowed a fraction. "I looked into the records we have on the Shadow gang. Nothing connected to Adrienne."

"That's good," Zandra said.

"Records are only as good as the people who keep them," Torrin said.

Finn's friendly expression sharpened, but he said nothing.

"Any news on your end?" Zandra said to Torrin.

"Not so far. No one is talking. Usually, a couple of the guys are happy to have a few beers and chat about their latest misadventures. Not this time. When I spoke to them, I got dead eyes and silence. They've been told not to talk."

"Which suggests they're up to something they want no one else to know about," Finn said. "The Shadow gang always closes ranks when they've taken on a big job."

"What kind of job would make them do that?" Zandra said.

Finn took a sip from his beer. "It's usually handling stolen goods. If they get a big consignment, all attention goes to that. Any smaller, private jobs take a back seat."

"From what I've heard about their latest activities, they're getting more into people trafficking," Torrin said.

Finn scowled. "If you've got evidence of that, you need to pass it to Angel Force."

"No evidence, just rumors. It's happened before. They sent a truck of wood nymphs they captured to a client. It took them a month to round up the nymphs, and some were in a bad state. They took risks back then, so they must have been desperate to make the job pay. They were asking everyone for nymph contacts."

"Including you?" Zandra said.

Torrin nodded. "I didn't help. We all have lines we don't cross. Anyway, they'd ask, being all friendly and buying me drinks, but when I said it wasn't something I was interested in, they got mean and told me to keep my mouth shut if I wanted to stay alive."

"So, of course, you said nothing to anyone, including Angel Force," Finn said. "You helped them get away with those abductions."

"What would Angel Force have done? Formed a committee and talked themselves to death?" Torrin smirked, and his eyes flashed amber. "It would have been a waste of my time and the end of my life when the gang found out I'd snitched on them."

I watched the interaction with interest. They were peacocking for my witch.

"Besides, everyone knows the Shadow gang intimidates Angel Force. For all I know, some of the angels are in the gang's pockets. I'm always amazed at how much they can get away with around here. It wasn't worth my life to report it then worry I might be talking to a gang informant."

"There aren't informants inside Angel Force." Finn's clipped tone spoke volumes about what he thought of Torrin's idea.

"Yeah, well, I wasn't taking that risk." Torrin focused on Zandra. "All I'm saying is that the last time the Shadow gang shut everyone out was due to them running an operation under huge pressure."

"Did they complete the job?" Zandra said. "They handed over those nymphs?"

"As far as I know," Torrin said.

No one spoke. Those nymphs wouldn't have ended up in a happily ever after situation.

"It's been a while since rumors circulated about the gang doing something big," Finn finally said. "Torrin could be right. This is the lead up to their next trafficking operation. There's not a chance Adrienne would have been involved with that."

"Agreed. She's ditzy but never mean." Zandra's gaze went around the bar. "Do you think Osorin's murder had anything to do with the gang's plans? Maybe he didn't want to be involved in trafficking, so they silenced him. He could have been talking about going to Angel Force."

"It would have given the Shadow gang an excellent reason to blow his head off," Finn said.

"I heard what happened to Osorin," Torrin said. "You think he was getting in with the gang? I didn't think he had it in him. The guy was a marshmallow."

"Maybe." Zandra tugged on her hair. "I came to Crimson Cove to figure out what happened to Adrienne, but it seems like I've stumbled into something bigger."

"I found no connection between your mother and the gang," Finn said. "You're worrying about nothing."

Zandra sipped her drink, not looking convinced.

I hopped onto her lap and settled down. I hadn't said anything to Zandra, but I was worried about her missing mother. We had to keep digging into where she'd gone. And with the possible involvement of the Shadow gang, we needed to find her fast.

The conversation moved on after a few minutes, and I snuggled in Zandra's lap as she chatted with Finn and Torrin, flicking my tail to the music. I kept a close ear on the conversation, so I'd notice if she was flirting with either of them, but it was all polite and surface level.

After a couple of hours of talking and a few more drinks, the evening drew to an end.

Finn stood and pulled back Zandra's seat. "How about the next time, it's just the two of us? I could take you to dinner."

Torrin laughed. "You're worried about a little friendly rivalry if I tag along?"

"No, but I'm not buying you dinner as well, and I plan on taking Zandra somewhere nice."

"Cheapskate."

I was settled on Zandra's shoulder, and she tensed as they bickered over her.

She waved a hand to get their attention. "There's no point fighting. I have my gorgeous cat familiar and my work, so I'm too busy for anything else.

Definitely too busy for romantic dinners with anyone."

Both guys looked crestfallen.

Maybe Zandra thought she was too busy for romance, but I'd make sure she had time for everything. Romance, me, new friendships, and her work.

We left the bar, and I curled my tail around her shoulders. "You could have given them both another chance."

"To do what? They didn't have information about Adrienne. Finn found no link in his records at Angel Force, and Torrin couldn't get answers from his contacts."

"What about their other qualities?"

"Crime solving and fixing vehicles?"

I huffed in her ear, making her squeak. "Companions to have fun with."

"Fun comes later. Mystery solving first. Agreed?"

I licked her ear until she tickled me into submission and scooped me into her arms like I was a baby. I pretended to hate it, but I secretly enjoyed being coddled.

Zandra looked down at me. "Agreed? Guys come and go, but I have to focus on what's important."

I wrinkled my booping snooter then nodded. "Agreed."

But I would still make sure my favorite witch got to enjoy herself. All I had to do was solve the mystery of Adrienne's disappearance and ensure Osorin's murder didn't lead the Shadow gang to our door.

Chapter 13

A fishy dish

The next morning, I had an early start. I'd crept out of bed, found some breakfast, having masterfully knocked over the dried treat box and given myself a healthy portion of Magnificent Meow Fishy Medley chews–all the nutritional needs to make the fur gleam, purr perfect, and eyes bright–and I was navigating the door, when Zandra shuffled out of bed.

"Where are you going? We don't start work for another hour and a half." She stifled a yawn.

"You'll be busy doing paperwork on that stinky panda first thing, so I thought I'd go sightseeing."

"On your own?"

"I want to make sure we haven't missed anything exciting in Crimson Cove."

"The place is so small, it's hard to miss anything, exciting or not."

"I won't be long. I'll meet you at the office later."

"If you're sure." She opened the door for me. "You don't need a cute sweater to keep out the chill?"

I ignored that comment. "You won't miss me. You've got those three new fosters to check in on after you've done the paperwork, and you need to look in on Archie. My super powers won't be required for any of that."

"Okay, super cat. Have fun. I'll see you later."

I dashed up the stairs, and after successfully opening the main door with my clever paws, I was outside in the fresh morning air.

I hadn't been totally honest with my wonderful witch, but the tiny omission was for her own good. I was planning on taking in some sights and smells of Crimson Cove, but I also had a mission to complete and a curiosity to fulfil.

My paws took me to Bites and Delights, and I was pleased to see it open. There were only three customers inside, all staring at the chalkboard full of delicious sounding treats, so I slipped in unnoticed.

My whiskers twitched as I saw the handsome bald cat in the window again. Although his eyes were closed and he was flat on his stomach, his ears were up, suggesting he heard my approach.

I hesitated before speaking, simply taking a moment to admire the view. All that smooth, silky skin on display was a treat.

He cracked open one eye. "I know your smell. You were here the other day."

For once, I felt temporarily tongue-tied. I pulled my attention from his magnificent form. "Greetings. I'm Juno. Do you live around here?"

"Nice to meet you, Juno." His voice had a slightly rough edge to it. "You must be new to Crimson Cove."

"I moved here recently with my witch. I'm looking for someone who has local knowledge to help with a few questions." I sounded so oddly formal. Maybe I'd been out of the dating game for too long.

"I'm Elijah. I'm as local as they come. I've been here forever." He stood and arched his back, stretched out his front legs, and did a full body stretch.

I was so captivated by those enticing movements, I forgot it was my turn to speak.

When he finally stopped stretching, he looked at me and curled his tail neatly around his paws. "What information are you after? I've lived here on and off most of my life, so if it's anything interesting, I'll know about it."

"Let me treat you to breakfast, and I'll tell you everything I need."

His nose twitched. "I never turn down a breakfast offer from a beautiful lady."

I was glad of my fur, so he didn't see my full body flush. I trotted to the counter, putting an extra fizzle of sass in my step, and let Sorcha know we wanted a deluxe plate of salmon bites and to put it on Zandra's tab, and then headed back to Elijah.

He was still on the window ledge, but there was room for both of us and our food, so I was happy to stay there. It was also out of earshot of anyone else, so we wouldn't be disturbed when I questioned him.

"You're bonded to that dark-haired witch, aren't you?" Elijah said. "The pale one who frowns a lot."

"Zandra Crypt. And she only frowns sometimes. She's a powerful witch and has immense potential. It's why I chose her."

He inspected one paw. "Potential is problematic."

"What do you mean?"

"I always pick older magic users because they've already found their magic groove. The younger ones often shoot off course. You don't want your witch turning to the dark side. Looking at you, I imagine you're a clean magic using familiar. All sparkles and fizz."

I wrinkled my booping snooter. "You know nothing about me. I've had my moments." I once had the ability to remove mortal hearts with a simple stare. That power had been taken when my magic was deemed inappropriate by several tedious councils. I only ever used that talent on particularly deviant individuals maybe once or twice a year.

"There's a little bad cat under that innocent demeanor, is there?" Elijah rumbled a purr in his broad chest, making my toe beans tingle.

"Wouldn't you like to know?"

"Yeah, I reckon I might."

Sorcha brought over our salmon bites, and Elijah was gentleman enough to allow me to go first, so I could select the most succulent morsels.

After we'd tucked in, I sat back and washed my face, giving my food time to digest before I went back for more. "I'm interested in the Shadow gang. I'm also interested in a resident of Crimson Cove, Adrienne. She used to live in an apartment near here and worked part time in the bakery. I'm also curious about Osorin Greenbow's death."

"You're interested in a lot of things. Why?"

"Why don't you tell me what you know, and I'll tell you what I think."

He chewed on a piece of salmon before swallowing. "I know Adrienne. She used to come in here. I haven't seen her for a while, though."

"Any idea where she went?"

"I don't know her well. She gossiped with Sorcha all the time. Mainly about work and guys. Something wrong with her?"

"I hope not, but she's my bonded magic user's mother, and she's worried about her."

"Interesting. I can't tell you anything about where she is. Not much help, am I?"

"You could still be helpful. What about Osorin's murder?" I said. "You look like a cat who has his ear to the ground. Have you heard who killed him?"

Elijah sat back and enticingly rubbed a paw across his ears. "I knew Osorin. Slimy little guy. And that enormous hellhound of his is scared of his own shadow. I heard the hound ate him. That's what killed him."

"Archie didn't touch Osorin, and he's been in a bad way since he died. I'm worried Archie may not survive since the bond was cut so swiftly."

We bowed our heads for a moment, both aware of the pain Archie would be experiencing.

"I feel sorry for the guy. No one wants to lose a bond like that. Sure, some bonds erode over time, the magic user changes, or our magic evolves and no longer fits, but to lose the connection because your bonded magic user's head explodes... how do you get over that?"

I stiffened. "You know a lot about Osorin's death, although a second ago, you said Archie had killed Osorin. I mentioned nothing about heads being blown off."

He huffed out a gruff laugh. "You're smart and cute. I was testing you to see what you knew about the murder. Of course, none of us would eat our bonded companion. And it's no surprise I know things. Crimson Cove is a small place, and people come in here to talk. I like to listen. You hear all kinds of fascinating things when you fake sleep."

"Has anyone talked about who may have killed Osorin?" I said.

"There's been speculation, including several people who think he did it to himself. Osorin wasn't the smartest wand in the wizard's armory. He made mistakes and lost money on bad investments. Not that he had much to begin with."

"Did you know my witch discovered his body?"

Elijah grimaced. "How did she handle that? Is she the squeaky type or not bothered by gore?"

"She handled it like a professional."

"It sounds like you've got a good one. I have to ask why you're interested in Osorin. Were you friends?"

"We've had dealings with other branches of Angel Force, and their methods aren't always thorough. Archie deserves to know what happened to Osorin."

"Dealings? Have you been in trouble with the angels? Are you a bad girl?" His gaze ran over me.

I purred at him. "Play your cards right and you'll find out. I must ensure Angel Force does a proper investigation, especially since Osorin was associated with the Shadow gang, and they make things difficult when people ask questions."

"He was?"

"It's what I've figured out. Tell me if I'm wrong."

He considered the question. "No, you're not. And I see why you're joining the dots and linking Osorin's death to the gang."

"What do you know about them?"

"I know a familiar who's in the group. Well, his bonded magic user is part of the gang. If you like, I could arrange a meeting, see if he'll talk."

I had to stop myself from bouncing on my paws. "That would be perfect."

"I'd say you're pretty perfect. Although I suppose a good-looking cat like you has a wonderful guy and a basket full of kittens somewhere."

"Perhaps. You're interested?" It never paid to look keen, and I was definitely keen on this delicious pint of warm, full fat milk.

"A guy sees a good-looking lady, and he wants to know more. And you're the best looking cat to walk through those doors in a long time. Of course, I'm interested."

"You're not answering my questions out of the goodness of your heart, then?"

"That's not my sole motive. You also bought me breakfast." Elijah ate another salmon bite and pushed the plate my way. "What do you say? Want to tread on the dark side for a while and see if we can dig up dirt on the gang?"

"I'm not afraid of a little darkness. Introduce me to this familiar." I knew this gorgeous bald hunk would be useful. I'd have this mystery solved by the end of the day, and then I could have a much-needed romantic interlude. It had been too long since I'd been gently held and snuffled.

"I need time to arrange things, but the guy owes me, so it won't be a problem. Meet me back here at noon."

"I look forward to it." We finished the salmon bites in a companionable silence, occasionally commenting on people coming in and out of the café.

Although I'd have loved to have gotten to know my potential new love interest better, I had to check on Zandra. I also wanted to freshen up before my next meeting with Elijah and make sure every fur gleamed.

"I really should get going," I said.

"Don't be late back. Missing you already." Elijah leaned forward and delicately licked the left side of my mouth. "You had a small piece of salmon just there."

I felt the flush right down to my toe beans. I hopped down and headed to the door.

"Hey! White cat. Juno! Over here."

I looked around to see who was hiss-whispering at me. A chunky gray cat with a missing ear tip was squashed under a table. His ears were down and his pupils dilated.

"Do I know you?" I said.

He jerked his head up. "Shush. Come over here, so no one overhears me."

I looked around, but no one was paying us any attention. I walked over to him. "What do you want?"

"You're in terrible danger."

I glanced over my shoulder, but there was no imminent threat heading my way. "Why do you think that?"

"You were talking to Elijah." The cat peered around the edge of the table leg. "Don't trust him."

"He seems trustworthy to me. He told me everything I needed to know, and he's even arranged to help me with a delicate situation."

The gray cat shook his head. “You don’t know him like I do. He’s awful. He’s a bully. You see my missing ear tip? He did that to me.”

“What did you fight about?”

“There was no fight. He jumped me and beat me up in an alleyway. He bit off part of my ear to teach me a lesson.”

“A lesson about what?”

“Not to talk about things I don’t understand.”

“Were you gossiping behind his back?” I looked at Elijah. He was dozing in the sun.

“Don’t draw attention to us, or he’ll come after me again.”

I inspected the ear wound. It was old and must have been done some time ago. “When did this attack happen?”

“Last year. It was late, and I was walking back from a friend’s house. Elijah jumped out of the shadows and got me.” The gray cat shook, and a tiny whimper slid out of his mouth.

“How do you know it was Elijah if it was so dark?”

“Do you know many hairless cats? It had to be him. Besides, I recognized him. He got in my face to make sure I knew who he was.”

“Then you must have been gossiping about something important to be attacked.” I wasn’t sure Elijah had jumped this unfortunate creature. He was most likely making it up to draw attention to himself. It was common for males to do that around me. He wanted to be seen as important and belittle anyone else to discredit them. These juvenile tactics didn’t fool me.

The gray cat stretched out a paw, almost touching me. “Believe me. Elijah is a bad cat.”

"I don't. And he isn't. He's charming."

"What are you doing here?" Tinkerbell strutted over, her nose wrinkled as if she smelled something bad.

"Not that it's any of your business, but I just had a marvelous breakfast with a wonderful cat. I was leaving when this... individual accosted me." I flicked a paw at the gray cat.

Tinkerbell glanced at him. "Cowering as usual, Sammy?"

"It's Elijah. He's been coming in every day. He's up to something."

Tinkerbell rolled her eyes. "You're a wimp. He only has to look at you funny and you shake."

"You would too if he'd jumped you in an alleyway."

"Yeah, I don't believe that story. You're making it up because you have no life."

Sammy lowered his head. "Why does no one believe me about Elijah?"

Tinkerbell hissed at him. "Scram. Get out of here and stop bothering people. Sorcha doesn't want you hanging around, and neither do I."

Sammy squirmed back, his hackles rising. "I don't want trouble. But when I saw Juno talking to Elijah, I had to warn her."

"How do you know my name?" I said.

Sammy wriggled back some more. "People talk, and you're new in Crimson Cove."

"Keep out of my café and stay away from Sorcha. No one wants you around here. You're worthless. Go on, get." Tinkerbell raised a vicious murder mitten, claws out.

"Stop that," I said. "Maybe Sammy is lying, but you don't have to hurt him."

Sammy backed away, wriggled between two chair legs, and dashed off.

"You can go, too," Tinkerbell said to me, her claws still glinting.

I turned and strutted away, refusing to respond to such crassness. Besides, I had something more important to focus on. I was about to infiltrate the Shadow gang with the most handsome cat in Crimson Cove.

Chapter 14

Never trust a cat who oils up

After a brief check in with Zandra to make sure her morning had gone well and the animals were behaving, I'd made my excuses again, spent an hour grooming, and then headed back to Bites and Delights to meet Elijah at noon.

He was waiting outside and had a glorious sheen of oil on his skin. He must have prepared for our date, too. He strutted over and rubbed his cheek against mine in way of a greeting.

I was taken aback by his forwardness. Face rubbing after one brief meeting! But he was a confident cat and sure of what he wanted. And he wanted me. I had no objection to that.

"Are you sure you want to do this?" Elijah said. "The gang doesn't go easy on anyone who interferes in their business. Familiars get treated badly if they're caught snooping where they shouldn't."

"You sound scared."

He chuffed out a laugh. "Nothing scares me, angel, but I don't want your delicate sensibilities disturbed."

"I'll let you know if my delicate anythings get disturbed."

"I'd hate for that glossy coat to get messed up."

I tilted my head. "Would you groom me if it did?"

He bumped his side against mine as we walked away from the café. "You'd better believe it. And I'd explore every inch while I did."

I flicked my ears. There was a fine line between confidence and cockiness, and Elijah had just leaped over it. I'd have to watch myself with this one.

We made it to the edge of Crimson Cove when Elijah stopped. He looked around. "You sensing that?"

"What?"

"We're being watched." He peered over his shoulder. "If I had fur, it would be standing on end. My cat senses are tingling."

"I sense nothing. Why would anyone be watching us?"

"The two best looking cats out together, of course we'll get attention."

I snorted a delicate laugh. "You're very sure of yourself."

"Why not when I look like this? Come on, hot stuff. I'll tell you about Crimson Cove and all the fun you've missed out on."

We walked for thirty minutes, and during that time, I barely said a word. Elijah filled in the silence with amusing anecdotes about Crimson Cove, and they all involved him. He was funny, charming, but overconfident. Every story he told had him as the hero.

I took it all with a large pinch of catnip, but his tales were entertaining, nevertheless. And my many dalliances with gentlemen in the past—those with two legs—had shown they exaggerated when they wanted to impress, so I didn't take it to heart Elijah was embellishing to make a good impression.

"You think you'll stick around Crimson Cove for long?" Elijah said.

It was the first question he'd asked me since we began our walk. "I want to, but I need to convince my witch this is a permanent place for us."

"You don't want to go to a big city? There's so much more going on."

"I like the quiet. And Zandra's already had plenty of adventures in her young life. It's important she doesn't lose focus."

"On what?"

I hesitated. Few people knew about my former life or what had happened to me thirty years ago, and I didn't trust Elijah enough to share such a personal story or how Zandra would help me get back what I'd lost. "On becoming the greatest witch ever born."

"Is that her ambition or yours?"

"We share the ambition. Zandra just doesn't know it yet."

"I love a female with high aspirations." Elijah rubbed his face against mine. "We're almost there. There's still time to back out."

"I'm going nowhere."

We'd left Crimson Cove and were entering a warehouse district. Many of the buildings we passed were empty, the road littered with potholes and trash.

"The Shadow gang operates out of this location?"

"It's a cover, so they can keep things on the down low and not draw too much heat. Over the years, they've suggested to other businesses that this is the wrong place for them to set up shop. They always make it worth their while to leave."

"They pay them?"

"Yeah, something like that. The district is all theirs, so they can come and go as they like and no one asks questions."

"The angels must visit and investigate their criminal activity. If the Shadow gang's location isn't a secret, they'd still need to be careful how they operate."

"Angel Force." Elijah snorted and shook his head. "They know to keep out of the gang's way unless they want trouble in Crimson Cove."

"You mean the arrangement the gang has with the town?"

"It's more of a silent agreement. The angels let the gang do what they like, and they make sure there's no trouble to deal with. If the angels poke around, the crime figures go up in Crimson Cove. It took Angel Force a while to work that out. They kept arresting gang members and then having to deal with all kinds of robberies, theft, violent disturbances, and arson. Not too bright, those angels."

"It sounds like an unpleasantly convenient arrangement," I said. "What about the residents?"

"They're the same as the angels. And who doesn't want a quiet life? So long as people keep their noses out of the gang's business, they're not troubled."

"Unlike Sorcha Creer. She told us about the fake body parts. I also heard about the very real tongue left in her bed."

"Sorcha must have needed to be taught a lesson. And it worked. She hasn't bothered the gang since it happened."

"How do you know that?"

"She's still alive, isn't she?"

"You're okay with their intimidation tactics and thuggery?"

"I couldn't care either way. Here we are." Elijah trotted ahead of me. "There's a back way in, so we can get inside unnoticed. Then I'll tell you everything about the gang while we watch them in action and wait for my buddy to show up." He hopped onto an overturned wooden crate, landed on a window ledge, and slid through a broken window.

I copied his moves and entered a dark, damp corridor. Elijah hadn't waited for me but was walking ahead. I hurried to catch up with him.

"This is the headquarters. It's where they plan all their operations," he muttered. "Keep quiet, just in case anyone's wandering around."

"You know a lot about the Shadow gang," I said.

"My buddy likes to talk, and it pays to stay informed. This way." Elijah led me to the end of the corridor. He hopped onto the stair rail and scaled it until he reached a ceiling with missing chunks of plaster. "You sure you can handle this, sweetheart?"

"I'll be fine. You just worry about not falling off that beam." I nimbly leaped and joined him.

"We crawl from here along the ceiling rafters. It'll take us to the main room where they hang out. Keep it quiet, though. They hate being spied upon."

"You don't have to keep telling me." I crept along on my belly, ignoring the dust and cobwebs. My grooming efforts would all be undone. Muted voices reached my ears. "Is that them?"

Elijah nodded. "Let's go see what they're talking about."

We crawled for another couple of minutes until I spotted light shining through a hole in the ceiling. We stopped by the largest hole, and I peered through. There were half a dozen guys below. Most were sitting around drinking beer, and a couple were playing pool.

"Is that all of them?" I whispered to Elijah.

He looked up from the hole. "They're the key players. There are four permanent gang members. The rest come and go. They recruit as they need. Sometimes, if they have a bank job, they get in an expert on explosive magic or a safe breaker. They hire the expert, pay them well, and cut them loose. They keep numbers to a minimum to stop people talking."

"I know that Anan and Koku Shadow are two of the key gang members."

"Yeah, two brothers. They formed the gang, along with two school friends, Emmett Brownstone and Lewis Jollop. They're all down there. Koku's the stocky guy dressed all in denim with dark hair. Anan's the taller, dark-haired one. Emmett and Lewis are playing pool."

I studied Emmett and Lewis. They were smaller than the others, wiry rather than muscled. Emmett had a skinhead, and Lewis wore a black baseball cap.

"They're always together. These four are the brains behind the thefts, abductions, ransoms, and dodgy spells this gang deals in."

"You really know a lot about them. Have you ever worked for the gang?"

Elijah peered through the hole. "Not directly."

"Your bonded magic user has, though?"

"Now and again. I stay out of things when it's gang related. You know what it's like. If our bonded magic user puts themselves in danger, we have a disgustingly overwhelming urge to protect them. And I enjoy being alive. I don't want to die protecting anyone."

I wrinkled my booping snooter. That was hardly a noble sentiment.

He reached out a paw and touched mine. "I'd make an exception for you."

I slid my paw away. "Of course you would." I'd do anything to keep Zandra safe. I wouldn't stay out of any situation where she could be in danger. Elijah had a skewed view of what it meant to be a true familiar.

He twitched his tail as if he sensed my judgment and didn't like it.

"Rumor has it the gang is planning something big. Would you know what that is?" I said.

"You shouldn't listen to rumors. They're always false."

"This one sounds accurate. Their behavior changed recently, which suggests they're building up to something. There are concerns it could be people trafficking. They did it with some nymphs not so long ago."

"I heard about that. It's not true. At least, I saw nothing like that going on. And who wants to deal with nymphs? Too flighty and squeaky."

Elijah's elusive answers were getting annoying. "Where's your friend?"

"He must be running late."

"He'll be here soon, though?"

"I reckon."

"Is there a way I can talk to the gang directly?"

"About what?"

"Where Adrienne is. Zandra is worried she could be mixed up with the gang."

His eyes were wide as he stared at me. "You want to ask them if some wonky witch got in their way and they did something to keep her quiet? How many lives do you have?"

"More than you'll ever believe."

"No one gets to speak to the gang unless they want them to."

"What about their familiars? Would they be open to talking if your friend doesn't show up soon?"

"Doubtful. You know what we're like. Familiars protect their bonded magic user at all cost. If you poke around and ask the familiars about murder, they'll close ranks. Besides, only two of them have familiars. Emmett and Lewis lost theirs ages ago, and Koku doesn't look after his. He leaves her in a cage most days. She's gone insane."

I sucked in a breath. "How cruel. What about Anan's familiar?"

Elijah's head shot up, and his eyes narrowed. He leaped away. "Someone followed us."

I scrambled after him, along the beam, and back into the corridor. Elijah was chasing Sammy! And although Sammy was sprinting away, Elijah was gaining on him.

I raced after them. Elijah's expression had suggested murderous intent when he'd realized we'd been followed, and although I didn't know this chunky gray cat, I didn't want him injured.

Elijah snarled and grabbed Sammy's tail, drawing blood with his claws.

Sammy howled and sped up.

Elijah landed on Sammy's back. Sammy flipped over, slammed Elijah into the floor, and raced off.

Elijah jumped up, shook his head, and darted after him.

"Stop! There's no need to hurt Sammy," I yelled.

"There's every need. He's a snooping snitch. Everyone knows what happens to snitches."

"Maybe he got curious about what we were up to and tagged along. He doesn't mean any harm."

Elijah turned on me, and the cold rage in his eyes made me slow. "I hate snoopers. He has no right to be here. I knew we were being followed when we left crimson Cove. It was him. And he needs to pay."

"Why? He hurt no one." I raised my chin. "And if you don't like snoopers, then you don't like me, because that's what I've been doing. And you've been helping."

Elijah turned and trotted after Sammy. "You're different."

I ran along beside him. "Am I? Why do you hate Sammy's behavior but don't mind me doing exactly the same thing?"

"Because you're prettier. Besides, I wanted to make you smile by taking you on an adventure. Some kitty cats dig the danger. It gets them all excited."

I increased the distance between us. "You know why I need to learn about the Shadow gang. This is important to my witch. It's not about my pleasure."

"Whatever you say, honey. Let's catch the snooper and teach him a lesson."

I dropped back as Elijah raced off. I should have listened to Sammy. I'd let my heart lead in this situation and was no longer sure it had been the right thing to do.

"Come on, or I'm leaving you behind," Elijah yelled.

I hurried after him. I had to make sure he didn't hurt Sammy. He'd already injured the poor cat's tail, and he clearly had no intention of stopping until he'd taught Sammy a painful lesson.

I rounded the corner to discover Elijah by an open door.

"Hurry. He went in here. We can corner him."

"We don't need to corner him. You've scared him enough. He's learned his lesson. I'm certain Sammy will never follow you again."

"He's got more education coming his way. Follow me." Elijah dashed into the room.

I sped after him, determined he wouldn't injure Sammy. When I entered the room, I came face-to-face with a dozen narrow-eyed, mean-looking cats. "Who are you?"

"These are my friends." Elijah stood at the front of the group.

"Is Sammy in here?"

"No, he's long gone. A true scaredy cat." Elijah stepped closer. "Now, it's time I got to know you better."

I backed away and bumped into a muscular black cat with a stump for a tail. He shoved me and hissed a warning.

I glared at Elijah. "Sammy told me you couldn't be trusted. I should have listened to him."

"Yeah, princess, you should, but it's too late now. You're not leaving this room until you've told me everything you know about my gang."

Chapter 15

A hero's reveal

I looked for a way through the wall of fur and claws, but there was no way out. "Your gang? You're involved in the Shadow gang?"

"Sure am. And you don't snoop on the gang and get away with it, no matter how shiny your fur is." Elijah hissed at me.

"I needed information for my witch." I hissed back at him, while keeping a close eye on the other cats. They were scruffy, underfed, and needed a long soak in the tub.

"Anyone who pokes around in gang business has to answer to me."

I stood proud. "You're Anan's familiar, aren't you?"

"We've been bonded for years. I go everywhere with him. Do everything for him. I'm his eyes and ears in Crimson Cove." Elijah puffed out his chest. "When I heard you and your witch were poking around, I made myself known to you. I knew you wouldn't be able to resist my charm. And you made it so simple. I didn't need to do any work. You came to me."

I bared my teeth. "Which was a mistake."

"Not for me. You practically begged for an introduction to the gang. I knew then this was serious. Now, you're answering my questions. And if I don't like the answers, you're not getting out of here alive."

"We'll see about that." I cast a translocation spell. The room wobbled, the floor slipped from under my feet, but the spell faded. I was still in the room full of mean, foul smelling cats.

Elijah waved a paw in the air. "We don't like people creeping in and out uninvited, so there are wards around the building. You can't use magic whenever you want. The boss doesn't like it. Only a few magic users get to flaunt their powers in here. And you're not one of them."

I looked over my shoulder. The muscled black cat still barred the way out, and the door was closed. I turned back to Elijah. "I meant no harm. My witch was worried, so of course, I must help her. You know how demanding our bonded magic users can be."

"You both want to bring down the Shadow gang. You want to stop us," Elijah said.

All the cats hissed.

"No! If the gang has nothing to do with Adrienne's disappearance, then they'll be left alone."

"And if they did? Will you and your tiny witch bring us to our knees?" Elijah laughed, and the other cats joined in, causing an echoey, high-pitched chitter to bounce off the bare walls. The sound sent a trickle of panic to the tip of my tail.

"We can negotiate. If any member of the gang sent Adrienne away or scared her into leaving, we can figure out how to bring her home. She's terrible with money, so if she owes anyone anything, we'll pay off her debts," I said.

"This isn't about money."

My whiskers twitched. "But Adrienne is connected to the Shadow gang for a specific reason?"

"I'm asking the questions. Tell me about your connection to Angel Force. We've worked hard to keep them out of our business, but you and your witch seem intent on dragging them into this mystery by asking about Osorin's missing head and the runaway witch. Why do you want to upset the happy balance in Crimson Cove?"

I squared off with Elijah. I was done with playing nice and dealing with his intimidation tactics. "There is no happy balance. The residents of Crimson Cove are sick of having thugs controlling them. They want freedom, not oppression."

"Freedom, not oppression," Elijah mimicked. "You don't care about anyone here. You've only lived here for five minutes. This is our home, not yours, and we built this place up from nothing. Before the Shadow gang got involved and pumped money into the economy, this was a backward little place. It was dying. The gang set up businesses, put people in jobs, and everything changed."

"Illegal businesses and dodgy money."

"Not important. People aren't scared of us. They're grateful, and they look the other way because we're their only hope. If we go, the money goes, and they lose their jobs, homes, and everything they care about."

"They look the other way because of your threats and intimidation," I said. "People don't want your crooked money. They can manage on their own."

"You know nothing about this place. But I'll tell you one thing for free. We own Crimson Cove. And you, your witch, and the angels aren't getting in our way."

The cats all hissed their agreement.

I planted my paws and stared at him. "We're going nowhere."

"Neither are we," Elijah growled out.

The cats behind him moved into fighting crouches, as if they'd received a secret signal to get ready. There were twelve cats behind Elijah and the chunky black guy behind me. The numbers weren't on my side, but I'd fought worse and had plenty of skirmish experience while on four paws.

Elijah stepped forward, and the cats behind him tensed. "Submit to me and you live. You can be my plaything. I'd love to mess up that silky white fur. Submit, swear allegiance to the gang, and you stay alive. So does your bonded magic user, provided she stops asking questions about Osorin's murder and Adrienne."

"I'd rather give up eating salmon." I sparked a spell between my paws and launched myself at Elijah. I slammed into him, hitting him with magic and extended claws. He yelped and tried to pull away, but I clung on tight, and we rolled into the mass of cats.

I raked my claws down his oily sides in a swift movement. How did I ever consider this monster attractive?

Elijah snapped his teeth in my face, and I jumped back to avoid being savaged.

The other cats formed a circle around us, content to watch the fight rather than join in. At least, for now.

Elijah stood on his hind legs and shot a spell my way. I threw myself to the side and dodged it. It hit one of the watching cats. There was a squeal of distress, and the cat dropped to the ground. He was dragged away, no one bothering to see if he was alive.

"You're using illegal magic." I eyed Elijah's paws warily.

"Are you going to tell the angels?" He thrust out another spell. I dodged, and so did the watching crowd. "Oh, and just so you know, the wards don't affect my powers. You aren't so fortunate."

We kept circling each other, waiting to see who'd make the next move.

"I'll wipe you out, and then I'm going to Crimson Cove and destroying your witch. She'll never see Adrienne again," Elijah snarled.

"You don't threaten my witch." I shrieked a battle cry and thrust another spell at him. My rage made me unfocused, and the spell skimmed Elijah's head and slammed into the floor. The draining wards tugged at my already distorted power. It wouldn't be long before I had nothing left.

He jumped at me, and we rolled around, a tangle of oily limbs, claws, and teeth. Elijah ripped out chunks of my beautiful fur and almost got his teeth in my ear, but I head-butted him, raked my back claws down his stomach, and leaped away.

My skin tingled where he'd pulled out my fur, and there was a deep cut on my front leg, but I wasn't stopping. Elijah had lied, deceived me, and been rude. But worst of all, he'd made a direct threat against Zandra. That was unforgiveable. No one did that and walked away.

Elijah circled me again, but this time he was limping, and there was blood dripping from his stomach. "You're more trouble than you're worth," he wheezed out.

"I'm glad you've noticed. I made a mistake by trusting you and letting you bring me here, but you made a bigger one. No one hurts Zandra."

"That messed up witch is trouble, too. The gang has eyes on her, and they don't like what she's brought to Crimson Cove."

"The chance to bring you down, you mean? She's afraid of nothing. Zandra has more power in her little finger than you have in your entire body and all these cats combined. You should tremble before me because I'm bonded to her."

He tilted his head, his gaze running over me. "Is that why you're weird?"

"I'm not weird. I'm magnificent."

"Your magic. It's old and distorted. Those spells you're hitting me with taste of an ancient past. A magic stamped out a long time ago because it was too dangerous. Even the wards aren't slowing you."

They were, but he didn't need to know that. "Then you know better than to test me if I hold a power so ancient and deadly."

"I don't think you're even a real familiar. What are you?" For the first time since we'd met, doubt flickered in Elijah's eyes.

I bared my fangs at him in a catlike smile. "Oh, sweetheart. If you knew the true me, you'd never have done this, because you'd know you wouldn't survive. Now, you rollover, show me your stomach, and I'll see if I have a thread of benevolence in this perfect body."

He snorted. "Whatever. Boys, get her."

I barely had time to brace as the troop of angry, rancid smelling cats launched at me. I couldn't even finish casting a shield spell before they were upon me. Teeth, claws, and fangs bit and scratched, tearing out my fur and shredding my skin.

I yowled as I twisted and turned, slashing, biting, and firing out magic. My spells were powerful, but every time I blasted one out, it lacked punch. And Elijah had sensed why. He knew there was something odd about my powers. I'd once been unstoppable, but not anymore. This was a fight I could lose.

Sharp teeth dug into the scruff on the back of my neck, and I was yanked off my paws. A second later, another set of teeth latched onto my throat.

"Well done, lads. Hold her. Let's see if she has any final words." Elijah strode over, his injuries already healing. "You can beg for mercy, darlin'. Let's see if I have any benevolence in me today."

"I'd never beg anything from you."

The teeth around my throat tightened, and a trickle of warm blood slid down my skin. That would be a pain to get out of my fur after this was over.

"You won't even beg for your witch? Imagine the grief she'll feel when I deposit your broken body outside her apartment. Think about the tears she'll shed because you're gone. Isn't that worth begging for?"

He'd found my weak spot. With the risk of death surrounding me, I keenly felt the strong tug of my bond with Zandra. I couldn't lose her. I had too much to fight for. And I'd never want my witch to grieve for me. She deserved every happiness.

"Too scared to talk?" Elijah said. "You're not so special. Your magic is weird, but there's nothing unique about you. You're a puffed up pretty kitty with an ego. And it's time we deflated that." He raised a paw.

The lights went out.

There were several loud thumps, a chorus of pained howls, and bodies fell to the floor. At least, it sounded like fluffy bodies hitting the floor. Even my cat vision failed in the pitch black, so I had no idea what was going on.

The teeth attached to the back of my neck and my throat vanished. I kicked out in the darkness to protect myself from anyone coming back for a second bite.

A light spell appeared over my head, and I came face-to-face with Sammy.

He was shaking, his nose wobbling and his tail flicking back and forth. "Hurry! We only have seconds before my magic dies. I'm not strong enough to hold it for long with the draining wards in place, and there are too many cats to control."

A quick look around the room showed the gang of cats were unconscious, although some were already stirring. "You're doing this?"

He nodded, his shaking intensifying. "Please, we have to leave. My magic is fading fast."

Sammy didn't need to tell me again. He must be using all his magic to subdue these cats. I'd underestimated this guy. I raced to the door, caught hold of the handle, and tugged. It took several seconds to get it to move, but I finally got the door open. I shoved it with my head to make a large enough gap to get through and ran out.

Sammy wasn't with me. I poked my head back into the room. He was frozen to the spot, a bundle of shivering fur standing in a puddle of what I hoped was perspiration.

"Come on!"

"I can't move. Too scared."

"If you stay here, they'll kill you when they wake." I raced over to him. "You must move."

"Leave me. I'm no good to you."

I nipped his side. "Don't be a martyr. You saved my life and knocked out a horde of mean cats. All you need to do is one more tiny thing to keep this excellent track record up."

"What's that?" The words croaked out of him.

"Come with me, my hero."

He blinked at me. "You... you think I'm a hero? Your hero?"

I nipped him again. "Yes! And I won't have you standing here like a quivering idiot. Don't make me change my mind about you. Let's go."

Sammy took a faltering step then another.

I ran behind him and nudged my nose up his butt. "Move it!"

He squeaked and dashed out of the room.

Sammy had an appealingly musky smell I'd not noticed before. I'd been so enamored by that slippery bald cat that I hadn't seen the quiet champion in the room.

"Keep going. Down the railing and through the broken window. Once we're out of the building, I'll translocate us out of here."

He made it onto the railing, but shook so badly, he fell off.

I jumped down and joined him on the wobbling stairs. "You'll be fine. Just hold that spell in place. We have to put distance between us and the cats. We're too weak to fight if they catch us."

Sammy drew in a shuddering breath. "I won't let them hurt you. I saw what they were going to do to you, and I had to stop them."

I nudged him as we hurried down the stairs, avoiding the holes in the boards. "You did an incredible job. Down the stairs, through the window, and then we're free. Got it?"

He nodded, leaning against me as we dashed to the foot of the broken staircase. We reached the window, and I had to help Sammy with a boost so he could get onto the ledge and through it.

I followed him, jumped to the ground, pressed a paw against his side, and translocated us to the animal control office.

Zandra was pacing when we arrived. She turned and gasped before wrapping me in a huge hug. "You're alive. What happened to you? Is that blood on your fur? All of a sudden, it felt like I was choking, and I knew you were hurt. Juno, where were you?"

I buried my face against her neck, breathing in her reassuring scent. "I'm fine. My injuries will heal."

"What's going on?" Her voice quivered, her arms so tight around me, the hug almost hurt.

I pulled back and licked her cheek to reassure her. “I visited the Shadow gang. I think they know something about Adrienne.”

Zandra’s expression turned from confusion to anger. “You could have been killed. Why do something so dangerous?”

I struggled out of her grip and dropped to the floor beside Sammy. “I was... tricked. I’ll explain later. But it would have been impossible for me to be killed. I had a new friend with me. Sammy saved my life.” I rubbed my cheek against his.

He wavered on his paws but flicked his tail and gently rubbed back.

Zandra dropped to her knees in front of him. “I owe you for saving Juno. Whatever you need, it’s yours.”

“We can sort that out later,” I said. “The cats we fought will tell the Shadow gang we’re onto them, so we don’t have much time. If we don’t figure out how to get them to talk, we won’t get answers about Adrienne’s disappearance or Osorin’s murder.”

Confusion crossed her face. “You fought with other cats? I’ve missed so much. I should have been with you.”

I pressed a paw on Zandra’s arm to get her to focus and stop her panic. “Do you trust me?”

“Always. But you’re injured. You need to rest and heal, not go up against the gang again.”

“Later. Zandra Crypt, do you trust me?” I repeated.

We locked eyes, and she nodded. “I do. What’s the plan?”

Chapter 16

A meeting with darkness

It was dusk when we finally made it back to the gang's lair. Zandra hadn't been able to get out of work for the afternoon, and she'd insisted I recharge my magic before we returned to the warehouse. Although I'd objected, I had felt drained and needed a good hour of grooming and brushing before my fur was back to its old self.

And although I was concerned about my witch's safety by involving her in this mission, we worked better together and would always look out for each other.

She'd used a translocation spell to bring us here, along with Sammy, who was crouched beside me, alert for any movement from inside the warehouse.

"I forgot to thank you," I said to him. "If you hadn't caused that distraction when we were fighting Elijah, I wouldn't be here."

He glanced at me but then looked away. "I didn't want them to hurt you. Elijah's rogue gang of mean cats always bullies people."

"How did you do it? You knocked out all the power and subdued an entire gang. I don't mean to offend you, but when we first met, you didn't strike me as a cat who had mastery over his abilities."

"You don't think I have power?"

"You must, but the way you behave, I figured your abilities were limited. That was wrong of me. I apologize for being so quick to judge you."

Sammy was quiet for a few seconds, his gaze on the warehouse. "I have power, but I don't have a bonded magic user. She died a year ago. Once our bond was severed, my magic became unstable, so I'm never certain what will happen when I use it. Sometimes, it works fine, but it also spectacularly backfires. I'm scared to use my ability in case I hurt anyone."

I pressed my paw against his side. "Every sympathy for your loss. It's so hard to lose a bonded magic user."

"You've lost someone?"

"I've chosen to leave, but that doesn't mean I don't feel their absence. Zandra is the first magic user I've stayed with for longer than two years. We've been bonded for more than a decade."

His gaze slid to the ground. "I think about her every day. She loved the woods in Crimson Cove and was always outside exploring. She enjoyed communing with nature, and I was happy to go along with her."

"What was her name?" Zandra looked over, her eyes full of sympathy.

"Rachel. She was a healer and would gather ingredients from the woods for her potions and lotions. She was popular in Crimson Cove for her healing. Everyone liked her. She was kindness. It shone out of her. She liked to make people feel better."

"Rachel would have been so proud of you today. You did an incredible job saving me from Elijah and his thugs," I said. "Maybe it's self-doubt holding you back. When I left my former bonded magic users, it took me time to trust myself when I had no one to look after. I didn't have a focus for my power."

"I got lucky helping you," he whispered.

"You got brave. You are brave." I sniffed his ear.

"You'd have done the same for me," Sammy said. "I'm just glad I followed you from the café. I wondered if I dared to. Elijah is always threatening me to stay out of his way. I knew he'd beat on me if he caught me."

"It's because he's intimidated by you. You have such a magnificent coat and are a strapping cat, so of course he'd want you to stay out of his way. None of the females would look at him when you're around."

Shock entered Sammy's eyes as he stared at me.

Zandra chuckled. "Juno is right. You're a handsome cat. And your coat shines in the moonlight."

I nodded. I was grateful for Sammy's help, but it was more than that. He'd selflessly rescued me when he hadn't needed to. We barely knew each other, but he'd put his life on the line for me. That showed a strong and noble character. Perhaps I could overlook his fluffiness and we could become more than friends.

"What's your connection to the café?" I said to him. "Do you live there?"

"Sorcha took pity on me when she learned about Rachel dying. They were friends, and she didn't want me wandering about with no home, so she temporarily fostered me. Of course, Tinkerbell hates it. She tolerates me because Sorcha scolds her if she's mean. But I know she wants to be the only cat in the café. I don't blame her. Sorcha makes amazing food."

"You should usurp Tinkerbell. She's so gross about Sorcha. She doesn't value their bond," I said. "You'd make Sorcha a much better familiar. And with your power, you'd be an incredible team."

"Oh! I'd never do that. Not after what Tinkerbell went through."

"What happened to Tinkerbell?" I said.

"You don't know about her?"

"I know she's uppity and has no respect for Sorcha."

"She has an interesting past. It—"

"There's someone coming out of the warehouse." Zandra ducked behind the shipping container we were using to shield ourselves from view.

I focused on the door and saw Anan and Koku.

"That's the two Shadow brothers I told you about," I whispered to Zandra. "Anan's in charge. Koku is his right-hand man. There are two more, Emmett and Lewis. They're the key gang members we need to watch out for."

"Got it." Zandra was quiet as she watched them. "Do you really think they had something to do with Adrienne going missing?"

"It wasn't confirmed, but it was something Elijah said. He said her disappearance wasn't about money, but I couldn't get him to tell me more."

We watched in silence as Koku and Anan checked half a dozen shipping containers on the other side of the yard. They opened each door, shone a light inside, and shot out a spell that blanketed the container.

"What have they got in there?" Zandra whispered. "Stolen goods?"

We kept watching until they returned to the warehouse and went inside.

"Let's go see what's in those containers," Zandra said.

After having a good sniff around to make sure there was no immediate danger, I led the way to the containers. We kept to the shadows to make sure no one looking out of the warehouse would spot us.

As I got close to the first container, a faint whiff of decaying meat drifted past me.

I lifted my nose and sniffed deeply. "Sammy, what can you smell?"

He joined me in a bout of rapid sniffing, his cute little nose flaring as he sucked in air and exhaled. "It smells like meat left on the counter in the sun. It's nasty."

A scraping sound from inside the container we were sniffing had me tensing.

"Have you found something?" Zandra said.

"Is there a lucrative market for transporting meat?" I said. "Whatever is in these shipping containers has gone off. The gang can't be looking after their cargo."

"Meat! Are you sure?" She stared at the container.

"What if they're killing protected animals? There's a black market for yeti meat in some parts of the world," Sammy said. "I even heard of one strange group who eats nothing but gnome flesh."

"I... that can't be true," I said.

He tilted his head. "It could have been gnocchi. Is that a sort of gnome? Kind of crunchy?"

I gave him a gentle pet. "Potatoes and gnomes taste very different."

"They can't make much money by transporting carcasses," Zandra said. "You're sure that's what you're smelling?"

There was another soft scraping noise close by. Just as I stepped forward to investigate, a bright light shone behind us.

"Hey, what are you doing back here? This is private property."

My nose had been so overwhelmed by the foul stench from the containers, I'd missed the smell of this new arrival. Lewis stood in front of us, a torch raised so it dazzled Zandra. He also had a spell sparking on his fingers, and I knew he'd throw it if we fought him.

Zandra glanced at me and nodded. "Hi. I was looking for someone. I thought she might be here."

"Who? There's no one here. This place is abandoned," Lewis said.

"Apparently not, since you're here."

"I'm security. And you're trespassing. What were you doing with the containers? You didn't try to get inside, did you?"

"We didn't realize we were causing any issues. We'll leave," I said.

Lewis shook his head. "You're going nowhere. Come with me."

I scrambled up Zandra's leg and onto her shoulder, pressing my booping snooter against her ear. "We can take him. It's just one guy."

"Or not. This is a chance to get inside," she whispered. "I have to talk to this gang about Adrienne. They know what happened to her. I'll make them tell me."

"They could kill you."

"We're going. All I want is information. If they have nothing to hide, it won't be a problem."

"Move it. The boss will want to know about this," Lewis said.

"What if you don't like the information they give you? What if they've done something bad to your mother?" My gaze remained on Lewis to make sure he did nothing dumb.

"Don't make me force you to move," Lewis said. "The boss hates anyone poking around in his business."

"Then take me to see him, and I'll explain everything." The determined set of Zandra's shoulders revealed she'd made her mind up, despite me trying to talk her out of this crazy plan.

Lewis seemed surprised we were so willing to go with him. "You first. Through that door to the right."

We passed him, Sammy staying by Zandra's side. I was proud of my new friend. When I'd met him, I'd assumed he was a scaredy cat, but Sammy was showing what a brave companion he'd make.

Lewis stayed behind us, directing us along a dank corridor and into the room where I'd seen the gang when I'd spied on them.

Anan and Koku were in there, as well as Emmett.

"Boss, I found a trespasser poking about outside," Lewis said. "She claims she's looking for someone."

Anan strode over, walking like a squat-limbed primate with his long arms dangling and his knees bent. "I know you. You're the new witch in town. What brings you to our palace?"

"A missing person. I heard you know something about her disappearance." There wasn't a trace of nerves in Zandra's voice.

"If someone's missing, you should speak to the angels about it. Although, I've heard you've already got experience of that." Anan got too close to Zandra for my liking.

I gave him a warning hiss to ensure he respected her boundaries.

He smirked at me but didn't move back. "So, who's missing?"

"A relative of mine. Adrienne. I wondered if she'd done business with you. I know she needed money."

"You're talking about that cute, ditzy witch who works at the bakery? The one that got kicked out of her apartment by Lennie."

"That's the one. How do you know her?"

"I know everyone in Crimson Cove. I wouldn't be such a successful businessman if I didn't keep on top of who's who." His gaze traveled down Zandra and back up again. "You must be Adrienne's sister."

Zandra shrugged. "I'm someone who cares about her."

"Cute. Let's have a drink and talk about what we can do for each other."

"Or we skip the drink, and you tell me where Adrienne is."

"You heard that, boys? This witch is giving me orders."

The others chuckled, but there was no humor in their eyes as they watched us. My attention flashed from Anan to the rest of the gang. I didn't want to miss if anyone made a wrong move toward my witch.

I looked down at Sammy. He was shaking. Now wasn't a time to show weakness, but I could understand why he was nervous after what he'd done to all those cats. They were somewhere in the warehouse and would be furious to find us back in their domain.

Anan crossed his arms over his barrel chest and clicked his tongue. "What's so urgent you need to find Adrienne?"

"You must have family," Zandra said. "You'd do what you had to do to help them if they were in trouble."

"Trouble! Now you've brought trouble into the mix. This gets better." He inspected his nails. His hand had the same black tattoo as the other gang members. "I'm not close to most of my blood family, so I made my own when I came to Crimson Cove. They're more effective in getting me what I need, and they don't ask annoying questions."

"Think about your family here, then. If one of your guys was in trouble, you'd want to help, wouldn't you?"

Anan waggled a finger in Zandra's face. "Nice try, but you're going about this wrong. You're appealing to my decent, respectable side, and I don't have one of those. Tell us why you're really poking around."

Zandra's shoulders tensed under my paws, and I tensed, too. Anan wasn't letting this go.

"I already have. I need to know what happened to Adrienne."

"Did you try to get into any of the containers outside?"

"She was looking at one, boss. I stopped her before she got too close," Lewis said. "I checked, and the lock was intact. She saw nothing."

"I hate people prying into my business." Anan caught hold of Zandra's wrist, making me hiss again. Even Sammy joined in this time.

Zandra stared down Anan, not wincing despite his tight grip. "You made this my business by involving someone I care about. All I want is the truth, and I'll leave you alone."

"Why should I tell you? If you don't like the truth, you'll snitch to the angels. I've heard you've been getting friendly with them, especially the weird half-demon. Like to play with fire, don't you?"

"It's hard not to get involved with Angel Force after finding a dead body. What do you know about Osorin Greenbow's murder?" Zandra yanked her arm away from Anan.

"Oh, this is how it's going down. First off, you accuse me of doing something to sweet little Adrienne, and now you're pinning Osorin Greenbow and his missing head on us. It seems you don't value your life."

"I value the truth. And your intimidation tactics won't work on me," Zandra said.

Anan smirked again. "Yeah, I've heard about your amazing connections to the Crypt witches. But I did some digging, and you're not related to them. You were the result of an infidelity by your old man, and he has no Crypt witch power. Those witches took pity on you and adopted you. For all I know, you could be a basic witch. A powerless witch. A witch I could destroy without any magic."

"There is nothing basic about my witch," I growled out. "Show respect. She's the most powerful magic user you'll ever have the good fortune to meet."

The whole gang chuckled again.

"Is that so?" Anan said. "Show us what you've got, witch."

The soft patter of fast moving paws on concrete drew my attention, and I grimaced as Elijah appeared. His eyes narrowed the second he saw me, and he dashed to Anan's side.

"Don't believe what they tell you. That's the cat I brought here. The one who wanted to snoop on you." Elijah kept away from us, his gaze darting around.

Anan grabbed Elijah and held him out in front of him. "This cute ball of fluff swayed you to be disloyal to me?"

Elijah went limp in Anan's hands, his tail and paws hanging low. "No, I was testing her to see what she wanted. She was asking questions about you and what your latest job was. I told her nothing. I didn't even tell her I was your familiar."

Anan shook Elijah then dropped him. Elijah landed nimbly on the floor, but his tail was limp as he scuttled away. He no longer looked like the magnificent cat I'd first seen but a scared, intimidated familiar who was being mistreated by the magic user who should protect him.

I hissed out a silent promise to stop this cruelty.

Anan laced his fingers together and cracked his knuckles. “We had nothing to do with Adrienne going missing or Osorin’s head going ker-splat. You made a mistake coming here and demanding answers.”

“And your mistake was messing with someone my witch protects,” I said.

Zandra rested a hand on my side. “Do you have alibis for the time of Osorin’s murder? It was—”

“We know when he exploded. We were all together when Osorin died. Isn’t that right, Lewis?” Anan didn’t turn his head to look at his buddy.

Lewis stuffed his hands in his pockets and rocked back on his heels. “Whatever you say, boss.”

“We were having breakfast.” Anan nodded. “Yeah, that sounds right. All together, all eating, not anywhere near that dump of a place Osorin called home.”

“I suppose you’re all each other’s alibis?” Zandra looked around the group, her gaze hard.

“It’s convenient, isn’t it?” Anan said. “We look out for each other.”

Zandra clearly didn’t believe them, and neither did I. They were covering for each other, but we had no way of proving it.

“Osorin was a jerk,” Emmett said. “I’m surprised someone didn’t blow his head off before this.”

“Zip it,” Anan said.

“You always said he was a loser.”

Anan strode to Emmett and shoved him over. “Keep your mouth shut.”

Emmett jumped to his feet, his fists clenched as he glared at Anan.

Anan swung the first punch, and the room exploded into chaos. Koku and Lewis dashed over to pull them apart, giving us an opportunity to escape.

Zandra didn't hesitate. She turned and raced out of the room, scooping up Sammy to make sure he didn't get left behind.

"They're getting away," Elijah yelled.

I shuffled around and shot him in the butt with a spell, knocking him down. He may be mistreated, but he didn't have to act like a cretin all the time.

Zandra kept running until we were outside the warehouse then cast a translocation spell to take us back into the center of Crimson Cove.

She puffed out a breath as she set Sammy down and petted me. "That gang knows what happened to Adrienne and Osorin. We can't let them get away with this. We have to know the truth."

"What do you want to do?" I said.

"Keep prodding. I don't care how long it takes to get to the truth, but I'm finding out what happened to Adrienne, why the Shadow gang killed Osorin, and we're making sure they pay."

And I'd be prodding right beside her. If Zandra was taking a stand against the Shadow gang, she'd need all the support she could get.

Chapter 17

A rotten offering

We were back at Bites and Delights the next morning, getting breakfast. Vorana had left the house early to pick up a collection of rare books from a seller an hour's drive away, so our choice of breakfast at home had been cold cereal and milk or burned toast. We both decided a short walk to our favorite café to enjoy waffles and salmon would be more fun. Of course, I had the salmon.

"The Shadow gang has to have a weakness." Zandra sat back and pushed away her empty plate. "Someone must be willing to talk about what they do."

"From everything I've heard, they have the town under their thumb. They don't cause trouble with the locals and keep the businesses going, and in return, everyone turns a blind eye to their bad behavior," I said.

"It's wrong. There must be another way. Crimson Cove is pretty enough to attract visitors, and it has the beach nearby. This town doesn't need gang money or support to thrive."

"You could have a job convincing people of that. If they're used to the gang being around, there'll be resistance to change."

"Not if the gang has started messing with residents." Zandra picked up a knife and played with it. "Juno, what if Adrienne's dead?"

"They wouldn't be stupid enough to kill anyone who lives here." I didn't like to say anything to Zandra, but I'd had this thought more than once. Adrienne had admitted in her letter to Zandra that she'd gotten in such serious trouble she had to vanish. What if she hadn't been able to get away before the gang caught her?

I didn't share this concern with Zandra. There was no point in worrying her, and it was clear she was already thinking the same thing.

"We need to start with people who dislike the Shadow gang. Sorcha must be one of them after what they did to her," Zandra said.

"Maybe they did enough to silence her. You need to be careful who you talk to. Pick the wrong pair of ears, and they'll blab to the gang."

"Does that matter? I'm already on their radar. Anan knew about us moving here." Zandra shuddered. "It's creepy, thinking he's been keeping tabs on us."

"Elijah said we were being watched. He was probably the one doing the watching, the sneak."

"I'm not sure whether to feel concerned or flattered. My magic isn't that incredible, despite what you always tell people."

"It is. You're the most powerful magic user I've ever met." Of course, I excluded myself from that description. It was only fair on Zandra.

"I wish I felt that power more often. My magical evolution has ground to a halt. I got to this level, and it hasn't improved for ages. Tempest told me magic grew with you, and the older you get, the more powerful and skilled you become. I'm getting forehead wrinkles but no more power!"

"You're at a disadvantage because you aged up so quickly using a spell. You missed ten years of magic evolution. Your magic is playing catch up."

Her bottom lip jutted out. "Will it always do that?"

"No, you're a fast learner, with more abilities than you realize. Your power will come. It'll just take a little more time."

"Maybe we don't have time, especially if the Shadow gang comes after us."

I hissed softly, and my hackles lifted. "They'll never hurt you. I'll make sure of it."

Sammy scuttled over. He was low to the floor, and his ears were down.

My heart did a little skip of happiness. I'd thought about him overnight and was prepared to consider him as a suitor, despite the gray fluff and inclination toward timidity.

He looked up at me, his brow crinkled and nose quivering. "I've got a message for both of you. I went to Vorana's to tell you, but you'd already left."

"Sammy, what is it? Is something wrong?" I said.

"You need to go to the alley behind the café immediately. There's someone there who has to talk to you."

"Who is it?" Zandra said.

"Emmett. He looks bashed up. I've been sitting with him for a while after I found him passed out. I thought he was dead when I first sniffed him out.

He smells bad. When he came to, he said he had to see you."

I glanced at Zandra. "It must be gang related."

We dashed away from the table, out the back where the washrooms were located, and through an emergency exit.

Emmett was propped against a brick wall. He had one arm wrapped around his ribs, and his right eye was so puffy it was sealed shut.

"Anan did this to you, didn't he?" Zandra kneeled beside Emmett while I circled around to the other side with Sammy.

Emmett nodded then winced as he moved. "The guy's lost his mind. And he's messing with something he shouldn't. He has to be stopped before it's too late."

"You came here to tell me that?"

"I figured you were the only one who'd believe me. You weren't scared of Anan yesterday, and no one ever stands up to him. If you do, this happens." He pressed a hand against his side and groaned.

"He's a bully and a thug. Of course I'll stand up against him," Zandra said. "Why did he beat you so badly?"

"Anan thinks I want the top position in the gang, but I'm not interested. I've never been interested in leading." Emmett coughed and groaned, taking a few seconds to compose himself. "I can't say a single thing right to him. Everything I say makes him fighting mad."

"Do you know what he did to Adrienne?" Zandra said. "She's my mother. She wanted me to believe she'd gone on a vacation, but I found a letter she left me. It revealed she's in trouble, and I think that trouble has to do with the gang."

He nodded. "It does. I can't tell you more than that, but she got mixed up in things she doesn't understand. And she didn't realize how dangerous Anan was. She even dated the lunatic."

Zandra's eyes widened. "They were a couple?"

"It wasn't serious. Anan never gets serious with anyone, but he can switch on the charm when he needs it, and Adrienne fell for it. Then something went wrong. I don't know what, because Anan rarely shares, but they argued. He even sent Lewis after her to warn her to keep quiet."

"About what? Did Lewis hurt her?"

"No, but she knew what was coming for her. I guess she didn't get away in time. There's nothing you can do to help her now."

"I'll do whatever I have to do to get her back," Zandra said. "Tell me where she is. Adrienne is still alive, isn't she?"

"Maybe. Kind of. I... I can't tell you everything."

"What does that mean?"

"I'm not here to talk about missing people. Not my problem."

I pressed a paw on Emmett's thigh and zapped him with a warning spell. "Reveal what you know about Adrienne, or you might get a beating from me as well as Anan."

Sammy growled and slashed out with his murder mittens.

Emmett grumbled and tried to move his leg, but I pressed harder to prevent him from moving. "Fine, fine! All I know is Anan said no one walked away from him, and she'd get what was coming to her. Then Adrienne disappeared."

Zandra gripped Emmett's shoulder. "Is she dead?"

"When Anan wants revenge, he takes his time. He enjoys pushing people to the edge, shoving them until they break, and destroying what's left. That's what he did to Osorin. Poor sap."

I sucked in a breath. "You saw Anan murder Osorin?"

"I saw nothing, but Anan and Koku hated Osorin, and they always messed with him. I didn't mind the guy, even though he was a loser, but all he wanted was to be in the gang. Anan gave him the worst jobs and claimed they were an initiation. If Osorin passed the tests, then he was in the gang. Of course, the tests never ended. They just got worse."

"Did Anan tell you he killed Osorin?" Zandra said.

"He never came flat out and confessed to it, but it was him. He was so smug about it and didn't stop laughing when you found Osorin's headless corpse and almost got arrested for murder by those dumb angels."

"How did he do it?" Zandra sounded a little breathless.

"I don't know. I remember Koku and Anan chuckling about some prank they'd pulled on Osorin. They gave him this test to see if he'd pull it off. They told him, even though everyone would see him doing something illegal, he wouldn't get in trouble. I wanted to ask what they meant, but I didn't dare. As you saw last night, Anan hates anyone standing up to him."

"An illegal prank Osorin wouldn't get in trouble for?" Zandra said. "What could it be?"

"Only Anan has the answer, and he doesn't talk. And even if the angels find evidence to say he was involved, he's got us backing him and giving him fake alibis."

"Why do you support a killer?" I said.

Emmett shrugged. "It's all I've known. I've been in the gang since I was a teenager. I met Anan and Koku at school, and they took me under their wings. I wasn't the brightest kid and took a while to grow big. It made me a target for bullies. One day, Anan stood up for me, and no one touched me after that, so I've always felt like I owed him."

"Not anymore?"

"There's no point. Anan turned on me because he thinks I'm after his job. He gets like that, all paranoid and suspicious. There's nothing I can do to convince him otherwise."

I shifted my paw off Emmett's leg and stepped back to join Sammy. "He wants you dead?"

"I know he does. He signed my death warrant last night, so it's too late for me. But I figured you both might be brave enough or crazy enough to stop him. Anan's reign must end."

"And you want us to go up against Anan?" I said.

"You're the only ones around here who would."

"How do we know you're not setting us up?"

"I'm out of the gang, so I have nothing left to lose by speaking to you."

"You told him that's what you planned on doing?" Zandra said.

"No! I wouldn't be breathing if he knew where I was. I snuck out first thing, as soon as I regained consciousness. When I realized what he'd done to me... well, nothing could change that. I'm already dead. But you can stop him from hurting anyone else."

I wasn't sure what Emmett meant by being already dead, and from the expression on Zandra's face, neither did she. Sammy also looked confused.

"Would you go on record to Angel Force about what you know about the gang?" Zandra said.

"No way."

"But you've got evidence all over you that Anan attacked you. That would put him behind bars and remove the danger."

"The angels are too slow to respond to serious threats. By the time I'd given them a statement and they'd investigated, Anan would have gotten to me. Anyway, it doesn't matter. I haven't got long left."

"You'll recover from these injuries," Zandra said. "If healing magic isn't your specialty, I can help. We could get you to the apothecary."

"These bruises and cracked ribs aren't the problem."

"I don't understand. Why do you think it's too late for you?" I said.

"You'll know soon enough." Emmett dragged himself up and leaned against the wall. "You're my only hope. You need to get the evidence to convict Anan and make sure he's put away. Make sure the Shadow gang is pulled apart."

"Help us do that. I see you want to change and stop what the gang is doing. We can work together," Zandra said.

Emmett pushed away from the wall. He leaned over and coughed dryly. "I have to get things in order. I'm running out of time. I can feel things changing. Good luck." He limp-ran away, pausing at the end of the alley and feeling around in his pockets. He dropped something then looked either way before disappearing.

"That was weird," Zandra said. "What does Emmett expect me to do with that elusive cry for help? Only the angels can arrest Anan."

I trotted to the end of the alley to see what Emmett had dropped. My booping snooter wrinkled, and I recoiled.

"What is it?" Zandra hurried over with Sammy.

I held my breath to avoid inhaling the gross scent. "A rotting finger."

"I've got a surprise for you." Zandra strode up to Finn as he left the Winding Spells magic store.

I was beside her, taking shallow breaths to stop breathing in the decaying wafts drifting from her pocket. After we'd discovered the rotting gray finger Emmett had left behind, Zandra had wrapped it in several tissues and placed it in a plastic bag.

We'd decided we needed help so had tracked down Finn. Sammy had stayed at the café, looking unwell after the discovery of the body part.

"Will I like it?" Finn's grin faded when Zandra didn't smile. "I'm guessing not?"

"You guessed right. And I can't show you out here. Have you got five minutes?"

"Sure. I've just finished my shift. I only had a half-day today. We can go back to mine. My apartment is a couple of minutes from here."

"Let's do that. This surprise involves the Shadow gang."

"Right this way." Finn strode along beside Zandra, his gaze full of curiosity. "Should I ask what you've been doing hanging about with the Shadow gang?"

"Probably not. But it's nothing illegal. And I had Juno and her new friend Sammy with me to make sure I behaved."

"My witch always behaves impeccably. She never breaks the law or cast spells she shouldn't." That was my story, and I was sticking to it. Even when Zandra was wrong, she was right.

Amusement crossed Finn's face. "Let's get inside and see what my surprise is." He took us into a ground-floor apartment in a converted early twentieth century red brick house. The window ledges had a fresh coat of white paint, and the steps were newly swept.

"Nice place. You run the animal rescue from here?" Zandra said.

"No, I rent barns and a field on the edge of town. Can't have a flatulent hellhound messing up my pad." He led us to a dark green front door and unlocked it.

"You've been to see Archie again?"

"Yep. That hound is still feeling so sorry for himself. And all the stress is making him badly gassy."

"I keep saying grief does weird things to people," I said.

"No kidding. You'll have to deep clean the pens at this rate. Poor guy can't keep it in." Finn strode into an open-plan white kitchen with nothing on the work surfaces. He placed down the bag he had in his hands and turned to Zandra, his eyebrow arched.

Zandra pulled out the bag containing the finger and held it out to Finn.

He stared at it. “I was going to offer coffee, but I have a feeling whatever’s in there will be stomach churning. Especially if the smell is anything to go by.”

“It’s decaying fast,” Zandra said.

Finn peered closely at the bag. “What is it? A dead animal?”

“Emmett dropped it when he ran off,” Zandra said. “He got beat up by Anan. The guy was a mess when he showed up around the back of Bites and Delights, asking to see me and Juno.”

“Why you? And why leave behind whatever that is?”

“That’s the mystery I’m figuring out. And weirdly, Emmett wasn’t worried about his physical injuries. There was something else on his mind. He said he didn’t have much time and needed the gang to be stopped.”

Finn sucked in a breath. “Has Anan put a kill order on Emmett? He does that when he falls out with someone.”

“He didn’t mention a kill order but said he needed to get his affairs in order and asked me to stop the gang.” Zandra jiggled the bag.

Finn still stared at the disgustingly fragrant bag. “He wouldn’t come to the angels, would he? He must see good in you.”

“Maybe not good, but I always get the job done.” Zandra wiggled the bag again.

“Go on, show me what’s inside.”

"Have you got gloves? Picking this thing up wasn't exactly a joy."

"Washing-up gloves?"

"They'll do," Zandra said.

Finn grabbed the gloves from the sink, and Zandra put them on. She unrolled the bag, rifled carefully through the tissue, and extracted the finger.

Finn grimaced. "Emmett's finger fell off?"

"I don't see how this finger could be his."

"You think he was carrying it around?"

"Maybe he's attached to a rotting finger," I said. "It could have been a friend's finger. He was looking for something in his pocket before he ran off and may have dropped it without meaning to."

Finn shook his head. "The only friends Emmett has are in the gang. Or they were. Go back a few steps. How did you get involved in this situation with Emmett?"

Zandra placed the finger back in the bag. "We may have visited the gang's home. The old warehouse on the edge of town. And I may have accused Anan of abducting Adrienne and killing Osorin."

A snort of surprise came out of Finn. "And you're still standing?"

"Anan was as surprised as you by the accusations. I got the impression few people stand up to him."

"If they do, they don't stand for long. Anan takes down anyone who goes up against him. How did you get out?"

"We got lucky," Zandra said. "Emmett said something Anan didn't like, and they fought. It gave us a chance to get away."

"Did Emmett cause the distraction so you could escape?"

"No, it wasn't intentional. He was trying to get Anan's approval," I said. "From what Emmett told us when he showed up at the café, Anan has a problem with him. Emmett could have said anything, and Anan would have attacked him. Probably breathing too loudly would have caused a fight."

"So after he got attacked, Emmett came to get help from you and left that finger." Finn jabbed a digit at the bag.

"Or Juno could be right, and he dropped it without realizing. He was in a hurry to get away," Zandra said.

"It doesn't look dried up, so it's a newly rotten finger. Hold on, I've got something I can use to test on it and see what we're working with." Finn disappeared into another room, most likely his bedroom, and returned a moment later with a small glass beaker and a vial of red potion. "Put the finger in here. A couple of drops of this will show if there's magic attached to the body part."

"You're an alchemist?" Zandra put the finger in the beaker.

"I dabble. It's a hobby. Along with grave robbing and scaring small children. At least, that's what Bertoli tells everyone." Finn dabbed a few drops of potion on the finger. A swirl of black mist drifted off it, and he recoiled. "It's ghoul! We don't have ghouls in Crimson Cove. We haven't seen any here for almost a year."

"You've got some now." Zandra wafted a hand in front of her face to disperse the foul mist. "And those ghouls are linked to the Shadow gang."

Finn peered at the fizzling finger. "But how, and why? They're thugs and thieves, not ghoul creators. It takes a special kind of scumbag to turn people into ghouls."

"If the gang is creating ghouls, we need to catch them in the act." Zandra tapped her hand against her thigh. "I want to stop them. They've done something to Adrienne, and they'll keep hurting people."

"You've got proof?" Finn said. "If you have, I can send a team over to arrest them."

"Only Emmett's word, and he won't talk to you." Her mouth twisted to the side, and she got a look on her face that meant we were about to do something risky.

"Would you be up for a stakeout to see if we can find out more?" Zandra said.

Finn looked up from the beaker. "You want help from Angel Force, or would this be an unofficial stakeout?"

"Will the angels be quick to respond if we share this information with them?"

"They're only ever speedy if someone leaves cookies in the break room. Then it's every angel for himself."

"Then let's keep this between us for now. If we find nothing useful when watching the Shadow gang, we'll reconsider. But if we get proof they're the ultimate ghoul creating scumbags we think they might be, you'll get a gold star to pin on your wings."

"That sounds painful." Finn stroked his fingers across one wing. "If I get caught, I'll be in trouble. I could lose my job."

"You could help bring down some bad guys and stop them from making more ghouls." Zandra waggled her eyebrows. "You'd be the hero. Bertoli might even stop being such a jerk to you."

"Bertoli is a jerk to everyone." He grinned. "I'm in."

And so was I. I was happy Zandra was working with Finn. She preferred to operate solo, but a new friend was welcome. And I had a feeling Finn would be good for her. Maybe even better than good.

A half-demon, half-angel was an asset we needed to go up against the Shadow gang and come out the other side unharmed.

Chapter 18

A ghoulish discovery

The sun had dipped below the buildings by the time we were back at the warehouse. Zandra had brought Finn with her, and I'd brought Sammy.

We'd been watching the warehouse for half an hour, and Koku, Anan, and Lewis had arrived fifteen minutes ago. There was no sign of Emmett. He'd most likely fled for fear of reprisal after snitching on Anan.

"Whatever Anan did to Emmett, it must have been off the charts awful." Finn's tone was low and quiet, even though we were tucked out of sight, far back from the warehouse.

"When I saw them in action, they weren't exactly being friendly to each other," Zandra said.

"That's the way they do things. They fight for fun. It must have been something unforgiveable for Emmett to turn on Anan and then ask for your help."

"Maybe Anan turned Emmett's girlfriend into a ghoul. The finger he dropped was hers," I said.

"The gang members don't have girlfriends. It's against the rules. It's always bros before... well, ladies. If a girl ever gets in the way, Anan puts a stop to it. He doesn't want his crew to have distractions that prevent them from being committed to him."

"She could have been a secret girlfriend," Zandra said. "Emmett fell for someone but didn't tell Anan because he knew what would happen. Anan found out and got revenge. Emmett's heart got broken, so he turned on him."

"And then carried his ghoul girlfriend's finger around as a love token?" Finn grimaced. "That's too disturbing even for Emmett, and he's a twisted son of a gun. This gang never breaks rank. You don't think Emmett was setting you up, do you? Anan sent him to see if you'd return to the warehouse."

"Why leave the gross finger behind?" Zandra said.

"Because he knows you're nosy and would have to find out where it came from."

Zandra nudged him with her elbow. "A curious nature is no bad thing. Besides, Juno asked Emmett that same question, but he really seemed done with the gang. I believed him. He wants them brought down."

"And he thinks you can do it?"

"Of course my witch can do it." I raised my hackles and hissed at Finn for his disrespectful comment. "Zandra is the most powerful witch you'll ever meet. She can do anything she sets her mind to."

"Thanks for the ego boost, Juno." Zandra shook her head. "I'm still growing into my powers, despite what my fluffy sidekick tells you."

"You seem powerful enough to me. And you're not scared of taking on a group like the Shadow gang. Don't underestimate yourself," Finn said.

"I'm always telling her that," I muttered.

"Hey, you two, no ganging up on me." Zandra wrinkled her nose as she glared at me.

While Zandra and Finn continued to talk about their powers, I nudged Sammy, and we headed to the shipping containers. The smell of spoiled meat still drifted out of them.

"Someone badly needs to take out the trash," Sammy whispered.

"It smells like the finger we found."

"It's coming from this container." Sammy's little nose crinkled as he sniffed along the bottom of the door.

A soft thump against the side of the shipping container made me jump back.

Sammy leaped in front of me. "Whatever's in there, it won't get you."

I rubbed my face against his to show my appreciation for his heroic behavior. "You would, wouldn't you? We barely know each other, but you've already helped me twice. You're a good cat, Sammy."

He lowered his head but flicked his tail. "And you're a beautiful cat and so smart. Loyal to your witch, too. I hope I find a magic user almost as amazing as Zandra. I miss not having anyone."

"She is special. You'd be lucky if you did. Maybe I can help you find someone. What do you look for in a bonded magic user?"

"Kindness is important, a good heart, a warm bed, and generous with the treats."

I shrank against Sammy and hissed when I spotted Elijah trotting out of the warehouse. He headed around the side of the building on his mean little paws.

"What is it?" Sammy leaned against me, his hackles raised, even though he hadn't seen Elijah.

"An annoyance, and one I intend to deal with." I despised that evil, furless cat, and I was angry with myself for being betrayed by my fickle heart.

"You're growling," Sammy said. "Is it something I did?"

I nuzzled him to show this had nothing to do with my favorite chunky gray cat. "I've just seen Elijah. Let's follow him and see what he's up to."

"Is that a good idea? You know how mean he can be. He could catch us."

"And if he does, you know I'll protect you, too. Relationships are never one-sided. We look out for each other."

He gave a happy chirrup. "Let's go deal with Elijah."

I checked Zandra was still content with Finn then slunk through the shadows with Sammy, following Elijah. When I caught sight of him again, he was heading through an open external door.

We waited a moment then went inside. We entered a plain gray corridor with minimal lighting. Elijah had reached the end of the corridor and turned left into a room.

I nodded at Sammy, and although he was shaking, he kept up with me as we headed along the corridor.

I peeked into the room Elijah had entered. It looked like a giant coat room. There were dozens of jackets, long and short coats, purses and wallets, and different sizes of bags laid out on tables. And they were being sorted by an unhappy looking Emmett. A very gray, sickly Emmett.

After a quick nudge to get Sammy moving, we ducked into the room and hid behind a pile of pallets.

"Hurry up," Elijah snapped as he stalked around Emmett. "The shipment is getting restless, and we need to pawn anything of value before we leave. The contact is waiting."

"I'm going as fast as I can. I'm struggling."

"Work harder, or Anan will teach you another lesson. Don't think he's forgotten you ran out on the gang. You're lucky to have any sort of life."

Emmett dumped down a bag he'd been looking through. "After what Anan did, what did he expect from me?"

"He taught you the lesson you deserved."

"I didn't deserve this." Emmett held up his hands. They were gray, and he was missing two fingers on his right hand.

"What's wrong with him?" Sammy whispered. "He looks half-dead."

"And he smells like those shipping containers." A worrying thought entered my head. Was the gang mass producing ghouls?

"Is he sick?"

I wrinkled my booping snooter. "I think he's turning into a ghoul. Let's get out of here. Zandra needs to know about this. And I have a bad feeling I know what's inside all those shipping containers."

Sammy dashed after me as I raced along the corridor and back outside.

I ran up to Zandra. "Emmett's inside the warehouse."

Her eyes widened, and she scooped me up. "I didn't know you'd gone inside. Did anyone see you?"

"No. But I've figured out what's in those shipping containers." I sucked in a deep breath. "They're full of ghouls."

"Ghouls! Why do you think that?" Finn looked at me, his forehead wrinkled and disbelief in his eyes.

I curled my tail around Zandra's neck. "Because of the finger Emmett left behind. It was his finger. It must have fallen off when he ran away."

"And he's lost another finger since then," Sammy said. "He's gray, and his veins are black. He's definitely turning into a ghoul."

"And the finger smells the same as the contents of those shipping containers," I said. "We have multiple ghouls to deal with."

"That's what Emmett meant when he said Anan signed his death warrant." Zandra shook her head. "Anan can turn people into ghouls. Is that new?"

"It must be. Although it's not the kind of magic you evolve. He's got to be messing with some shady dark spells to achieve that level of twisted magic," Finn said.

"Why get into the ghoul trade?"

"Cheap labor. Ghouls never complain when you put them to work, they don't need rest, they definitely don't get benefits, and they do as they're told. If they don't, you dump them and leave them to decay."

"Emmett was sorting through wallets, purses, and clothing," I said. "They're taking the belongings of those they're turning into ghouls. Elijah said they're pawning anything valuable before shipping out the ghouls."

"So Anan doesn't want them for himself," Finn said after a few seconds of silence. "I know there is an underground market for ghouls. It's usually dark magic users who want them. They don't trust people, so they recruit ghouls to work for them."

"A slave army of mindless ghouls who don't listen to conversations or gossip would be the perfect workforce for people who have a lot to hide," Zandra said.

"It's also a workforce that eats flesh and can go rogue if they're not properly cared for." I'd seen plenty of ghouls over the years. They could be stable and productive, but leave them to get hungry, mistreat them, or let them wander without instruction, and they turned into flesh eating killing machines.

"There's only one way to find out if that's what the Shadow gang is doing." Finn's gaze went to a shipping container. "We need to see inside those things."

"Juno, Sammy, you watch the warehouse and make sure no one sees what we're doing. We'll open a container," Zandra said.

I didn't want to leave Zandra, but she had Finn with her, and so far, he'd done nothing to make me doubt him. I kept half my attention on the warehouse and the rest on Zandra as she headed to the shipping containers with Finn.

They walked around one, and Finn tried the lock. There was a small flare of magic, and they broke it open.

"Are you ready?" Finn said, his hand on the door.

Zandra sparked magic on her palm. "Let's see what's inside."

Before Finn could open the door, a mass of gray, stinking bodies swarmed out. They staggered about, their eyes black and limbs a mottled gray with prominent black veins on display.

One ghoul, a small old man with a bald head wearing only suit pants and a tie, lunged at Zandra, his teeth snapping too close to her face.

"Look out! They're hungry." Three ghouls tackled Finn, and they hit the ground.

"Sammy, keep watching the warehouse." I raced away and launched at the ghoul trying to bite Zandra. I sunk my teeth into the creature's ear and almost gagged as the taste of rot and death filled my mouth. But I wasn't letting go. Not when Zandra was in danger.

She blasted the ghoul away with a spell, and I leaped off as the creature staggered back and hit the ground with a squelchy splat.

A wave of hot, red magic shot out of Finn, and the three ghouls attacking him were vaporized.

I stared at the ash floating in the air. That was not angel power he'd just used. But I couldn't get distracted. There were more ghouls coming for us.

"They haven't been feeding them," Zandra yelled. "They're starving and desperate."

Finn yelped as a giant of a ghoul standing almost seven feet tall tackled him from behind. The ghoul had hold of Finn's wings and was yanking one off.

Zandra blasted the ghoul with several spells before he let go, but he was still standing.

Finn turned, one of his wings hanging at an odd angle, and vaporized the ghoul with another red blast of magic.

It was time to show these ghouls we meant business. I dug into the deep well of ancient power inside me. As always, the well felt sludgy and reluctant to stir into action, but I kept digging and forced it to life.

"Everyone stay out of my way," I yelled as magic shimmered on my paws and flooded out of my eyes.

Finn had never seen me in all my magical glory, so he stood staring rather than ducking for cover like any sensible person would.

Zandra tackled him, and they hit the dirt a second before my magic flared and captured the ghouls in an icy bubble of primal power. It wavered and bent, desperate to break, but I held on by sheer force of will. These ghouls were a danger to my witch, and they had to be stopped.

I herded them back to the container, magic blazing out of me. Every step was an effort, and every movement weakened me, but I gripped onto the power. Zandra's life depended on me succeeding.

I glimpsed Sammy through a haze of magic. He stood at the edge of my bubble, adoration in his eyes. The confidence and love shining from him was the push I needed. I dug into my power and forced the last of the ghouls into the container before slamming the door shut.

My legs wobbled as I pulled back my magic. Zandra locked the door on the shipping container as I sank to my belly. I needed rest and food and then more rest. A week in bed should see me right.

There was a high-pitched squeal and a yelp, and I leaped up. Elijah was rolling Sammy in the dirt, his teeth attached to one of his back legs.

Despite being exhausted and wanting to pass out nestled deep in Zandra's bed, I wouldn't give Elijah the pleasure of hurting Sammy.

I screeched a hissing battle cry, dragged up my magic again, and joined in the catfight. I bit the first lump of bare flesh I found, which was Elijah's skinny tail, and dug in tooth and claw, holding on tight, leaning back, and yanking him away from my chunky friend.

It took Elijah a few seconds to realize he'd received some new piercings in his tail. When he did, he let out the loudest caterwaul I'd ever heard and twisted around, trying to shake me free. The spell he thrust at me was off by a couple of inches, and it slammed into the dirt, scattering stones everywhere.

But the distraction allowed Sammy to get away. He rolled over several times until he flopped onto his belly. He had a deep cut on his nose and was missing another chunk of ear. Poor baby.

Elijah twisted and writhed, but I wasn't letting go. He deserved everything he got from me. I let go of his tail for a second, only to reattach myself to his back.

He tried flipping me off, but that blast of magic he'd used on me must have taken it out of him because he stumbled and staggered to the side.

I clung on and growled in his ear. "Payback's a minx, isn't it? You deceived me. You hurt me, you've hurt my friend, and you tried to hurt Zandra. And that last one is unforgivable. We protect our bonded magic users. We do not betray them."

"Please, stop. Anan will kill me if I fail him." Elijah writhed and wailed beneath my savagery.

"You're as bad as him. You led me here to kill me."

"No, to teach you a lesson. If I hadn't done that, Anan would have whipped me and chained me up. He's a bad guy. I'm terrified of him. Please, I was only following orders."

As much as I wanted to destroy Elijah, I'd seen how poorly Anan had treated him, and no familiar deserved that. If familiars were mistreated, it changed them. They became cautious and scared. They stopped trusting, and their power grew as twisted as the bond they had with their magic user.

"If I spare your life, will you testify against the gang?" I snarled.

By this time, Zandra and Finn had joined us, and even Sammy had crept closer on his stomach.

"I'm too scared. If I tell you everything, my life is over," Elijah said.

I eased my claws out of his skin. I could be benevolent when I had to be. "You don't have much of a life. Anan is the wrong magic user for you. He's bad for you, and I can see you're scared of him."

"Everyone is scared of him," Elijah muttered, his shoulders hunched in sullen deference. "Even you'd be with all your weird power. No one can stop him."

"We can," Zandra said. "But we need your help. We need someone brave and strong to stand up against this gang and stop them once and for all. We've already found the shipping containers containing the ghouls, so we know what Anan's doing."

"He'll challenge anyone who stands against him. He threatened to turn me into a ghoul if I didn't do everything he demanded." Elijah sank onto his belly.

"He did that to Emmett, didn't he?" I kept him pinned with my weight, just in case he tried to escape.

Elijah dropped his chin onto the ground. "Yes. It's his new favorite threat. If any of the gang members disobey him, he threatens to turn them. Of course, none of them believed he'd do it. The gang is crucial to him. Anan needs his people around him."

"Maybe the magic he's misusing is making him feel invincible," Finn said. "He's got to be dealing with nasty stuff to gain the power to change people into ghouls."

Elijah nodded. "Anan's gone too far. The magic has turned him from a cruel, unfeeling person into a monster. It's almost like he's become a ghoul. He just wants to destroy. That's all he's interested in. I think... no, I know, the magic he's messing with has damaged him, and there's nothing anyone can do about that."

"Which gives you even more reason to help us," I said. "Elijah, we need you on our side." I hopped off him as a sign of trust, but one false pawstep, and I'd stamp on him again.

Elijah turned and licked his wounded tail. "If you go up against Anan and this goes wrong, we're all dead."

"It won't go wrong. If you're on the same team as my witch, you can guarantee victory." I ignored

Zandra as she shuffled her feet. She'd want to protest over that comment, but she'd only be lying to herself. She simply didn't realize how powerful she was.

"What's Anan planning on doing with all those ghouls?" Finn said.

Elijah heaved out a sigh. "He has contracts to create ghoul armies. He asked around and found there was an underserved market, so he's filling it."

Finn hissed out an angry breath. "An illegal market. This evidence will put him away for years."

"For the rest of his life, if we can prove he murdered Osorin, too," Zandra said.

"Do you know anything about that?" I said to Elijah.

"I know Osorin wanted to be in the gang, but they considered him a joke. They were always messing with him."

"Just messing? How far did they take it?"

Elijah didn't speak until I jabbed him with a murder mitten. "I wasn't there, so I didn't see what happened to Osorin. Anan said he was a nuisance and not worth keeping around."

"So he killed him?"

"No! I don't know. Maybe. Anan didn't take me on many jobs, so if he went to Osorin's house and killed him, he didn't tell me about it."

"Are you saying that because you're scared or because it's the truth?" I said. "If you're on this team, you have to be truthful."

Elijah hissed softly. "There is no team. You're just a band of misfits in over your heads. I need to get out of here. I've already told you too much."

"You're coming with us." Sammy marched over and yanked Elijah up by his scruff. "You're taking us inside that warehouse and showing us everything."

I became breathless, watching my handsome man tackle this oily cheater.

Elijah wailed and hissed but didn't fight back. He knew when he'd been bested.

"Take us to the room with the purses and clothing. They're from the victims, aren't they?" I said. "Everyone who's been turned into a ghoul?"

Elijah kept his head down. "Anan wanted to maximize profits. Not that the deadbeats we picked up had much going for them, but he planned to get everything he could out of this deal."

"If we're going inside, we should move," Finn said. "I'm surprised no one has been out to see what the disturbance was all about."

"They sent me to check," Elijah said. "And they'll miss me if I don't go back soon. I have to escape now. If they learn I've been speaking to you, I'm dead."

I rested a paw on the top of his head. "We'll look after you. You're a bad cat, but Anan's mistreated you for years. I saw the way he handled you and talked down to you. He has no respect for you. I understand why that made you bitter and cruel, but you can change. You can work with us. Be one of the misfits, too."

"Until Anan finds me and kills me."

I pulsed calming magic over him. "Not if you stick with us. But if you go it alone, then you're guaranteed not to make it."

He heaved out another sigh. "I'll go with you, even though it's a suicide mission. This way." He dragged his paws as if they were too heavy to move as he took us into the room where the victims' belongings were being sorted by Emmett.

Except they weren't. Emmett was on his back on the floor. His eyes were glazed and his limbs stiff at his sides.

We raced over, and Finn checked for a pulse.

He shook his head. "Emmett's gone. Why so fast? Ghouls can last for years if they're not mistreated."

Elijah sniffed Emmett's body. "The ghouls Anan made are supposed to last for at least a year. Anan must have done something else to Emmett. He's crazy enough to use even darker magic on someone who wronged him." His gaze kept darting around, and he was shivering.

Zandra found a blanket and covered Emmett.

"Everyone take a few minutes to look around the personal belongings. See if there's anything useful. Grab ID if you find it. There'll be families out there missing loved ones," Finn said.

We got to work. Zandra sorted through the jackets with Finn, while I checked purses and wallets with Sammy. Elijah remained out of the way, still shivering.

"They're scum," Finn growled out as he worked through the pockets of a large black overcoat. "They've picked the ghouls clean. There are gold teeth in a box over here. The Shadow gang has moved down in the world." His wings flared behind him, and rather than the pristine white of angel wings, they glowed a dull red and hot sparks came off them.

"Look at this." Zandra was leafing through a file she'd picked up. "These are the signed contracts for Anan to deliver the ghouls. There are a dozen names here."

Finn joined her and looked at the paperwork. "Keep hold of that. We'll need it for evidence so we can charge Anan and the others."

"Someone's coming!" Elijah darted to the door, Sammy hot on his heels.

"There's no one out there," Sammy said. "You're being paranoid."

"Anan and the rest of his gang are in the warehouse. They could come back. We should leave." Elijah's tail was between his legs.

"You're going nowhere." Sammy blocked the exit.

"If you won't let me leave, then I should find Anan and let him know everything is fine, so he doesn't get suspicious."

I didn't trust Elijah enough to let him go off on his own. He could have second thoughts and tell Anan we were here in the hopes of getting back on his good side.

"Leave it a few more minutes," I said. "We'll get all the evidence from this room, then we'll leave."

"You know, Emmett's body would be an excellent source of evidence." Finn stood over Emmett.

"We can't carry a ghoul out of here unnoticed," Zandra said. "And if we take him, Anan will know someone's been poking around."

"I could fly him out. Anan's dark magic will be all over Emmett. Angel Force will have everything they need to make an arrest."

"Elijah, what's this all about?" I studied a map of Crimson Cove on the wall. There were six red dots on it. They were locations of large stores in the town.

He scurried over to me. “It was a prank Anan and Koku made up for Osorin.”

“What kind of prank?” Zandra walked over and joined us.

“Anan didn’t say, but they were laughing about it. They said it would be an easy way to make money and get rid of a problem at the same time.”

“Osorin being the problem?” I said.

“Maybe. I know nothing about it.” Elijah backed away, but I stood on his tail to stop him from getting too far.

The door slammed against the wall, and I spun around to see Anan standing in the doorway.

His cold, hard eyes worked the room. “Elijah, come here.”

Elijah took a step forward, but hesitated and looked at me.

“Get your scrawny, useless body over here if you want to keep breathing,” Anan said.

“Leave him alone.” I stepped in front of Elijah. “You’ve hurt him enough. You’ve turned a once beautiful, loyal familiar into a coldhearted, mean creature. He wants nothing to do with you.”

“I suppose you’re his girlfriend.” Anan smirked. “Get out of the way, unless you want that fluff chargrilled.”

“It’s okay,” Elijah whispered. “I knew he’d catch me. This was always my fate. It’s too late for me.”

Anan stepped into the room. He was followed by ten other guys, Koku and Lewis among them. They spread out in a line, glaring at us like we’d stolen the last fishy treat that had been promised to them.

“I’d ask what you’re doing, but it’s obvious,” Anan said. “You couldn’t leave the ghouls alone, could you? You had to keep poking. Now you know the truth, it means you're never going to leave. Lewis, have you got the collar?"

Lewis lifted what looked like a dog collar with faint sparkles of magic on it. "Primed and ready to go, boss."

I backed away and turned so I could jump onto Zandra's shoulder. "That looks like the collar Osorin was wearing." My gaze was intent on the collar. The magic sparking off it looked unstable and made my insides tremble.

"You're right," she whispered. "What have they got it for? Is it a gang thing? Like the hand tattoo?"

I shook my head, my inner demi-goddess wailing at the darkness spiraling off that repulsive collar. "It's much worse than that. I think that's what killed Osorin."

Zandra's eyes widened, and she licked her lips.

"Not looking so confident anymore, are you?" Anan clicked his fingers. "Now, you put this collar on, little witch, and I'll tell you a final story before you die."

Chapter 19

A shiny revelation

"How about you get lost?" Zandra said. "No one is putting on that collar. We know what it does."

"How can you possibly know that?" Anan bared his teeth. "More snooping, I suppose?"

"We saw the same kind of collar on Osorin. That's how he lost his head, isn't it? I'm assuming it's remote activated, or the magic is timed to go off at a specific moment. You made him wear a collar and then killed him with it."

"Why would I do such a thing to a valued gang member?" Anan chuckled, and the rest of his gang joined in, the noise humorless and more like rough grumbles than laughs.

"Because you hated him. You thought he was a joke and got in your way." Zandra pressed a hand to my side. "Or you were using Osorin as a test subject. Put one of those collars on a person, and they'll do anything for you. If they don't, they die."

"Interesting theory. Let's test it on you. Lewis, Zandra needs the collar," Anan said.

I hissed and magic sparked off me, the wards tugging at it and stopping it from flaring out. "Stay away from my witch."

"Elijah, if you value your life, keep your girlfriend quiet and out of our way," Anan said.

Elijah shuffled back until he was next to Zandra, Sammy with him. Finn stood further away by the table of purses. "Juno's not my girlfriend. I don't deserve someone like her."

Anan rolled his eyes. "Just keep her quiet. I'll deal with you later."

I jumped off Zandra and leaned briefly against Elijah to show he had my support. "No, you won't. Elijah is with us now. He'd never hurt me. Keep your hands off him and stop threatening Zandra."

Anan whipped his fingers through the air and slammed a blast of black magic into Emmett's blanket covered body.

Emmett jerked like a zap of electricity had hit him. He rose from the floor and lunged, grabbing Zandra from behind.

She yelped as he lifted her off her feet. Lewis raced over and attempted to put the collar around her neck, dodging and ducking to avoid her flailing legs.

I threw myself at Lewis at the same time as Sammy and Elijah. I landed on Lewis's face and bit the end of his nose as my claws latched onto his ears. Elijah hung off one of Lewis's legs, growling and scratching, while Sammy bit Lewis in the groin.

Lewis shrieked, dropped the collar, and staggered away, taking us with him.

I summoned my magic, intent on obliterating Lewis.

"Let Lewis go, if you want your angel freak to live," Anan yelled.

I kept snarling and slashing, my battle lust raging, while my two fighting companions got to work on Lewis's lower section.

"Juno, stop!" Zandra's high-pitch focused my attention. "They've got Finn."

In the chaos, I hadn't paid attention to our angel comrade. I removed my teeth from Lewis's nose and looked up. Anan had clamped another collar around Finn's neck. It sparked with more unstable magic, and smoke drifted off it.

I got in one more good scratch on Lewis's ear before dropping to the floor. Sammy and Elijah joined me, and we dodged a flailing, yelping Lewis as he dripped blood and clutched his chewed parts while he staggered back to Anan.

Zandra took a step toward Finn, magic on her palm, but Anan waggled a finger. "Try to save him, and he dies."

"Go! I'll deal with Anan and his gang," Finn said.

"Sure, you will." Anan shoved Finn.

He hit the floor, landing on his knees. Finn grabbed the edge of the collar and tugged. Magic flared off it and smoke billowed around him.

"Don't do that!" Zandra said. "Remember the remains of the collar Osorin had around his neck? That caused the explosion. If you mess with it, it'll kill you."

Finn froze then slowly lowered his hands.

"Nicely worked out," Anan said. "I never liked getting my hands too dirty with the business of murder. There are always too many out-of-control body fluids spraying about when a person dies.

These collars are a great way to deal with troublemakers without being on the scene."

"You admit, you killed Osorin with one of those things?" Zandra watched Finn. His face was pale, and there was a tremor in his hands, but he was no longer trying to take off the collar.

"I confess to nothing," Anan said. "No one saw me there when Osorin died. Maybe he was having a bad day with his magic. It wouldn't surprise me. That guy was the world's worst idiot. The only thing I am surprised about is he didn't kill himself sooner."

"Angel Force has the remains of the collar that killed Osorin," Finn said. "Your magic will be all over it. And by trapping me in a collar, you've given us even more evidence."

"Sure, but you have to get out of here with your head attached to your body to be of any use to Angel Force. And I don't see that happening," Anan said.

Although I watched Anan and the rest of his gang closely, my attention kept being drawn back to the map on the wall with the red dots. I was familiar with the stores in Crimson Cove, and the ones picked out on that map were successful places that must make a lot of money.

I stuck my nose in Elijah's ear. "Is there any way you can bring down the draining magic wards?"

He nodded and slunk away. I didn't trust him, but I had to hope Elijah would do the right thing.

I nudged Zandra's leg with my head and then clambered up to her shoulder. "That wall map, the missing money, Osorin losing his head, and the collar, they're connected."

"Ignore that map." Anan glowered at his gang. "That was supposed to have been taken down before we moved on. Which moron forgot his job?"

The guys shuffled about and looked at each other to see if anyone would take the blame.

"What's the connection?" Zandra said to me.

"Anan used Osorin to rob the stores in Crimson Cove. They put him in a collar, so he could plead his innocence and play the part of a victim when he got caught. At least, that's what Anan told him."

"Keep your mouth shut, fluffy," Anan growled out.

"Is the hardware store on there?" Finn said. "That was the place most recently burgled. And the pawn shop."

I nodded. "They are."

"Did you use Osorin to steal from those stores?" Zandra said to Anan.

"I have no idea what you're talking about." Anan's smug expression revealed the opposite was true.

"You do! You killed Osorin. Was he a test subject, or was it another way of bullying him?"

"It was never bullying. Osorin was always so eager to please," Anan said. "He'd do anything we told him. If he wanted to rob some stores to prove something to us, that was his business."

"Osorin couldn't pour water out of a boot even if the instructions were on the heel." Elijah had returned from wherever he'd slunk off to and stood next to Sammy. "He'd have never come up with the robbery and magical collar plan on his own."

"You keep quiet," Anan growled.

Elijah cowered low on the floor. "It's true. Osorin did everything you told him. And you said that the collar was a fake and it wouldn't explode."

"And you just signed your death warrant," Anan said. "You're a traitor. No one betrays me and gets away with it."

"If I'm about to die, I may as well tell them everything I know."

Anan's scowl grew thunderous. "Elijah, don't say another word."

I hopped down and slowly blinked at the bald cat. "Do the right thing. We can destroy Anan and everything he stands for."

Elijah nodded and scurried to the map. "After robbing the hardware store, Osorin went to the pawnbrokers."

"Quiet!" Anan roared.

Although Elijah quivered, he kept going. "Rumor has it a diamond had been brought in, and it was worth a lot of money."

"Was there a diamond found at Osorin's house?" Zandra looked at Finn.

"No. No diamond and no money from the robberies."

"Cat, you are dead." Anan pointed a finger at Elijah. "Boys, get that mongrel."

I flared magic around me, making the gang pause. The wards were gone, and my power was enjoying itself for once.

Zandra's magic blasted out strong and pure and slammed into the group of hovering goons, knocking them back. "You made Osorin wear a dangerously unstable collar and then rob those places, but something went wrong. What was it? Did he fail to get the diamond? Or did he keep it, so you got payback?"

"Get up!" Anan yelled at his stunned gang. "Deal with this witch."

"Osorin didn't work alone when robbing those places." Zandra blasted the gang again, sending them scattering. "He kept trying to connect with someone on his snow globe, but they wouldn't pick up. That someone was you."

Anan's angry glare was still on Elijah. "You've got nothing on me."

I stepped forward. "Wrong. You've practically confessed to the murder, and we have the collar. There are also shipping containers of ghouls outside, and all the personal possessions of the people you've taken and turned are in this warehouse. I expect you also have the money and the diamond Osorin took from the stores. You have scumbag criminal stamped all over you."

"What money? What ghouls? And I never got to see that wretched diamond." Anan shrugged.

I tilted my head. "Oh! You're telling the truth. Osorin hid it from you. It's still in the one place you'd never think of looking. I know exactly where that diamond is." Laughter bubbled out of me.

"Where?" Anan snarled. "It's mine. That cheat took it, and he thought he could get away with it."

"That's confession enough for me," Finn said.

Anan whacked Finn on the side of his head.

"Juno, where's the missing diamond?" Zandra said.

I hurried over and stood up her leg. "Our furry hellhound friend with the digestive issues has the answer to that question."

Her mouth dropped open. "Archie has the diamond." Zandra pointed to her stomach.

I nodded.

"You're lying! Trying to distract me. The diamond is gone. It probably wasn't at the pawnbrokers." Anan shoved Finn to the floor and pressed a foot on his back. "This is a waste of time. And when Angel Force gets here and picks through the pieces, there'll be nothing left to show what happened. The ghouls are about to be shipped out, and all of their personal possessions will have been pawned or sold. Anything not valuable will be burned. This warehouse won't be standing in half an hour. We'll leave no clues behind. Just confusion."

The collar around Finn's neck flared, and he groaned and sank down. "Something is wrong with this thing."

"It's ready to explode," Anan said. "And there are more explosives around this building. You're my trigger. When that thing blows, it'll take off your head, kill anyone here, and detonate the rest of the explosives."

I gestured Sammy and Elijah over to me. "We need to stop that from happening."

"I don't know how to stop an explosive device," Elijah said. "I knew it was a mistake sticking with you."

I dug my claws into his cheek. "Be more like Sammy. Stop giving up because things are hard. If we're quick, we can sniff out the explosives and stop them. We all have magic. Use it."

Elijah squirmed under my clawed grip. "Fine! I'll try."

"You'll do more than try. You'll succeed. Sammy, are you with me?"

Sammy rubbed his face against mine. "Always."

I booped my nose against his. How had I overlooked such a brave, unstoppable creature? "We wait until Anan is distracted, and then we move."

"You should all get out of here." Sweat trickled down the side of Finn's face. "This collar is getting hot, and Anan's crazy enough to use it."

"Thanks for the compliment. And I am. But I won't be here to see the fireworks. I have orders to fulfil. And ghouls wait for no man. Well, they do if you order them to. That's the great thing about ghouls. They don't answer back, and they never cause trouble. You could learn from them."

"You're not sending those ghouls anywhere," Zandra said. "We found your contacts. We know who paid you."

Anan smirked at her. "My ghouls are hungry. They need a feast before we send them to their new lives, and I know just the banquet they should dine on."

Horror hit me like a goblin war hammer. I couldn't leave my witch to deal with the explosives if they were sending in the ghouls.

Anan rubbed his hands together. "Lewis, Koku, let's go unleash the ghouls. The rest of you keep watch. Guard the door. No one leaves. If the angel moves, rip his wings off. I'll send in some backup."

They disappeared, and a few seconds later, a ragtag army of skinny familiars appeared. There were two cats, three dogs, and a fanged rabbit. They all snarled or squeaked in anger when they saw us.

A momentary flicker of doubt trickled through me. This gang was big, motivated by fear, and desperate to get out alive. They'd fight hard and dirty to stop us from escaping.

I looked at my small, white paws. They were so pretty, but sometimes I wished I wasn't trapped in a cat's body and my power wasn't so unstable. Most of the time, I made the best of every situation, but looking at the wall of hatred and anger, I needed my true powers back. Every time we got into danger, I realized how much I lacked and how little I could offer Zandra.

As if she sensed my distress, Zandra lifted me from the floor and settled me on her shoulder. "Elijah and Sammy, keep an eye on the gang. If anyone looks at you funny, yell." She walked away until we were out of earshot of the others, set me on a table, and bent until we were at eye level. "What's wrong?"

"I'm worried about how I'm getting you out of this. I need to defuse the explosives, but we can't get out of the room."

"You do know we're connected, right? Or did you get a knock to the head I missed?" Zandra scratched between my ears. "I can feel your panic. There's something you're not telling me. Is it a problem with your magic?"

"My magic is perfection. So is yours."

"Nice try, but neither of us is perfect. Far from it." She glanced over her shoulder. "We can do this. If we work together, we're all powerful, aren't we? That's what you're always telling me. I have this incredible power I don't understand, and you have something special, too."

"Nothing compared to you."

Zandra's sigh drifted across my fur. "I know you don't lie to me, but you omit and keep things from me, and in all the years we've known each other,

I haven't figured out why. I'm not pushing now. It's the wrong time. But I'm here whenever you're ready to tell me."

I wrinkled my booping snooter. The time was drawing close to reveal everything to Zandra. How would that change our relationship? Would my awesomeness intimidate Zandra? She might not want a cursed demi-goddess as a familiar.

"Is that a good silence, or have you fallen asleep with your eyes open?" Zandra said.

"It's a thinking silence."

"Maybe pause the thinking for now. We have to defeat this gang of bullies, stop Finn from getting a gruesome makeover, and put down a ghoul army. Are you with me?"

I leaned my forehead against hers, my love for my wonderful witch erasing my concerns. "Always. Let's deal with this gang, save Finn, and stop the ghouls."

Chapter 20

Ghouling around

Zandra stepped back from the table, a gleam of amusement in her eyes. “If you’re still worried, you shouldn’t be. I took Vorana’s advice, and I’ve been studying magic.”

My ears flicked. “What? When? Why didn’t I know about this?”

“I’ve been doing it at night when you were sleeping. I sorted through the chest of magic items Adrienne left me, and I’ve been reading the spell books and tuition manuals. Some of it went over my head, but a lot made sense. And I’ve been practicing. I’m not afraid of an army of ghouls and the thugs who control them.”

I raised my chin and puffed my cheeks, so my whiskers bristled. Sneaky, wonderful, perfect witch. “If you’re not afraid, neither am I.” I hopped onto her shoulder.

“The ghouls are coming!” Sammy said. “I feel the floor shaking.”

“And I can smell them,” Elijah grumbled. “I don’t want to be ghoul meat.”

Anan entered the room, clutching a glowing lump of rock. Blotches of gray covered his hand and forearm. His face was covered in sweat, and he was gritting his teeth.

"Boys! String up the angel. The ghouls can have him first once we let them in, but don't let them kill him. I'm considering keeping him. A half-angel, half-demon ghoul will be of interest. Someone will pay handsomely for such a unique specimen."

"Keep your filthy ghoul magic away from me." Finn got to his feet and backed away, sparks of red magic shooting from his wings.

"You let loose that demon power, and you'll be dead in seconds." Anan splayed his free hand and whispered boom then gestured three gang members over to Finn.

There was a brief tussle, but with the threat of his head getting detached from his body, Finn put up little resistance. His arms were tied, and the ropes thrown over a beam in the ceiling. He was hoisted and left dangling in the air.

After giving my head a firm pet and keeping a hand on my side, Zandra stepped forward. "If you kill a member of Angel Force, you'll have every angel hunting you. Angel killers aren't popular."

"This fine specimen won't be dead. I'm just giving him a new purpose in life." Anan chuckled. "Besides, turning people into ghouls makes them more productive, better than the misfits and wasters we took for this job. And there was plenty of choice in Crimson Cove. You should join them. You and your misfit crew are a good fit for my ghoul army."

"There's nothing wrong with being a misfit." I glared at Anan. "Is that why you killed Osorin? He tried to be a good person, and you stopped him."

"Hah! Osorin has never done a good deed in his life. And he only came to you because he was desperate. Osorin has always wanted my role in the gang. I simply showed him why I was in charge and he never would be."

"That's a confession," Zandra said.

Anan laughed. "And who will you tell that I just confessed to murder? Your angel freak friend? He won't listen to you. He'll be too busy eating your brains. Osorin wasn't important. His days were numbered when he turned against me."

"By hiding the diamond from you?" I said.

Anan shrugged. "There never was a diamond. He wasn't smart enough to cheat me."

I knew otherwise. "But you killed him, anyway?"

"Lessons must be learned."

"Can you smell that?" I said to Zandra as the waft of spoiled meat grew stronger. "The ghouls are waiting to attack."

She nodded, her attention on Anan. "You're scraping the barrel, trading in the undead. Not exactly a quality product."

"Don't let the vampires hear you say there's anything wrong with the undead, or you'll end up on their bite list." He cracked his knuckles. "Would a vampire turn into a ghoul? That would be an interesting experiment. Maybe next time."

"You wouldn't go up against a vampire. They're not scared of thugs."

"Then why do the local vamps not bother me if they have nothing to fear?"

Zandra's top lip curled, her anger making her hot as I perched on her shoulder. I wanted to caution my witch not to taunt Anan too much. He was unstable, and madness glinted in his eyes, but whatever she said wouldn't give us an easy ride out of this unpleasantly fragranced situation.

"The vampires around here are nothing. They just want a quiet life. That was why it was so easy to take over Crimson Cove. Everyone here is weak and worthless. It was barely a challenge to turn people into mindless drones." Anan glanced at the waiting gang. "Now, it's your turn. Send them in."

I pressed against Zandra's cheek. "Don't let them bite you."

"Don't worry about me. Go! Keep an eye on Finn. He can't protect himself."

"I stay with you."

"You fight better when you're not watching over me."

"I will always watch over you." I hesitated, knowing it would be easier to fight at ground level, then nuzzled her ear and leaped to the floor to stand with Sammy and Elijah. "Keep clear of the ghouls' teeth. That's how they'll infect you with the magic that turned them."

Sammy was by my side, and although he was trembling, he stood firm. "I won't let any of them touch you."

"No sacrificing yourself. When this is done, you're taking me on a date. And I don't date ghoul."

His head whipped around. "You want to date me?"

I licked his cheek. "Of course. I only ever date heroes." I glanced at Elijah, who cowered and trembled. I wasn't sure how useful he'd be in this fight, but I had to hope he'd do the right thing.

He caught me looking and gave a single nod, his head lifting as he silently accepted the challenge.

The rank smell of decay filled the air as the ghouls' stamping feet grew nearer. The gang members who'd left with Anan dashed in. They each carried large electrified cattle prods. The ghouls were right behind them. Their teeth snapped, and their blunt nails clawed the air. They were in a wretched state. Many were missing limbs or had head wounds. Anan hadn't been gentle when he'd captured them.

"Meet my army," Anan said. "And they're all under my control."

The rock in his hand glowed, and the shadowy darkness crept further up his arm.

I focused on the rock. That was what controlled the army. Whoever held that rock held sway over the ghouls. I had to get it from Anan.

"Sammy, Elijah, I need you to help me do something important." I gathered them close. The gang members held back the ghouls with the cattle prods, while Anan strutted in front of them, and the rag-tag band of mean familiars shied out of his way. "We need to get that rock from Anan. It must hold dark magic. That's what's controlling the ghouls. Zandra needs it."

"You're right. That's how he does it," Elijah said. "Anan was away for days doing some crazy deal with a dark magic user. He came back and brought that stone with him. It hasn't left his pocket. He must have traded big to get his hands on such powerful magic."

"We have to distract Anan and snatch the rock," I said. "If we don't control the ghouls, this whole town will be lost."

"We!" Elijah shook his head.

"Yes. It's the only way this will work. We do this together." I hissed at him. "Don't back out now."

"I'll grab the rock," Sammy said. "I'm an excellent jumper."

"Maybe you were when you were five pounds lighter," Elijah said.

We both swatted him with our murder mittens.

"Ouch! Fine, you're a great jumper. It's still a dumb plan."

"Not if we work together. Elijah, pretend you want back in with Anan. Run toward him, begging for forgiveness," I said.

"I don't beg for anything."

I swatted his cheek. "It's acting! We'll chase after you and then you jump at him and knock the rock from his hand. If that fails, we'll jump him, too. One of us will get that rock. Whoever gets it, return to Zandra and give it to her."

"Hey, what are you three plotting? No time for talking. We have ghouls to defeat," Zandra said.

I looked up at her and smile-blinked. "We're getting you control of the ghoul army."

"You mean the glowing rock Anan keeps waving about?" She shook her head. "It's too dangerous to tackle him."

"I'll be fine with my friends backing me up. You ready?" I fixed Elijah with a hard glare, knowing he was the weak link in this snatch and grab mission.

"I'll do it, since I owe you one." Elijah drew in a deep breath as he turned away from me. "Anan, I made a mistake. I want back in with you."

Anan sneered as he glanced at Elijah. "You've defected to the other side. You're no good to me."

"I know things about this group. Juno told me stuff, so I can tell you their weaknesses." Elijah inched toward Anan, his tail down in a gesture of submission.

The snarling familiars leered at him, although most of them looked more scared than angry now Anan was in the room. He really was a monster.

"Not interested. I'm breaking the familiar bond. It was never that strong, anyway. I'm getting something more powerful. You've never been any good to me, you gross bag of bones."

"I can change. I'll do anything to show I'm loyal to you. You name it, and it's yours." Elijah was getting closer to Anan. He was almost within pouncing range.

It was time for me and Sammy to react.

"You traitor! You won't get away with this." I raced toward Elijah, Sammy beside me. I shot out a warning blast of magic to make sure the mangy group of familiars didn't try anything.

Anan laughed. "No one wants you, Elijah. I'm done with you, and you've just turned on the only people who gave you the time of day. You've lost it all. Better you roll over, expose that bald belly, and let the ghouls gnaw at you."

"Please, take me back. I'm sorry. Sorry I ever met you." Elijah launched into the air. He was aiming at Anan's chest, but whipped his rat-like tail against Anan's hand, and the rock slipped from his fingers.

Elijah bounced off Anan's chest and hit the floor.

Anan roared. He dived for the rock.

I sprinted ahead and jumped at the rock, but Anan got there first. He shoved me away with a whip sharp spell that made me dizzy.

Sammy landed on Anan's hand and bit down. He yelped and whacked Sammy with the back of his free hand. Sammy squeaked and flopped onto his side. He didn't get up.

I raced over, my eyes rolling and unable to see straight. I wouldn't make it in time. Anan had his foot raised over Sammy's head.

Elijah landed on Anan's face and bit his forehead. Anan yelled and staggered back.

He grabbed Elijah and tore him off his head, leaving a trail of blood behind. "That's the last time you betray me." He lifted him like a football and tossed him in the air, straight at the ghouls.

A tall ghoul with only one arm grabbed Elijah in midair, caught him, and took a bite.

The horrifying scene took seconds, but it felt like the world had stopped turning and everything happened in gut wrenching clarity. The ghoul took one bite of Elijah and dropped him.

I lost sight of Elijah through the mass of rotting, swaying legs, but he wouldn't have survived that bite. And even if he had, he'd turn ghoul.

I grabbed Sammy's front leg in my teeth and dragged him to a safe place behind a stack of pallets. There was nothing I could do for Elijah, but I could save Sammy. Elijah had sacrificed himself for Sammy. He'd seen what Anan was about to do, and he'd done the noble thing. It was a small comfort, but Elijah had died for a good reason.

Anan looked around the floor, muttering to himself.

The rock! He must have dropped it again when fighting with Elijah.

I spotted it behind him and dashed toward it, but Anan suddenly turned and reached for it. He only got halfway before a spell zapped him in the butt, and he went flying and faceplanted on the floor.

Magic sparked on Zandra's fingers. Her face was pale and her eyes wide as her gaze locked with mine. "Never do anything like that again. I almost lost you."

I grabbed the rock, almost dropping it as the taste of burned toast and vinegar flooded across my tongue, and raced back to her before dropping it into her palm. "You'll never lose me, not when we work together. Now, you control the ghouls."

Zandra looked at the rock and then at the ghouls. Her gaze turned to the anxious faces of the remaining gang members. "Let us go. Release Finn, take the collar off him, and we can all walk out of here alive."

No one moved, other than the guys with the cattle prods, who occasionally shoved back an over enthusiastic ghoul.

"You heard me. Unless you want me to set those ghouls on you, you'll do as I say." Zandra held out the rock. "I control them."

"Don't listen to her." Anan rolled over and shooed away the hovering familiars. "She has no control over them."

"I do. I have your rock." Doubt drifted through Zandra's words, but she stood firm, the rock held out.

"But you're missing a vital ingredient." Anan staggered to his feet, one hand rubbing his zapped butt. "I spent a week with a dark witch, and she infected me with the magic I need to control the ghouls. That rock is an anchor, the thing that lets me give them orders they understand, but without having the right amount of dark magic simmering inside you, that's just a basic rock you're holding. And you're just a basic witch."

Zandra licked her lips, her hand lowering. Her gaze grazed me. She was scared.

But we hadn't been defeated. If dark magic was what was needed to fire that rock to life, I could offer it to her. "Use me."

"For what?" Panic flickered in Zandra's eyes.

I scrambled onto her shoulder and lowered the barrier I always kept in place. It contained the darkest parts of my history. My demi-goddess days hadn't always been full of lightness. I'd been in brutal battles, defeated demons, and had more than my fair share of encounters with dark witches.

And some of their magic had stuck to me, and I'd learned from it. I rarely used it, but this was one time when it would be handy. "Use my power."

Zandra gasped. "Juno! Your fur has changed color."

My beautiful, shimmering white fur was a dull matt black, and I smelled like ripe Brie as the darkness shifted within me and blossomed like a corpse flower. "Quick! I can't hold this power back for long. Only take what you need, and after this, you're getting a trip to a cleansing spa. I don't want this darkness to linger in you." I gritted my teeth, fighting the urge to absorb the toxicity and give in to a primal urge to destroy everything I saw.

Zandra kissed my side. “I love you, Juno. Remember what we have together and hold on tight. This ride is about to get bumpy.”

Chapter 21

Enter the darkness

Zandra shuddered as the dark power soared through her. What would she think of me when she knew how dark I was?

I had to trust my witch. She'd continue to love me, no matter what.

"Juno, no offence, but this magic is rank. You've been carrying this with you all the time I've known you?" Her shaking intensified.

"A little longer than that. Keep focused. Don't let it overwhelm you. If it gets too much, let me know, and I'll draw it back." Hopefully. I fought the darkness as it swept through me like a jagged blade of despair and rage.

"I'm good, for now." She lifted the rock and held it in front of her chest. "Ghoul army, I command you. Return to the shipping containers. Hurt no one."

The ghouls remained where they were. Several snarled, their attention on Zandra.

"Why isn't it working?" she whispered.

I let out an extra trickle of darkness. Whoever Anan got the power from must have been a particularly unpleasant deviant. "Try again."

"Ghouls! Leave this room. Don't harm anyone."

Again, they didn't respond, and they were getting angry.

I didn't know what else to do. Zandra had dark power racing through her, and we had the anchor that controlled the ghouls. This should work. The ghouls shouldn't be a problem.

A shuffling reached my ears. Sammy had dragged himself over and landed on Zandra's feet.

"Use my power, too. I can be useful." He wheezed out a breath.

"Thanks, Sammy, but you're injured. It would be too much for you." Zandra kneeled and petted him softly. "I appreciate the offer, though. We'll figure something else out."

Sammy groaned and shut his eyes.

He was a hero to the end. My Sammy would get a reward if he lived through this. Although from the paleness of the tongue hanging out the side of his mouth, I wasn't certain he would.

Anan slow-clapped. "Great show, but you've lost, witch. Give me back that rock and stop playing with powers. You know nothing about how to control dark magic."

Zandra's intake of breath was so deep, I rose several inches in the air. "You're right. I know nothing about dark magic, and I don't want to. I don't need twisted, dangerous spells to prove myself to anyone. I know my worth."

"Your only worth to me is as a snack for my ghouls." Anan grated out a laugh. "You need me if you want this ghoul army under control. They're growing restless, and my guys can only hold them back for so long before people get eaten. Hand over the rock and let the men get to work. Maybe I'll let them eat you first, so you don't get to see what they do to your angel friend and your familiars." He smacked his lips together.

"No one is getting eaten," Zandra said. "And although I know nothing about dark powers, I know all about goodness. And these ghouls need kindness." She slid her hand into her jacket pocket and pulled out a brilliant white opal.

"How are you planning on being kind to them? Kiss their wounds better and give them a glass of milk and a cookie?" That earned Anan a few chuckles from his gang, but most of them looked worried and about ready to flee.

Zandra turned her head a fraction, so her mouth was pressed against my fur. "I have no idea if this'll work, but this stone was in Adrienne's chest of magic. I read about it. It cancels out darkness and neutralizes power. If we combine the rock and this stone, do you think it'll give me control over the ghouls?"

I booped my nose against her cheek. "You know what you're doing. If you believe this will work, then it will."

The worry on her face cleared. She extended both arms and slammed the rock and stone together. There was a shower of brilliant light that filled the room, covering us, the gang, and the ghouls.

Zandra shifted her shoulders before settling in place and holding out a single stone. It wasn't gray or white, but it sparkled a pale green. It was beautiful. "Ghouls, leave this place. Return to your shipping containers and do no harm to anyone you meet."

The ghoul army shuddered. Their snapping teeth were silenced, and they stopped raking their nails through the air. They looked at Zandra and nodded. Someone's head fell off and rolled away. Slowly, they turned and shambled off, leaving a variety of gross body parts behind.

The gang members and their familiars darted out of their reach, but the ghouls weren't attacking. They were calm under Zandra's control. They didn't want to destroy and rip apart everything they saw. Being under Anan's command had made them like that. Now my wonderful witch was looking after them, we had the time to figure out a way to find them peace.

Once the room was clear, I saw what was left of Elijah, and my heart stuttered. He looked broken, wasn't moving, and there was an oozing bite wound on his side. I wanted to go to him, but if Anan saw him, he may exact revenge. Providing Elijah lay still and didn't draw attention to himself, he might make it through this.

The gang members shuffled around, then one guy broke ranks and raced to the door.

I shot out a paw and whacked him with a knockout spell. He crashed to the floor and didn't get up.

"If anyone else tries to leave, I'll bring back the ghouls," Zandra said. "They'll hold you if I order them to. And while they do, they may take a nibble or two. Do any of you want to be ghoul food?"

"You're such a do-gooding witch. It makes me sick, but that's your flaw. You'd never hurt us," Anan said.

"Shall we test that theory?" Zandra arched an eyebrow while I issued a threatening hiss.

"They're mine." Anan almost stamped his foot. Petulant fool. "I have clients waiting for those things. If you take them, I'm dead. They'll come looking for me and want their money back if I can't supply them with the goods."

"That's not my problem. This is your mess. You should never have turned innocent people into ghouls," Zandra said.

"They're no good for anything else. I cleared up the dregs of society. Crimson Cove should be thanking me."

"You may believe you picked the loners and those who wouldn't be missed, but there is always someone out there who cares," I said.

Zandra nodded. "We can't reverse the damage you've done, but I can tell everyone what happened to their friends and family. And when they find out it was you, they'll turn on the gang. Your days in Crimson Cove are numbered. Your rule ends now. Let Finn down, and hand yourselves in."

"I'd rather die." Anan bolted toward Finn. "Give me my ghouls, or the angel freak gets it. I'll activate the collar. He'll lose his head, and everyone else will be vaporized."

"Err... Anan. If you do that, the blast will kill us, too," Koku said.

"And destroy the witch, her bug-eyed familiars, and this angel." Anan yanked on Finn's leg.

"I am not bug-eyed." I flung out a restraining spell. It was still tainted with the darkness that rumbled through me, and the magic latched onto Anan like a spiked web and dug into his skin, drawing blood.

He yelled and dropped to his hands and knees, clawing at his skin.

I was enjoying watching his agony a little too much. I leaped like a winged gazelle on a caffeine high and flew across the room, landing on Finn. I dug my teeth into the collar and bit through it. Bitter magic filled my mouth, but I kept tugging.

"Juno! No! You'll set it off." Horror was etched across Zandra's face as she ran toward me.

With a final tug, the collar broke. I dropped to the floor, flipped the collar onto Anan's chest, encased Zandra, Finn, Sammy, and Elijah in the strongest shield I could conjure, and backed away from Anan. "Ready to sacrifice yourself and your gang? You'll be the only ones getting hurt."

Anan snapped his teeth at me, looking more ghoul than person. He gripped the collar, clearly warring with his desire to destroy and self-preservation, then tossed it into the corner of the room. He flipped over and crawled toward the door, my restraining spell making each movement slow.

"I suggest we obliterate him," I said to Zandra, the dark magic sending spikes of heat and cold through me. "Some people aren't worth saving."

"Juno! We've talked about this. No one gets obliterated." Zandra grinned. "Perhaps his gang will help us, though. What do you say, boys? Angel Force may go easy on you if you stop your leader from getting away. And I'm sure, if you share the information you have about his schemes, you'll receive leniency."

The gang shuffled about. Several of them took a step toward the crawling, defeated Anan. Their familiars matched their movements.

"If you don't help us, the angels won't think twice about throwing the full weight of their feathers at you if you assist in Anan's escape," Zandra said. "Why don't you men show us girls how it's done?"

I stood proudly on my witch's shoulder. "Will you protect your fallen leader or give yourselves a second chance at living a good life?"

The gang members exchanged glances. After a second of deliberation, they formed a circle around Anan with their familiars and stopped him from getting any closer to the exit.

As Anan roared his rage at the betrayal, I leaped off Zandra's shoulder, checked on Sammy, then dashed over to Elijah. There was a deep bite wound on his belly, and his eyes were closed. He was still breathing, but that breath was faint and his heartbeat rapid.

"Hold tight. We've got you. You helped us when we needed it, so it's our turn to assist you," I whispered.

His eyes flickered open, and he moaned. "Too late. A ghoul got me. After everything I've done for Anan, this is how he repays me. He never cared for me. Our bond meant nothing to him."

"Anan's a bad person, but you can be better than him. You've shown me that. Now, you need to be strong. The strongest you've ever been if you're going to survive."

"I'm dying, Juno. Let me go. I can't be a ghoul cat. End me."

"You won't be a ghoul. I won't let that happen."

His eyes shuttered closed. "I know you have weird magic running through that pretty body, but even you can't do anything about this. No one is that powerful."

I bumped him with my cheek. "Never underestimate an ancient, powerful female. When we really want something, we make it happen. You rest while we deal with the cleanup."

"Err... hey! Anyone bothered about the angel still strung up over here?" Finn said. "I could do with some help to get down."

Zandra dashed over and released him, while I pulled back as much of the dark magic as I could. Then I pulsed healing magic over Elijah to keep him stable. It wouldn't remove the ghoul infection, but it would slow things down and give me breathing room to solve this problem. And I had an idea of how to keep him from transforming, but it would take finessing and power.

Sammy hurried over, limping on one paw. "Is Elijah still alive? He should be turning gray and going grrrr by now."

"He is. Elijah has something to live for," I said.

"What? Anan slung him to the ghouls. Elijah doesn't have anyone else."

I hissed quietly. "Sammy! That's not kind. He has us. We're Elijah's friends now. We'll look out for him and ensure he doesn't get too grrrr on us."

Sammy squinted at Elijah. "After everything you've done to me, I should make sure the ghouls give you an extra bite. You're a bad cat."

"Ah! But you won't, because you're a kind cat. The sort of cat Elijah aspires to be. And a brave hero like you would never turn his back on anyone, no matter the history you have together," I murmured.

Sammy didn't look happy, but he nodded. "Sure. But you're making it up to me if you live, Elijah. No more bullying, got it?"

"But you're such an easy target." Elijah cracked open an eye and grinned.

Sammy harrumphed and stomp-limped away.

Zandra walked over, assisting Finn, who was staggering, his wings drooping. "Oh! Is Elijah..."

"He's alive. I'm just figuring out how to make sure he stays that way. How about Finn?"

"I'm able to speak for myself, thanks. And I've been better. My wing got bent out of shape. I won't be able to fly for weeks."

"You hate flying, anyway," Zandra said. "If you play up your injuries, you might even get a few days paid sick leave and a pass on flying duties for a couple of months."

"There's always a silver lining," Finn said. "Why didn't the ghouls attack? I was too high up to see what was going on."

"Because even the undead need to feel they're a part of something," I said. "The ghouls were terrified. Anan mistreated them ever since they were turned. Ghouls don't want for much, but the least they need is food, a safe place to stay, and to be free from threats and punishment. That was all Anan gave them, so their half-lives were fear-filled and miserable. Now Zandra controls them, they feel safe."

"But they're still ghouls. Mindless, flesh eating destroyers," Finn said. "I figured they'd have chewed on the jerks with the electrified cattle prods when they shambled away."

"Ghouls just want a quiet life," I said. "They don't want to hurt others."

"They always act like they do."

"Because it's always the bad guys who create ghoul armies and exploit them. What would happen if a good witch had a ghoul army?"

"Back that thought up and park it in the never going to happen row, fluffy pants," Zandra said. "I don't want an army of anything. Ghouls, gnomes, chipmunks, or cats. I'm happy looking after myself and you."

"So am I. I won't share you with anybody." I leaped on her shoulder and rubbed my face against hers.

She let out a sigh. "Good. From the way you were talking, I was expecting you to suggest we move the ghouls into the basement. That would be a squeeze."

"I have no plans to let any ghouls live with us." After this eventful day, I'd be arranging some quiet time with my witch. We'd go to a cleansing spa, have a proper break where we could chat all things witch and cat familiar, and then get back to our work in animal control and figuring out what happened to Adrienne. It would be business as usual.

Finn pulled himself upright, swaying as he inspected his bent wing. "You watch the gang while I contact Angel Force. I have arrests to make and evidence to gather. You good with that?"

Zandra nodded. “Sure. We’re not going anywhere.”

I nodded along with her. Our new home was a weird one, but it was our home just the same. And we fit in perfectly.

Chapter 22

An unwelcome clue

I was stretched out in a glorious patch of sunshine in the window of Bites and Delights. I was warm, my belly was full, and I had my handsome new friend, Sammy, beside me, snoring softly.

While we half-snoozed in the sunlight, I listened to Zandra as she sat at the table with Vorana. It was the weekend, so we had two days off, and Vorana had insisted she take us for a celebratory breakfast after learning we'd stopped a ghoul invasion in Crimson Cove two days ago.

Sorcha hurried over with a plateful of cinnamon and banana waffles and joined them at the table. "I wouldn't have believed all the rumors if you hadn't told us that tale. A ghoul army! Exploding magic collars! A hidden diamond! And Anan's cruddy gang taking people from town and turning them into ghouls. It's all so incredible, even for this place."

"We all knew how dark that gang could go," Vorana said. "You in particular."

"Don't remind me I've seen Anan's seedy underbelly. I much prefer finding chocolates on my pillow rather than body parts." Sorcha dished out the waffles. "But to kill Osorin in that way. That was cold. And what about all the people they took? Did any of them make it out?"

"Not that I know of. Angel Force has been working through the belongings found at the warehouse," Zandra said. "It'll be days before they've identified all the ghouls, but they're being looked after. They've been fed and are in secure storage with light and warmth. Their friends and family are being informed."

"I'm still in shock the gang took so many people," Vorana said. "Why didn't we miss them?"

"Because they picked on the vulnerable," Zandra said, "the people who slip between the cracks."

Vorana huffed out a breath, her normally sunny disposition hidden behind a sullen cloud of concern. "That's our fault. We should have taken better care of everyone who lives here."

No one spoke as they ate waffles and drank coffee.

"We weren't to know Anan's plans," Sorcha said. "But I agree. There were a few homeless guys who used to drop by to see if there were leftovers. I always gave them what I could, a mug of coffee or a sandwich, but I could have done more. I will."

"We all will," Vorana said. "I feel bad for sometimes shooing people out of the bookstore. They never bought anything and would linger for hours. I was relieved when they stopped showing up. Now I know why. My bookstore could have been their only refuge, and I didn't notice."

"It's a lesson learned," Zandra said. "And if Osorin had been treated a little kinder and his sister hadn't been so awful to him, he may never have looked to the gang for approval, and he'd still have his head."

The café door opened, and Finn walked in. He looked better than the last time I'd seen him. His wings sparkled white again, and the bruising on his face was gone.

He walked over and handed Zandra a small cactus in a plastic pot.

She stared at it. "What's this for?"

"I figured you weren't a cut flowers kind of woman. It's my way of saying thank you for saving me from being turned into a ghoul."

Zandra laughed and showed off the cactus to the others. "You got it right about the cut flowers. I've never owned a cactus, though. What do you do with them?"

"Leave it alone," Vorana said. "Cacti are independent, spiky, and they know their own minds. Don't over water it, keep it warm, make sure it gets enough light, and don't tinker too much, or it may stab you."

"Sounds like someone I know," I mumbled to Sammy.

He stretched out and flopped a solid gray paw over me. "I've been meaning to ask, would you be open to sharing Zandra?"

I tensed, and so did he. "With you?"

Sammy slowly removed his paw so I could turn and face him. "She's incredible. And she was so brave, standing up to the Shadow gang. Zandra didn't flinch when the ghouls came into the warehouse. Neither did you."

"I also didn't see you running away." I needed a minute to process. I was growing fond of Sammy but had no plans to share Zandra. She was my witch.

"True, I didn't run, but I was scared. It was easier to be brave when I was by your side." Sammy snuffled my nose. "I won't be any bother, and I'll stay out of the way. You'll barely know I'm around. It's the familiar-witch bond, you see. I miss it. And—"

I pressed a sun-warmed paw gently against his mouth. "Zandra isn't the witch for you. Your personalities aren't a match. She is wonderful but needs careful handling. You'd be too soft on her. You'd never tell her when she has a misstep."

His eyes widened. "Zandra gets things wrong?"

I glanced at her as she continued to fill in her new friends about the events at the warehouse. "She's younger than she looks and has a lot to learn. Zandra needs an experienced familiar by her side. Someone with more years of experience than I care to remember."

"What if I sneak into a corner of the basement? Or it could be a temporary bond, like you have with Archie. I get so lonely."

"No, Sammy. Besides, if you're bonded with my witch, it would make our relationship difficult. I never mix business with pleasure."

"Pleasure?"

"You haven't forgotten you're taking me on a date, have you? I've been waiting for two days for you to make a move."

He lowered his head. "We've been recovering after almost being eaten by ghouls. And you went away for a night with Zandra. And... I wasn't sure you meant what you said about me being a hero. I figured you were being kind because you felt sorry for me. I'm nothing special. Why would you want to date me?"

"You are special, but I had to prioritize my witch so I could remove the dark magic from her. She doesn't need that tainting her life. Our magic users always come first. They sometimes don't realize what we sacrifice to make sure they're happy."

He snuffled me again. "I wondered if you wouldn't come back. People always leave me. I always thought I'd have Rachel forever, but then I lost her. What if that's the story of my life?"

"You write your own story. Maybe along the way, people pick up a pen and add a side story or erase things you want to keep, but you're in charge."

"I am?"

"Yes, just like I am. And I know your main story isn't to be with Zandra." Zandra would look after Sammy if he asked her to, but I had an idea about his perfect new magic user. "Besides, if you bond with Zandra, we can't date. It would be too complicated."

He puffed out a slightly meaty breath. "Then I pick you. And I'll take you on that date. I know you love fish, and there's a quiet cove on the beach with the best saltwater fishing. The tide comes in and feeds the lagoons, and the fish get trapped. You can catch amazing fresh fish there."

"That's my kind of date." I rested a paw on his side and nuzzled him. "And we'll find you a new bonded magic user. If you feel ready for one, then we'll look. And I have someone in mind for you."

"You do? Who?"

Someone quietly clearing their throat had me peering over the edge of the window ledge. Elijah sat neatly, his tail over his paws. He wore a new collar with a tiny green stone set in it.

"I don't like to intrude on a private moment," he said.

Sammy rolled over and glared at him. "Then don't."

I patted Sammy's side. "How are you feeling, Elijah?"

"Good. Better. I've slept and eaten."

"Any urges to eat the living?"

He shook his head. "It's working. The collar is stopping me from getting any worse."

It had been a risky idea, but with Zandra's help, we'd forged a small piece of the combined ghoul control stone and a sliver of the cleansing opal onto a collar. Provided Elijah wore it and kept the protective magic topped up, he'd stay almost completely cat. He was still a little gray around the edges, and the healing magic on his wound had left a silvery scar on his side, but he was still himself.

"I'm happy to hear it. Was there something you wanted?" Although I didn't want Elijah dead, we were taking things slowly on the friendship front. Lost trust took time to rebuild.

"Just want to say thanks again. And sorry. Sorry to you, too, Sammy. You're not a fat loser. You're a good guy."

Sammy blinked slowly. "You think so?"

"I saw how you behaved in the warehouse. You were brave. I should have looked beyond the flab and dull gray fur, and—"

"That's enough!" I admonished Elijah with a hiss. "Sammy accepts your apology."

Sammy looked disgruntled but nodded.

"What will you do now Anan is behind bars?" I said.

"Finn has a bed for me at his sanctuary. I'm staying there until I figure things out."

"And your bond with Anan?"

"Gone. I severed it. Now I can give evidence against him to make sure he gets what he deserves." Elijah gave a quick nod. "Thanks again. And sorry. Again. I'll leave you to it."

We watched him limp-walk away. Elijah had a lot of healing to do, but I'd keep an eye on him and make sure he stayed on the right path.

An explosion of laughter from Zandra's table drew my attention.

Finn had settled in a seat and was entertaining them. "It's true. If Zandra hadn't rescued me, I'd be ghoul meat, or ghoul angel. It would have been humiliating. And if Juno hadn't figured out where that diamond had been hidden, poor Archie would have been in serious trouble."

"We need to keep Zandra and Juno around," Sorcha said. "If they can defeat a ghoul army and bring down the Shadow gang, they're invaluable. We can never let them leave."

"Agreed. You must stay," Vorana said.

"I support that." Finn grinned at Zandra.

"I don't know how long we're staying." Zandra's gaze met mine, and she nodded. "But we'll be here for a while. We've got plenty of business to take care of, and I'm enjoying my job with Barney, despite the dead body and a run-in with a criminal gang."

"I'm happy to have you as my lodger for as long as you want to stay," Vorana said.

"And you can't leave yet," Finn said. "We still have some loose ends to tie up with the Shadow gang."

"You've got my statement about what happened. They're all talking, aren't they?" Zandra said. "And you got the diamond safely out of Archie?"

"He's fine. The diamond is clean and in evidence, and the gang is talking. They listened to your advice about scapegoating Anan. And everything they've told us means Anan will never see the outside of a cell. Several of the gang members were unhappy when he diversified into ghouls. They wanted to break rank but were too scared to leave because they knew what would happen to them."

"They'd lose their heads like Osorin or be turned themselves," Sorcha said.

Finn nodded. "Anan had them so scared that they kept quiet. But thanks to Zandra and Juno, the gang's days are numbered."

"That calls for waffles," Sorcha said. "Or how about muffins? I have pecan cherry chocolate."

"Yes to both," Finn said. "I'm starving."

Torrin strode through the door. He smiled as he saw everyone at the table and strolled over. "Did my breakfast invitation get lost?"

"I messaged you," Vorana said, "but you didn't reply."

"Ah, I didn't get it. My snow globe got peed on by a long-eared baby kraken."

"Don't kraken live in water?" Zandra said.

"She's a hybrid, so she enjoys land and water. The little monster slid out, did her business, and fled back under the water. I've got my snow globe sitting in rice and hoping it hasn't been fried." Torrin grabbed a seat and joined the party. "Are the rumors true? Zandra, you brought down the Shadow gang?"

"With some help." She winked at me and Sammy.

"I'll have to take you for another drink, and you can tell me how it all happened," Torrin said.

"Maybe she's already been asked out for a drink," Finn said.

"By you? Don't you have spare haloes to polish or reports to write up in triplicate?"

Zandra shook her head. "Let's just have breakfast together and enjoy ourselves."

Torrin and Finn both shrugged. It looked like they had some unfinished business of the Zandra variety to tackle, despite her trying to put them off.

"I've just been to see Barney," Torrin said. "I've got a place for Archie, and I moved him in first thing. I left him to get settled, but he'll be fine. He was already making friends with a three-legged part hellhound and telling him all about the horror of passing a diamond from his butt."

"I thought you were taking him," Zandra said to Finn.

"We share the unloved critters between us. Torrin is one of the guys I tag team with, so we can always find a space. I'm dealing with all the gang familiars. They're a messed up, motley bunch, so I have no room for Archie. We figured it out between us."

"We've tag teamed with the unloved fluffies for a long time," Torrin said. "And Barney's happy with the arrangement."

"And Archie?" Zandra said.

"I'll be back soon." I gave Sammy one last nuzzle then hopped up from the delicious patch of sun and joined Zandra, settling on her lap, so I could hear more about Archie.

"He's still sad but better than the first time I saw him," Torrin said. "He asked me to say thanks for the bond. He appreciates someone still cares for him."

I gave the bond a gentle tug, so Archie knew we were thinking about him. "We'd never abandon a familiar in need. Finn, how did you get that diamond out? I figured Archie would need surgery."

Finn laughed, while Sorcha and Vorana looked repulsed. "A trip to the vet, some sedative, a few magic spells, and it sorted the problem. It was only a small diamond."

"Anan must have been crazy when he didn't get the diamond," Vorana said.

"Crazy enough to kill. Although I think Osorin was dead whatever he did. He must have realized that, so he hid the diamond inside Archie. Maybe he thought it would be insurance to keep him safe," I said.

"Anan has admitted he sent a guy to search the house. That's why the money was never found," Finn said. "Of course, they had no way of knowing where the diamond was hidden, or Archie would have been in danger."

"Archie should keep the diamond," I said. "Osorin gave it to him."

"Osorin hid stolen goods inside him. That's a different thing," Finn said. "It's evidence in a crime."

"I hope it's been given a good clean. No one wants a diamond that's been through a hellhound's digestive system sitting on their finger," Sorcha said.

"It's as good as new." Finn grinned. "How about those muffins?"

Sorcha rolled her eyes but headed off to grab an extra plate of goodies.

"All we need to do now is find Archie a permanent home," Zandra said.

"He can spend as much time with me as he likes. There's no pressure to move him," Torrin said. "And I've worked with Barney before on difficult cases, so I know these guys take time to adjust to another home."

"Archie can tug on our temporary bond," I said. "It's there. There's a place for him."

"But not in our basement," Zandra said. "No hellhounds allowed. He might eat my new cactus."

"Who got you that sad specimen?" Torrin inspected the potted plant.

"I did," Finn said.

"When I take you out, I'll get you real flowers," Torrin said.

"No! No flowers required. Although I did save Finn's life, so a cactus is an understated gift." Zandra arched an eyebrow at Finn.

Torrin roared a laugh, while Finn looked a little embarrassed.

"Name your gift, and it's yours," he said.

"Nothing. I want nothing from you. I'm just happy we made it out of that warehouse in one piece, the ghouls didn't hurt anyone, and the Shadow gang is finished in Crimson Cove. That's reward enough," Zandra said.

I snuggled on her lap as the group chatted and ate together. Sorcha came back with muffins and waffles, and Zandra spent the next half an hour surrounded by her new friends.

I'd been right about Crimson Cove. It was the perfect place for us. Sure, there were challenges, and there'd be more to come. We still hadn't figured out where Adrienne was, Zandra needed to be less spiky around new people, and I had to figure out where Sammy fit in my life, but it was progress in the right direction.

Soon, perhaps sooner than I'd expected, I'd call on Zandra for help with my own problems. Using my powers in this battle had drained me more than it should. And the darkness buried in me couldn't be contained forever. I needed to get back to what I was. But I had the time, and with Zandra by my side, we were unstoppable.

With that comforting thought, I snoozed on Zandra's lap until the food was eaten and everyone started heading off.

Zandra went to the washroom, and I was about to go back and snuggle with Sammy in the sun when I spotted Finn waiting by the door. He was looking at the washroom where Zandra had gone, then he looked at me.

Rather than going over to Sammy, I trotted to the door. "Is something the matter?"

Finn's mouth twisted to the side, and he rubbed the back of his neck. "I came here to tell Zandra something, but she was in such a good mood, I didn't want to ruin her day."

"What is it?"

"Not in here." Finn opened the door, and we stepped out together.

He looked back inside the café. "The angels finished sorting through the belongings the gang took from the people they turned into ghouls."

"That can't have been easy. How many were taken?"

"A hundred and twenty-five. At least, that's all the individual identifications we found. We've tallied most of the ghouls with their ID, but there are a few we may never match. We'll be releasing information to the local press soon and hoping people will come forward and name the ghouls. Some of those ghouls were so far gone, their features are unrecognizable, though."

"I'm sorry to hear that. What did you want to tell Zandra? Anan hasn't escaped, has he?"

Finn tipped back his head and stared at the sky for a few seconds. "Nothing like that. There's no easy way to say this, so I'll show you." He reached inside his jacket and pulled out a clear plastic bag. Inside was a tasseled yellow purse.

I stared at the purse, and my stomach dropped to my paws and bounced back again. "That belongs to Adrienne."

Finn nodded slowly as he tucked the purse into his jacket. "Her ID is in there. I'm sorry to say this, Juno, but I think Anan turned her into a ghoul. I don't know how to tell Zandra, though. It'll break her heart."

My happiness faded as I looked back into the café. Zandra was at the counter, chatting to Sorcha and laughing about something. "Have you found Adrienne? Was she in one of the shipping containers?"

"There was no sign of her anywhere, and she isn't any of the ghouls we haven't paired with ID. They're all male."

"Could she have escaped before they changed her?"

"It's possible." Finn grimaced. "I think it's more likely she was turned, too. Maybe Anan sent some ghouls out early. I want to be certain before I tell Zandra, though. I owe her."

My fur bristled as a hot rage flickered through me. "What are you doing to find Adrienne?"

"Talking to the gang members and checking their logs to see if there were any early shipments."

"And?" I stepped on his foot and glared up at him. "You must do more. Everything you can to find the truth."

Finn jerked back. He must have seen the rage firing inside me, although it wasn't aimed at him. It was aimed at this new problem. "I can't keep this from Zandra for long. She has a right to know. I just don't want to give her another mystery to solve, not when she seems so happy."

"For now, we stay silent. Zandra has been through a lot," I said.

"For how long?"

"Until I say otherwise and you know everything about Adrienne." I glared at him until he nodded.

I gritted my teeth and growled, making Finn back away. We'd solved the mystery of Osorin's murder, defeated the Shadow gang, and stopped the ghouls from invading Crimson Cove, but there was a bigger mystery that wasn't over yet.

A mystery I had to solve, even if it broke my witch's heart.

About Author

K.E. O'Connor (Karen) is a cozy mystery author living in the beautiful British countryside. She loves all things mystery, animals, and cake. When she's not writing about mysteries, murder, and treats, she volunteers at a local animal sanctuary, reads a ton of books, binge watches mystery series, and dreams about living somewhere warmer.

To stay in touch with the fun mysteries:

Newsletter:
www.subscribepage.com/cozymysteries

Website:
www.keoconnor.com/writing

Facebook:
www.facebook.com/keoconnorauthor

Afterword

Intrigued to explore Juno and Zandra's origin story, and discover what happened when they first arrived in Crimson Cove to look for Adrienne?

Then join the Magical Misfits Crew and grab an exclusive FREE story – **Every Witch Way but Meow**.

Sometimes it takes a magical cat to solve a problem...

A mysterious message, a missing parent, and a new start.

When my witch is troubled, I'll do everything to make things right. And when a message from her chronically ditzy mother jangles her nerves, a trip to Crimson Cove is needed.

Arriving in the quaint, up-and-coming magical town unveils puzzles, opportunities, and problems. And I sense change coming when we uncover a chest of magic, encounter a klutz with a heart, and make a life-changing decision.

If you'd love to join the Magical Misfits Crew, grab your FREE copy of **Every Witch Way but Meow**, and let's solve the puzzle together.

And if you'd like to stroke my silky white fur, I'm always happy to oblige.

Get your copy here: https://dl.bookfunnel.com/rxtbdntz7o

Milton Keynes UK
Ingram Content Group UK Ltd.
UKHW041519030823
426277UK00004B/202